GW00393040

SIR THOMAS
THE HESITANT
AND THE
TABLE
OF LESS VALUED
KNIGHTS

LIAM PERRIN

For Kelly & Abby
My love and my joy.

With special thanks to:
Steve the Diagnosticator, Chris the Cognoscente, Amy the
Ameliorant, and Lee the Longstanding

Copyright © 2013 Liam Perrin
All rights reserved

First Edition, March 2013
Second Edition, September 2018

ISBN: 1727102185
ISBN-13: 978-1727102185

Ordering and contact: liamperrin.com
Cover illustration by J. Caleb Clark

One of the last paragraphs in one of the last volumes of
*The Merlin Continuation of the Old French Arthurian Post
Vulgate* by Lacy & Asher reads:

Know that there were three kinds of tables there. The first was the Round Table. King Arthur was companion and lord of this one. The second table was called the Table of Errant Companions, those who went seeking adventure and waited to become companions of the Round Table. Those of the third table were those who never left court and did not go on quests or in search of adventures, either because of illness or because they had not enough courage. These knights were called the less valued knights.

I shall now set the record straight.

Liam Xavier Perrin, LVK
March 7, 1990
Somnia Salvebis

Dear Reader,

My name is Liam Bartholomew Perrin. My father was Liam Horatio Perrin, and my grandfather was Liam Xavier. This book comes to you by way of my late grandfather, LXP. Dad (Liam Horatio) knew he was dying two winters ago, and one of the last things he gave me was a plain, dented lockbox with my grandfather's monogram.

Dad said, "Here," and shoved it at me. "I wouldn't open it if I were you.

"Your grandfather was a crazy, old coot," he said.

The lockbox sat on my desk for weeks next to a picture of the two of them on a fishing trip when Pop-pop was young and Dad was a boy. In the picture, Dad holds a sixteen inch bass by the gills. Both he and the fish look grim. Pop-pop has his hand on Dad's shoulder. Pop-pop is beaming.

The lockbox sat on my desk unopened for so long because there was no key to go with it. I would pick it up from time to time and think about Pop-pop while I tipped the box, listening to the contents shift inside. I ruined two letter openers and a butter knife trying to jimmy it open.

Finally I took it to a friend's, set it up on a stump out back, and shot a hole in it with his revolver. I holstered the gun and retrieved the target to discover that I now had a plain, dented, locked box with a hole in it. I took the box to a locksmith.

Inside were stacks of scribbled notes and clippings, a partial manuscript with a bullet hole ripped through it, a scrap of wood, and a ring.

The ring is silver and stone-less. It bears the letters "LVK" and a crest. Above the crest is the word *Somnia*, and below it, *Salvebis*. The scrap of wood is cut from something larger. A phrase is carved crudely into the scrap. It reads: "Bane was here."

I took the box and its contents home, brewed a pot of coffee, and read my grandfather's story.

It was clever. It was fun. It was unfinished. Most intriguing of all, Pop-pop seemed to think it was true. He'd been a part of something, and he wanted the truth finally told. Apart from the ring and a handful of newspaper clippings, it would have been easy to believe Pop-pop was losing it. But there it was: that ring.

I've spent the last two years finishing LXP's story. It's a story about a secret society, but not the kind you usually read about or see on TV. This is a kind that's more overlooked than secret, per se. It's the story of the young man who set the bar for all of them: Sir Thomas the Hesitant. The setting is Camelot, but the story is not, for instance, about how Sir Thomas and Sir Philip the Disadvantaged rescued Percival and the Holy Grail, or how Ox the Monosyllabic and Dedric the Diplopian foiled Morgan's plot and saved both Gawain and the Green Knight. It's not about Arthur, Guinevere, or Merlin, although they are all part of Thomas's tale.

It's the story of what made Thomas who he was. At its heart, it's the story of a young man growing up and learning what it means to be a hero, a *true* hero, in a world that doesn't always make sense. His heart and his deeds inspired an order that spanned centuries and long outlived those whom it initially served. It inspired me to finish my grandfather's work, and I hope it inspires you too.

I dedicate this work to my late grandfather, Liam Xavier Perrin, the last Less Valued Knight.

Liam Bartholomew Perrin
February 5, 2008

INTRODUCTION

"I really don't think this is a good idea," says a person.

"Nonsense, you'll be fine," replies another.

People have been speaking those phrases at each other for as long as they've been speaking. Neanderthal women encouraged their mates this way when they wanted them to taste-test a new brightly colored berry or when their Neanderthal family had outgrown their starter cave and needed to move into a swanky new cave presently occupied by a T-Rex or a big, nasty, pre-historic cave bear.

The phrases reportedly constitute the exchange between Adam and Eve when God showed up asking what had happened to His apple tree. In fact, those two phrases form the gist of the sacred documents of several of the world's major religions:

Supplicant: "I really don't think this is a good idea."

Deity: "Nonsense, you'll be fine."

It can be shown that the encourager is correct roughly forty-eight percent of the time and incorrect equally as often. The remaining four percent depend on semantics: Encouragers tend to employ much more flexible definitions of the word "fine".

Just about midway through history between King Saul handing David a helmet and pointing him at Goliath ("You'll be fine!") and the crew of Apollo 13 strapping themselves to a rocket pointed at the Moon, all the young men in what was more or less Britain were packing up and heading for knightly tryouts at King Arthur's place. One young man in particular, Thomas of Fogbottom, soon to be called The Hesitant, turned to his mother and said, "I really don't think this is a good idea, Mum."

To which she replied, "Nonsense, you'll be fine."

Like every other case where those fateful phrases have been spoken at each other, Thomas had about a fifty-fifty chance of doing fine. Plus or minus two percent. And depending on what you mean by "fine".

But lest we get ahead of ourselves: Thomas hasn't protested yet, and his mother, at this moment, would in fact advise Thomas against the idea she'll shortly embrace. At this moment, all is well. Or, at least, as well as can be expected. The land is dying. The ground lies fallow. The livestock languish. Thomas's family has been eating a kind of bread made from things you would be surprised to know a person can eat. Suffice it to say Thomas's mother is rather creative in the kitchen, though "creative" isn't the word Thomas would use.

There's an evil Baron around the bend and up the hill who owns these lands and has storehouses full of real grain. He could open those storehouses and feed the people who work his fields. He hasn't. And no one's asked. He's rather scary in a throw-you-in-the-dungeon-and-let-you-think-about-how-good-you-really-have-it sort of way. He's got a strong sense of boundaries, meaning there's a line on one side of which there's everything that's his, and on the other side there's everything that's anyone else's. He respects that line, and makes sure his people respect it too. The problem is all the stuff anyone would want is on his side of the line.

There's a point, however, where even an evil Baron isn't scary enough to keep a man's empty stomach looking at things objectively. The stomach looks at the Baron, then looks at the swelling storehouses and says to the man, "Go for it. You'll be fine."

Someone who is not Thomas is going to head up that hill soon to talk to the Baron, but here we're getting ahead of ourselves again. At this moment, Thomas is standing in the Baron's stable with his eyes closed and his arm outstretched. He's supposed to be using that shovel and wheelbarrow over there to collect all the... Let's call it "fertilizer". But Thomas has a dream, and being a dream and doing what dreams do, it tends to take Thomas away from the practical tasks essential to a community's well-being. Instead it whispers to him of grander ways of tending to said well-being – ways that involve more accolades for Thomas and less direct contact with fertilizer.

Thomas dreams of being a hero, and in Thomas's time, where Thomas lives, this means being a knight. He's got his eyes closed and his hand outstretched because he recently heard a story that described how one of these hero-knights came by his noble and loyal steed. The steed, said the story, chose the knight, not the other way around. Thomas is waiting to see which noble and loyal steed will choose him.

CHAPTER I

MY KINGDOM FOR A HORSE

Even with his eyes shut tight, the day was bright enough that Thomas could make out forms shifting and moving around him. His ears picked up little sounds his brain normally ignored: his breath, straw sliding under hooves, leather creaking. Thomas, hand stretched out before him, began to slowly turn.

"Noble steed and loyal friend," he said. "At the start and at the end..." Thomas took a deep breath, shut his eyes tighter, and whispered, "Choose me."

There was a nicker and then clearly the sounds of a horse walking straight toward him. Thomas's heart pounded. A head nudged his one raised hand and snorted. He smiled and opened his eyes.

When Thomas imagined a horse, certain images came to mind. He imagined trotting through town, galloping through forests, flashing between trees, hurtling creeks and crevices, knocking armed enemies flat. The animal under Thomas's hand might've handled the trotting through town part adequately, years ago, but it was doubtful.

Thomas slumped and his smile slid sideways. "Booker," he said.

Booker was aging, gray, and not the kind of animal any artist was ever going to paint underneath a knight. He was small for a horse, carried a big belly, and always seemed to have something coming out of his disproportionate nostrils. Flies love horses in general, but Booker was special. Flies loved Booker the way seagulls love the beach.

"Booker, this is serious. You're messing it up." Thomas patted him on the shoulder. When he turned to lead him to a stall, he spotted his brother in the doorway. Thomas froze.

William Immanuel Farmer. A year older, a head taller, and a species apart. Life for William just seemed to work. Mum and Dad loved him, girls adored him, everyone wanted to be his friend. He worked the same stables as Thomas, but always seemed to be clean. On the rare occasion when he wasn't clean, even the dirt on him was somehow endearing.

William put down a bucket and began to clap.

"Good show. At the start and at the end, eh? I know something you're going to get in the *end* if you don't get all these horses back in their stalls."

Thomas's face went bright red. He hated when it did that.

At the sound of William's voice, Solstice whinnied and went to him. Solstice was the opposite of Booker. Solstice was big and strong and snow white. He looked like he stepped out of the painting into which Booker would never be painted. This was the horse Thomas had hoped would move under his hand. But Solstice was beautiful, and everything beautiful loved William.

"What were you doing anyway?"

"Nothing," said Thomas, and tried to mean it. Most of the Farmer family didn't go in much for dreams, despite the fact that William was theirs.

2

William sized him up. "Alright then, if it's that way. But you're going to get us all in trouble with the Baron if you keep messing around. Dad will have your hide." He led Solstice to his stall. "So cut it out."

"Why are you dressed like that? Are we going to Mass?"

William had on a full-length brown robe, with a hood. Full-length robes weren't for working stables. Full-length robes, as far as Thomas could tell, were for impressing God, your neighbors, and girls. And not necessarily in that order.

"*We're* not going anywhere," said William, and clammed up.

While Thomas hated talking about Thomas, William loved talking about William. Failure to immediately divulge his plans with the merest prodding was, for William, unheard of, and made Thomas dreadfully curious.

"Well, then, where are *we* not going?"

William looked up the hill. "Nowhere."

Thomas looked up the hill too, then quickly back at William. "You're not."

"I am."

"You can't!"

"I have to. We're starving Thomas. All of us. Look at the fields. Someone has to do something. The Baron has to see that. He has to care about *something*."

"Oh he cares alright, cares about his treasure. He'll throw you in the dungeon William. He's not like us. The fields are proof of that. He *doesn't* care."

William just kept looking up the hill.

Thomas tried another tack. "What do Mum and Dad think?"

William didn't reply.

Thomas waited, and William still didn't say anything. He just looked at his foot and kicked the dirt a little. Which, when you grow up with someone, get beat up by them fairly regularly, and get tricked into bad bets that result in you doing their chores for a week more often than you care to admit is practically the same as just coming out and saying it:

"You didn't tell them," said Thomas now both shocked and fascinated.

William continued to say nothing which confirmed to Thomas he was right.

"I have to tell them," said Thomas.

"You won't."

"I will," said Thomas. William was beginning to scare him.

"It doesn't matter. I have to try."

Thomas shot a look up the hill at the Baron's keep, as if it were a wild beast you had to keep your eye on. "Don't do it William." And then Thomas used a word seldom spoken between brothers.

"Please," said Thomas, "don't do it."

They looked at each other. Thomas knew saying "please" meant admitting he cared – a dangerous thing for a boy his age to do.

William hugged him and walked off toward the castle.

Thomas watched him go. He couldn't believe what he was seeing. What did William think was going to happen? Did he think he could charm the Baron?

He's going to get himself killed.

The thought settled on Thomas with a cold chill. Frantic, he rounded up the remaining horses and raced down the hill toward their home on the other side of the village.

Brown fields. Skinny, dizzy cattle. Small, scraggly weeds. It all flew by in a blur. Thomas leapt a low wooden fence and picked up his pace on the hard-packed road that ran from the Baron's hilltop fortress to the village below.

More brown. Less cattle. More weeds. One of the last cows opened its mouth to say "moo" at him, but all that came out was a pathetic sort of "muh." And then he was careening through town.

Like the fields, town was mainly a blur of brown. Unlike the fields, it required a lot of dodging. The inhabitants of the town had a much wider vocabulary than the cows, and they used it to tell Thomas exactly what they thought of him as he bounced off brown carts, startled brown mules, and panicked brown-clothed people who dropped their brown bundles in the brown dirt.

Thomas tossed out apologies and tried his best to cause as little havoc as possible as he dashed up alleys and down side streets.

He rounded the final bend, prepared for a final sprint out of town, and stopped dead in his tracks when he spotted the peacock.

CHAPTER II

THE PEACOCK

Many people suspect the village of Fogbottom gets its name from the way the fog settles, especially in winter, at the feet of its surrounding hills and ridges. Others suppose this idea is correct, because they haven't been able to come up with anything better. Suffice it to say there isn't much that is terribly unusual about Fogbottom, and there certainly aren't any peacocks roaming about.

There was a pink-footed goose that got into Old Lady Applebutter's fruit cellar one Christmas. He didn't come out the way he went in.

In any case, the only reference Thomas had for a peacock was a collection of bright, mismatched feathers and an illustration carried by a traveling merchant who had wandered into town a few years ago. The merchant had also carried a frond as long as William. He said he'd received it as a gift from the one and only Uther Pendragon as thanks for locating a rare and exquisite gift for a lady friend. Uther, of course, had got it straight from the tail of a cockatrice, right before the lizard-bird caught sight of its reflection in Uther's smooth and polished shield and consequently turned itself to stone.

When Fogbottom's Parson told the merchant the frond looked like a rotting version of a leaf he'd seen on a palm tree in the Holy Land, the merchant said he'd never been so insulted, packed up his things and left the same day.

The point, of course, is that the man standing in front of Thomas, hammering the poster into the town's bulletin board, didn't look anything like, and was in fact not, a peacock, though he was quite colorful.

He wore a pair of thick wooden shoes painted green and decorated with stars, yellow britches, and a blue, knee-length doublet with wide short sleeves exposing a long-sleeved orange tunic beneath. A long line of silver buttons marched up the doublet's sleeves serving no purpose whatsoever. A yellow cape was fastened to his epaulets and a long pointed hood hung nearly to his derrière. A red tri-cornered hat topped off the ensemble, and a thick white plume topped off the hat. He was, of course, a herald, and he'd come from Camelot by way of several other villages where he'd delivered the same news, answered the same questions, endured the same gawking stares, and generally suffered for want of a good chamomile and a vigorous foot rub.

The peacock turned and cleared its throat.

"Hear ye, hear ye," it began.

The scene resolved itself in Thomas's vision with a nearly audible whoosh. He noticed for the first time a pair of armed guards to either side of the pea–... of the herald. They wore steel caps on their heads and a kind of tightly fitted drape made out of tiny metal rings that began under the cap, hugged the neck, ran down over the shoulders and trunk, then split and fastened around the thighs. Tapered short swords dangled at their hips, round shields hung on their arms, and boredom sat on their shoulders. Three gold crowns emblazoned the shields on a blue field.

Thomas's eyes came to rest on the emblem. "Camelot," he whispered.

"Look at all that metal," said a voice on Thomas's left.

He turned to find Smitty gaping unabashedly at the guards. Smitty was the village's farrier. If you collected all the iron in Fogbottom outside the Baron's residence, melted it and poured ingots, you'd have a handful of unhappy, shoeless mules and not much else.

In the time it had taken for Thomas to catch his breath and figure out what was going on, a crowd had gathered. Everyone who passed by stopped to gape at the spectacle, and word was spreading. People came out of every alley and byway to join the throng. Impromptu assemblies were nothing new for the Herald, but they were for Fogbottom. Church Mass would be the closest experience, but at Mass there were rules to follow and clear expectations.

While the Fogbottomtons busied themselves with figuring out where to stand and glancing at each other uneasily, the herald unfolded a tiny, hinged platform and stepped up onto it. It raised him about a foot above the crowd – enough for everyone to see his face. He unfurled a scroll and from then on paid it no attention.

"Hear ye, hear ye," cried the herald, "let it be known across the land and in all quarters that on the occasion of the wedding of King Arthur Pendragon, son of Uther, to the Lady Guinevere, daughter of King Leodegrance, one month hence, King Arthur does hereby pledge to suffer a request, one from each family, for all in his kingdom. Be ye neither ashamed nor hesitant in supplication, for the King wishes it be known that his Highness loves only God and his new Queen more than thee. Glory be to God, to King Arthur, and to Camelot."

The herald re-furled the scroll with a flick of his wrist, picked up his platform, and nodded to his guards. As they turned to leave, a man in the crowd cleared his throat and said, "Pardon, but what was it exactly, the part about the..."

The herald raised an eyebrow.

"So there's a wedding then?" asked the man.

The herald sighed.

"The king," he started, then paused.

Some members of the crowd nodded, so he continued, "is marrying Lady Guinevere." He paused again.

There was no reaction from the crowd.

"Arthur's true love."

"Aah," said the crowd.

"The wedding is one month from now, and the king is allowing one person from each family to appear before him with a request."

The Fogbottomtons eyed him suspiciously.

"Seriously?" said someone.

The herald nodded, "Seriously." Then he shrugged, picked up his platform, turned, and walked away.

"What kind of request, exactly?" shouted a woman.

Still with his back to them, the herald yelled, "Anything you want, within reason of course." He held up a hand in a dismissive wave and without another look, strolled out of town guards in tow.

The crowd remained, staring variously at each other, their feet, the poster the herald had left, and empty space. Then, slowly, it disassembled. One woman muttered as she departed, "Within reason, eh? That's a convenient clause isn't it? Who's reason I wonder? Not yours or mine I suppose."

"Probably King Arthur's reason," said her companion.

"And that's just it isn't it? What's a king to know about what is and isn't *reasonable*? If I had a farthing for every time a royal wanted to give me something reasonable..."

But Thomas had ears only for the herald's message which he was replaying over and over in his head. The rest of the Fogbottomtons had returned to the things they were doing, but Thomas remained rooted some distance from the poster. With the herald gone, and the town bustling about as usual, he could almost convince himself he'd imagined it all. But there, across the way, was the poster. He blinked at it, but it stayed put. Swallowing, he walked up to it.

Thomas, unlike most of his fellow villagers, could read fairly well. Of course, the poster had been made to be as widely comprehensible as possible, which is to say: There were lots of pictures.

One illustration in particular caught Thomas's eye. It was of a man wearing a crown, surrounded by a dozen knights whose suits of armor made the herald's guards look dangerously underdressed. The king had his hands raised and outstretched over a commoner kneeling before him. Behind the king were stacks and stacks of fruit baskets, bread boxes, and other unidentifiable but assumedly delightful treats. There were also sheep, oxen, and horses behind the king. There was also a very long queue of people behind the kneeling man. Rather than bringing gifts to the king, the supplicants were receiving gifts from him.

In the bottom, right corner there was a map with a castle in the center marked "Camelot." Several outlying towns were labeled with names unfamiliar to Thomas. Beyond them was a mark indicating, presumably, Fogbottom and the words, "You are here." An arrow pointed from Fogbottom to Camelot.

Thomas stared at that arrow for a long time. Then he walked home.

CHAPTER III

FAMILY

Thomas's young sister, Elizabeth Abigail, spotted him coming down the lane. "Thomas!" she shouted, and came skipping toward him. Mr. Farmer was out splitting wood for the hearth. He glanced their way and went back to his task.

"Any news from town?" she asked.

"Um, maybe," he replied.

She pulled him down to her by his sleeve and whispered, "Grandma lost her tooth."

"And that's her last one isn't it?" Thomas said with a wink while his mind raced trying to figure out how to broach the subject of the herald with his parents.

"Shh!" She patted her chest, and Thomas noticed a cord hanging from her neck and disappearing into her dress. "I've got it right here."

Thomas reeled back, horrified, "Got what? Her tooth?"

"Yes!" she said, and skipped to the door giggling. Thomas picked up an armful of wood and followed her in.

Grandma Farmer was snoring on a chair in the corner

under a pile of blankets. Mrs. Farmer was leaning over a pair of cooking pots that dangled above the fire. The cottage smelled of broth.

Elizabeth announced, "Thomas is home!"

Grandma Farmer sat up with a start. "Just resting my eyes," she said.

Mrs. Farmer said, "Good, he can help me with the soup."

Contrary to popular belief, most cooking in the Middle Ages was indeed edible and could be, on occasion, quite tasty. Men and women have tongues as far back as history records, so things that people eat tend to be if not palatable at least not repulsive – even when the times don't lend themselves to culinary refinement.

Thomas's time was one of those unrefined times. It is true that some of the best inventions arise from such environments. Unfortunately for Thomas, none of them arose from the environment of Mrs. Farmer's kitchen.

The bread could be chewed if you soaked it in the soup. The soup could be swallowed if you diluted it with the bread. That's about as clever as it got. We don't need to talk about the strained beans.

Thomas grimaced, but headed dutifully toward the soup.

There was something in there.

Thomas leaned as far over the fire as he could bear and peered into the kettle. He stirred from the bottom, and tried not to breathe the flavored steam rolling up past him and out the chimney.

There were definitely bits of something floating around in there.

"Mum," said Thomas not sure he really wanted to know, "what's in the soup?"

He didn't have to look, he could tell just by the sound of her voice that she was standing taller when she said, "Your father caught a hare this morning."

"Huh," said Thomas.

"What did you say?" said Elizabeth as one hand tucked the tooth back inside her dress.

"I said you father caught a hare this morning. Probably the only one left in Fogbottom."

"You're cooking", said Elizabeth, and each word came out of her mouth as if it was ashamed of being in the room with the others, "bunny soup." It wasn't so much a question as an accusation. Thomas stopped stirring.

The door opened, and in stepped Mr. Farmer with another armful of wood. He hobbled over to a basket near the fire, laid his logs on the stack, and turned to find Elizabeth glaring at him, brow furrowed, and lips tight.

"What?" said Mr. Farmer.

Elizabeth's chin began to quiver. Her eyes welled up, and then she burst into tears. She turned and climbed up the ladder to the loft, flounced down on her bed, caught her stuffed bunny up in her arms and cried to it, "Oh Alice!"

"What just happened?"

"There's something in the soup," said Thomas.

Mr. Farmer beamed. "I know! I couldn't believe my eyes when I went and checked the trap this morning and found a–"

His face froze. "Oh," he said.

"I won't eat it!" cried a small voice from above. "You can't make me!"

Mr. Farmer looked up the ladder, and for a moment Thomas thought his father might climb up there and talk to her. Then he saw the weight of the year's hardships settle on him. He slumped. He limped over to the table and sat down.

"Then you'll go hungry," he said.

"It's time she gave up that old, dirty thing anyway," said Mrs. Farmer.

The comment elicited a loud wail from Elizabeth, who threw herself down, buried her face in Alice and continued to cry.

Thomas resumed stirring the soup, though now he felt like something of a criminal by association. Elizabeth's muffled sobs grabbed his heart and squeezed.

Grandma Farmer snorted and woke herself up from another nap.

"What's for dinner?" she asked.

Elizabeth wouldn't come down. Thomas thought about trying to convince her it was chicken, but knew she'd ask where they'd got one and for that he didn't have an answer. They'd eaten their last chicken some time ago. It had been delicious.

It was horrible timing, but he couldn't keep it in any longer.

"Dad," said Thomas. He continued to stir the soup, not because it needed it, but because Mrs. Farmer required it. It also made a decent prop for pretending to be nonchalant, which Thomas now desperately tried to do.

Mr. Farmer grunted.

"There was a herald in town today."

Everyone stopped what they were doing. Even Grandma Farmer, who had been doing nothing, stopped doing nothing and started now to fidget.

Thomas stared hard at the soup.

"A *herald*?" asked Mrs. Farmer.

"The conscription's beginning then," started Mr. Farmer. "I knew it would come to this."

Mrs. Farmer faced Mr. Farmer. "You knew what would come to this?"

"The war! It's time we showed 'em what's for if you ask me."

"Show who what's for? What are you talking about old man?" Mrs. Farmer stared at Mr. Farmer as though she'd just spotted a bug in her bread – that is to say, with a mixture of exasperation and familiarity. Thomas wondered how she managed to pull that look off fresh every time the subject of the war came up. The particular conflict Mr. Farmer referenced had ended decades ago but lived on in his gimpy left leg. Mr. Farmer's injury served him sometimes as an excuse, more often as a medal of honor, but always as a reminder of:

"The French," he said, spitting the word out like it was some of Mrs. Farmer's hare soup.

"What did the herald say?" It was Elizabeth's voice. Thomas looked up to see her peering over the edge of the loft. Her eyes were puffy and red and her cheeks were stained with tear tracks. She rubbed at them and sniffed.

Grandma Farmer butted in, "I'm sure it was nothing important. Time for dinner!"

Everyone looked at her.

"Worth a try," she mumbled to herself as she shrugged and sat back down.

"The herald," said Thomas, "was there to announce King Arthur's wedding."

Elizabeth gasped.

"It's about time," said Mrs. Farmer.

"I knew he wasn't right in the head," said Mr. Farmer.

Mrs. Farmer glared.

"And," said Thomas, "he said because of the wedding, people could go to Camelot and ask for things, like I don't know, to be made a knight or something."

Thomas couldn't remember the last time his father had looked as closely at him as he was now. Mrs. Farmer slowly turned to face Thomas. Elizabeth's jaw dropped open with a nearly audible pop. Grandma Farmer looked from one person to the next.

In a voice that was clearly calmer than the owner, Mr. Farmer asked "What, *exactly*, did the herald say?"

❦

Mr. Farmer wanted to go to Camelot and ask for a sword. Mrs. Farmer wanted to go to Camelot and ask for a cow. Elizabeth wanted to go to Camelot and elicit a proclamation for the protection of wild rabbits. Grandma Farmer wanted nothing to do with any of it. She said the Baron of Fogbottom and his son were enough nobility for anyone for a lifetime.

Thomas thought they were all dreaming far too small. "Think of the things I could do for Fogbottom," he said.

"Well, I'm going and that's final," said Mr. Farmer.

"You can't go," said Mrs. Farmer, exasperated. "You can barely hobble across the yard. Unless you've been hiding a horse somewhere I don't know about?"

"Where would I hide a horse?" He said it like a man who clearly had plenty of hiding places, none of which, unfortunately, actually held a horse. "Well, you can't go either. Who would do the..." He gestured as he tried to find the right words. "...the things you do in the kitchen, and wash the clothes, and take care of Elizabeth – all those things you do?"

That was the closest thing to a compliment Mrs. Farmer was likely ever to get from Mr. Farmer. She blushed.

"Well *I'm* not going," said Grandma Farmer. "And if it was up to me—"

"Someone has to go," interrupted Thomas. "When will we ever get a chance like this again?"

Mrs. Farmer began doling out bowls of soup and setting them on the table.

"Royals marry all the time," said Grandma. "They have more true loves before breakfast than a normal person has in a lifetime."

Thomas had been breaking off hunks of bread and setting them beside the bowls of soup. He slammed the last one down. "Arthur's not like that!"

Mr. Farmer hit the table.

"Enough, Thomas! I know you want to be a hero. I know you want to dress up in shining armor and go save the world from... from what? Dragons? How about saving us all from your ridiculous notions? We can't eat dreams Thomas. We can't wear hope to keep us warm. Sometimes being a hero is as simple as passing on bread when there's not enough to go around."

Thomas quickly counted the hunks of bread and gave a mental sigh of relief when the number came out right.

Mr. Farmer took a moment to calm down.

"Talking to royals is always dangerous." As he spoke, Thomas was getting a horrible feeling of déjà vu. "If it's a job for anyone, it's a job for your brother. He can ask Arthur to appeal to the Baron to open up those storehouses of grain he's sitting on."

"Ah, there we go," said Mrs. Farmer. "If anyone can handle Camelot, it's William." An idea dawned on her. "Maybe William could be a knight," she said.

"But it was my idea," protested Thomas.

"Don't be silly Thomas," said Mrs. Farmer. "You're too young." Thomas and his mother both knew he was only a year younger than William. Thomas had to bite his lip though. The last thing he wanted was to be compared to William again. He never won that contest.

"Besides," she said, "Camelot is no place for a boy to be on his own." Thomas wanted to say that Camelot seemed like the perfect place for a boy to be on his own, but he kept his mouth shut and brooded. This hadn't gone at all how he'd hoped, but it wasn't far from what he'd expected.

They sat down at the table. Thomas stared at the empty space where William usually sat. The quiet, uneasy feeling he'd gotten earlier was now a great, big, dreadful feeling sitting on his chest.

Mr. Farmer noticed the empty space too. He chewed for a moment, swallowed and said, "Where is William, I wonder?"

An unidentifiable sound escaped Thomas. He clamped his hands over his mouth. Everyone looked at him.

"Thomas?" said Mr. Farmer who was now very calm which meant that inside he wasn't very calm at all. He put down his spoon. "Do you know something about where William might be?"

"He told me not to say." Thomas knew that wouldn't hold any water with his father, but now at least he could tell William he had tried to do his brotherly duty.

The cottage was dead silent. Mr. Farmer didn't move a muscle, but the temperature of the air around him went up a good five degrees.

"He-went-to-the-Baron-to-ask-him-to-open-the-store-houses-so-the-village-can-have-food," blurted Thomas. He cringed and shut his eyes tight.

Mr. Farmer said, "Pardon?"

Thomas opened his eyes and tried again, slower, "William said he was going to ask the Baron to open the storehouses so the village can stop starving to death."

Mr. Farmer raised his eyebrows, "Did he now?"

There was a thump behind them.

Grandma, who'd been snoring again, woke with a start. "Someone get the door!"

"There's no one at the door Grandma. Mum's just fainted."

Mr. Farmer had been proud at first. He'd revived Mrs. Farmer and reassured her William could handle himself. Mrs. Farmer would have none of it. She wanted Mr. Farmer to head straight up there and stop him. Mr. Farmer refused. "You've got to let them grow up sometime," he'd said.

"It's a horrible idea," said Mrs. Farmer, to which Mr. Farmer replied, "Nonsense, he'll be fine."

But time passed, and William didn't return.

When the sun set on the day after William's disappearance, Mr. Farmer stopped speaking. Mrs. Farmer pleaded with neighbors who expressed their condolences and politely declined to form a mob and storm the Baron's keep. While they all knew and loved William dearly, they preferred their heads attached to their necks, thank you very much. At dinner on the second day, there was a knock on the cottage door.

"Who's fainted now?" said a startled Grandma Farmer.

"No one's fainted," said Mrs. Farmer. "It's the door," she said, staring at it and wringing her hands.

Mr. Farmer set his jaw, strode resolutely to the door, and pulled it open.

It was a messenger from up the hill. He was dressed not unlike the guards that had accompanied the herald from Camelot, but the messenger's mail tunic was not nearly as polished, he lacked the steel cap, and the only color he wore was a kind of bib with the Baron's crest: a white crescent moon on a red field. His boots looked liked they'd been trying to fall apart for years, a process that had been forestalled by the addition of a buckle and strap at each potential breach.

"Mr. and Mrs. Farmer?" asked the messenger.

"Yes," they said.

"Parents and or Guardians of one, William Immanuel Farmer of," He paused, scanned the outside of the cottage and glanced up the lane. "...of this here cottage?" He was sweating.

"Yes," said Mrs. Farmer, and she choked back a sob.

"Your son has been imprisoned on the grounds of failure to comply. In the event of his execution, his effects shall be returned minus any charges due for services rendered relating to said internment. Good day."

As he turned to leave, Grandma Farmer shouted from inside the cottage, "Is that Wendsley Hunter I hear?"

Wendsley stopped. "Grandma Farmer?"

She appeared at the door and pushed a distraught Mrs. Farmer to the side. "Wendsley Cheston Hunter," she said and looked him up and down. "Look at you in the Baron's employ, all dressed up in his livery. I knew you'd turn out."

Wendsley blushed now and sweated even more. "Man's gotta put food on the table somehow, isn't that right?"

"Looks like the table isn't where you've been putting the food Wendsley." And then she poked him right in the belly just beneath where the mail tunic stopped.

Wendsley recoiled. This wasn't how an internment notice was supposed to go. "Now see here," he started.

"You see here," snapped Grandma brandishing her poking finger. "You take care of my boy William or I'll be talking to your nana next week at pots 'n kettles."

Alexander Shuttlecock's *From Fidchell to 12 Man Morris, A Complete Reference of Pre-Modern Lawn and Table Games* describes Pots and Kettles as an "odd activity involving, rather than symbolic markers, actual pots and real kettles. The problem with Pots and Kettles was that the participants usually played for keeps. Having lost their kitchen tools, the losers tended to die from the ingestion of undercooked meats while the winners were invariably accused of robbery and hung."

Wendsley recovered himself as best he could, nodded to Mr. and Mrs. Farmer, said "Good day" again and made off up the lane. He looked back twice. Each time Grandma Farmer poked in the air at him, and each time Wendsley picked up his pace until finally he was out of sight.

"When I was teaching that boy his letters I told his mum, 'This one could go either way.'" She shook her head and headed back to her chair. Mrs. Farmer huddled at the table sobbing. Elizabeth went and hugged her mum. Mr. Farmer stood in the open doorway, staring up the lane. He stood there for a long time.

"Winter's coming," he said, then stepped out, closed the door and headed to the wood pile to split some more logs.

Thomas stood in the middle of the cottage floor watching it all and feeling like he wasn't really there. He hoped it was all an awful dream. He hoped he'd wake up soon and life would be back to its normal, boring, uneventful self. It didn't happen. Instead, he went to bed later that evening and laid there feeling like the cottage had a big hole in it. Sometime before he was completely asleep, he realized that despite how frustrating it was to live in his brother's shadow, William had been *his* dream too.

"I really don't think this is a good idea, Mum."

"Nonsense, you'll be fine."

Thomas squinted through the window.

"What's Dad doing?"

"He's making a gift for you," said Mrs. Farmer as she stuffed hunks of stale bread into a satchel. She looked pale, and Thomas noticed her hands were shaking.

Mr. Farmer burst through the door holding up a squarish sort of flat thing made mostly of pine and held together with leather straps. He beamed at Thomas.

"What's that?"

"What's this? 'What's this?' he says. It's a shield, my boy. Wants to be a knight and doesn't even know the tools when he sees 'em."

Thomas took the shield from his father and turned it over. Sure enough, there was a strap on the inside for his arm so he could wear the thing. One of the pine branches was oozing sap.

"I tell you what, if we'd had gear like that at Bristlington there'd be a hundred men still alive to tell you you're looking at a fine piece of work. Fine piece of work, that is."

Mrs. Farmer handed Thomas the bag of bread and a tin of beans she'd packed. She tightened the straps on the pig leather jerkin they'd presented him with that morning, and Mr. Farmer showed him how to sling the shield over his shoulder for travel.

"I've got one more, hold on." Mr. Farmer went back outside. Shortly, they could hear grinding noises. It sounded as if something metal was being tortured.

Thomas looked at his mother. She smiled and wrung her hands. She still looked pale. Thomas stayed rooted to his spot, afraid of what Mr. Farmer was going to come through the door with next.

The grinding noises stopped abruptly and in came Mr. Farmer with the bottom half of a small kettle.

"Dad."

"Your helmet!"

"Dad," Thomas sighed. "It's a kettle."

Grandma Farmer hollered from her chair near the fire, "You aren't messing with my pots, are ya?"

"No ma'am!" Mr. Farmer hollered back, then put his finger to his lips and looked Thomas in the eye. He put the kettle on Thomas's head, closed one eye, then rotated the kettle a quarter-turn and said, "There."

He looked proud.

"Dad."

"Shhhh."

Mr. Farmer pushed Thomas out the door. Mrs. Farmer and Elizabeth followed.

"So," said Thomas, "suddenly this is a good idea? Me going to Camelot?"

"It was always a good idea," said Mr. Farmer. "It just hadn't found its feet yet."

Thomas pushed the kettle back up on his forehead where it had slipped down.

"What about a sword? Don't knights have swords?"

"Well you're not a knight, are ya? These things are for protection. You're not getting in any fights, and if you do get in one your job is to get out of it."

"Dad, there's going to be a lot of kids there going for knighthood and—"

"Exactly. A lot of dumb kids. You're going to appeal to Arthur for your brother. No more, no less. Got it?"

Thomas was not looking forward to this at all.

"Got it," he said.

Elizabeth threw herself at Thomas and hugged his leg fiercely.

"Don't worry, 'Lizbeth. I'll be back soon." Thomas had no idea if it was true, but felt like it was one of those things you're supposed to say.

She looked at him with teary eyes and said nothing.

Mrs. Farmer pulled her away, and Mr. Farmer walked Thomas a few paces away.

"Right then, keep yer chin up, don't take any guff and don't give none neither. You'll be fine."

Mr. Farmer said it like he was trying to convince himself. He patted Thomas awkwardly on his back.

Thomas spotted William's walking stick leaning against the cottage. He picked it up and started down the lane.

"You'll be fine!" yelled his mother.

"Depends on what you mean by 'fine' I guess," said Thomas to himself and followed the lane into the forest.

CHAPTER IV

A MISPLACED STONE

In the forest between Camelot and Thomas's home in Fogbottom, there's a spot where the road crosses a stream via a tiny bridge. It's barely wide enough for a cart's wheels, and a man could cross it in three long steps. A horse could leap it easily. A stream burbles below it, tumbling smaller rocks on a long, slow journey from mountaintop to ocean. Larger rocks make their way too, but require more forceful persuasion provided by the occasional spring flood and summer thundershower. But Thomas came here in autumn, and autumn is normally a different story. By then most folk, including Mother Nature, have settled down and things will tend to stay put for a bit. In autumn, a person can get a handle on how things lie before the world goes and gets itself all shaken up again.

In the water, just past the bridge on the downstream side, there's a particularly stubborn stone. The small rocks, the ones that tumble easily and occasionally appear even to float, might take a generation or two to move along their course. The larger, most reluctant rocks measure their trip in miles per century. No one knows exactly how long this particular stone has been sitting there, but all of the rocks further downstream, big and small, can tell you stories about the time they passed that stone. Most of the stories are not terribly exciting; they are rocks after all, and I wouldn't recommend trying to interview them all for the one or two tales that are worth hearing. A person could go crazy talking to rocks like that.

In any case, our stone didn't come from the mountaintop like most of its neighbors. In fact, it came from the same place as the other stones that were placed to make the bridge, as is evident by its color, shape and texture – a rough, gray, cube-ish sort compared to the stream's smooth, brown, rounded lot. There's also a rather conspicuous gap on top of the bridge's downstream wall which could lead one to believe the stone was somehow knocked loose, perhaps in a struggle or by a bored miscreant, and that it fell and landed at or close to its current position. These are all plausible theories that are nevertheless incorrect. This stone was left here on purpose. Nature has managed to budge it twice in its lifetime.

Further downstream, there's a fishing village. There's not much to say about the village, it's the kind of village you barely notice and soon forget if you're the sort of person who travels in order to get somewhere specific. One morning, a child in the village woke up early and was standing on the beach staring rapt at a bright red sky when he noticed three shapes on the horizon. They were Viking ships, and they were headed his way. The child yelled a warning, then knelt on the very spot he'd been standing and began to pray. As the morning aged, the villagers prepared to flee, but the child could not be persuaded to move. Finally, his father came and picked him up to carry him away. By now, the ships were all in a line just beneath where our stream empties into the sea via a small waterfall. At the moment the child's knees left the sand, a great wall of water, rock and debris flooded over the fall, smashed the ships, and drowned the Viking raiders to the last man. Back at the bridge, the misplaced stone flipped over once, onto its side.

As you can imagine, the flood was quite disruptive in regards to the forest creatures that made their living along the stream. Many went missing that day, including the only son of a royal toad family. Years passed, then one day a wise and learned toad, who'd spent many hours talking to rocks, came to the King and Queen and told them of the once-rolled stone near the man-bridge. On the spot, the King ordered a construction crew to assemble at the stone and heave it over. The toads flipped the stone from its side to its bottom, its second and final budging, and out popped the Prince of Toads none the worse for wear. He explained he'd been surveying the area as a site for his future court, and that it had really been quite comfortable swaddled in mud down there under the stone though dreadfully boring. He then requested some breakfast, which was brought to him immediately. The wise, old toad revealed that the whole affair had saved the Prince's life by protecting him from the machinations of his evil half-brother who wanted the crown for himself, and had died just the week before by choking on a dragonfly. The Prince became a great king in his time, and ruled justly and mercifully from his court on the stone.

As it turns out, something special had happened on the day the bridge was completed: An event inspired the wife of the bridge-builder to prophesy about the misplaced stone. As the builder was dropping the last stone, our stone, into place on top of the downstream wall, a black knight came upon him. "If you're finished with your labor, good sir, take arms and fight me for the glory of your Lady," he said, pointing at the builder's wife. The builder swallowed, wiped his hands on his shirt and looked at his wife, who clasped her hands to her mouth and shook her head in fear. A short grinding sound issued followed by a splash. They all turned to see a gap in the downstream wall of the bridge and a stone resting, upside down in the water below. "Um, I'm not quite finished yet, good knight, sir. If you could wait a moment?"

"I'm afraid I have an appointment. I beg your forgiveness good builder. I must retract my offer. And my apologies to you dear lady for I cannot afford your man the opportunity to heap glory upon you today. Sometimes these things just don't work out. Timing is everything you know, we're all very busy these days." And off he rode.

The builder and his wife sighed relief, and the builder made to fetch the misplaced stone. The wife rushed to stop him and made a great to-do about it. She went on and on about the stone, how it had saved the builder's life, how it was clearly a stone of stones and obviously enchanted. She said no one could touch the stone until "an innocent and one who would be king" had moved it. And there the stone would lie.

So you see, by the time Thomas came to the spot in the forest between his home and Camelot, where the road crosses a stream via a tiny bridge sporting a conspicuous gap on top of its downstream wall, the misplaced stone had already been emptied of most of its magic. But most is not all, and as the black knight would say, timing is everything.

CHAPTER V

THE SILVER WOLF

Thomas plodded along. He'd been traveling all day, and as the sun was setting and a full moon rising, he was still of the opinion that – well he wasn't quite sure what to think. He'd dreamt his whole life of one day being a knight and slaying dragons and rescuing princesses, and now it seemed like he could reach out and make that dream real, if only. If only William hadn't gone up that road to the Baron's keep. If only his parents would look at him for once instead of William. If only someone would believe in him. Of course now that William was in trouble, "Off you go, Thomas!"

Things had gotten very complicated very quickly. His kettle slipped down on his forehead and it set him fuming all over again. His shield was heavy and awkward and already starting to fall apart. In frustration, he took a swing at a sapling with William's walking stick and nearly tripped trying to keep the shield and helmet in place. He looked like someone pretending to be a knight, which was bad. He figured pretending to be something he actually wanted to be was just asking for it.

Thomas, son of a landless farmer, without a drop of royal blood in him, did not look forward to appearing at Arthur's court, dressed in pig skin and a few pieces of make-believe, the family fortune such as it was, and asking—

"You're not a knight," His father's voice echoed in his head. "You're going to appeal to Arthur for your brother. No more, no less. Got it?"

If only William hadn't gone up that road, Thomas thought, and he found himself right back in a big stewing pot of what-ifs.

Lost in aggravation, he found himself at a small stream. He slipped down beside the bridge that crossed it and used his makeshift helmet as a makeshift drinking vessel. As he drank, a stone in the stream caught his eye. It looked like it didn't belong: It was more like the stones that made up the bridge, and there was a conspicuous gap on the bridge's wall. Thomas picked up the stone and carried it to the bridge, slotting it into the gap where it fit perfectly.

Something came flying out of the woods onto the bridge and hammered into Thomas who had turned after dropping the stone in place just in time to be standing directly in the thing's path. There was fur, and a yelp, and a great tumble that carried both Thomas and the thing off the other end of the bridge and left them both sprawled in the road. Thomas laid still on his back for a moment, stunned, then rolled and propped himself up on one knee. He found himself eye-to-eye with a magnificent silver wolf.

The wolf was panting hard, and its left front leg was bleeding steadily from an odd, sawtooth-shaped wound. Despite its thick coat, Thomas could tell the beast was well muscled, wound tight and ready to spring. In the moonlight, its fur almost glowed, but the eyes were what caught Thomas's attention. There was more than beastly instinct behind those pale gray discs. He could read them as if they were a man's. Thomas shifted, slowly, trying to

29

appear non-threatening but positioned to defend himself. He had no intention of harming such a proud animal if it could be avoided, and he wasn't sure how the match would turn out if it were forced.

His posture must have communicated what Thomas wanted. The wolf relaxed ever so slightly and turned its attention to its previous engagement, glancing nervously past Thomas, back across the bridge. A growing rumble of hooves on ground issued from that direction, and the wolf backed a few steps down the road. And then it did a most startling thing.

It yowled. Only it wasn't so much a yowl as a plea. And it sure sounded to Thomas like the plea was the word "Help."

"Did you just–" said Thomas.

And then it was gone, racing as fast as its wounded leg would let it, into the woods.

A horse came galloping out of the trees on the other side of the bridge. Its mane flew. Its rider crouched. Moonlight glanced off helm, lance, and shield. It was a fearsome sight, half a ton of flesh and metal barely exerting itself and still moving easily twice as fast as Thomas could run. There wasn't a moment to think, and so, unencumbered by the kind of careful analysis that time affords and that generally keeps a person alive, Thomas swung his plank of wood from his back, brandished his walking stick, and squared himself in the middle of the road. On advisement from the self-preserving part of his brain, which was clearly stunned but scrambling to come up with something, Thomas shut his eyes tight.

There was a great tumult of whinnying, and yelling and pounding hooves and clanking metal in the general area in front of Thomas. A blast of dirt pelted him, stinging his skin where it was bared and sounding like a rain shower where it bounced off pig leather, wood, and kettle. A moment passed. When no impact came and Thomas determined his teeth were still inside his head, he opened an eye.

The rider sat tall in his saddle, looking down at Thomas, and made no effort to keep his amusement from his voice, "Lost your carnival have ye?"

Thomas swallowed, "My name is Thomas, Thomas of Fogbottom, and if it's the silver wolf you seek, I must petition you to give up your chase." An image of Elizabeth hugging her stuffed bunny, Alice, flitted through Thomas's mind, and he suddenly felt very foolish.

"You've seen the beast eh? I'm sworn to capture and deliver it. Give up this charade, boy, before you get hurt. Which way did the foul thing go?"

Thomas was clearly outmatched. The rider's helmet alone looked like it was worth more than all of Thomas's family's belongings put together. He carried himself well too. And though he showed no coat of arms that would indicate actual knighthood, he was clearly trained and born to it. Thomas tried to ignore the insults. He'd been treated worse, and was expecting a great deal more of these kinds of remarks upon his arrival at Arthur's court.

"Will nothing persuade you to give up your pursuit of that remarkable creature?"

"No. Now give it up, for my patience wears thin."

Thomas saw only two choices. He would either have to hand over the noblest creature he'd ever seen or stop the rider somehow. Handing it over seemed impossible, especially if Thomas had heard what he thought he'd heard. He could lie and say the wolf went in a different direction, but the rider would eventually discover it and then he would be after both of them.

Thomas had learned long ago by being William's younger brother that if you start something, you'd better at least try to finish it if you want any respect after. Though part of him couldn't believe what he was about to say, he figured now that he was in the thing the only way out was straight through.

"I can't let you pass." He knew he was in for it, but he felt proud nonetheless.

The rider shifted and said, "Well, isn't this a pickle?"

And with that, he trotted up next to Thomas, brought his pommel down on Thomas's head, and knocked him out cold.

CHAPTER VI

THE WEEPING GIANTESS

The first thing Thomas noticed was the smell. Or smells, rather – there were lots of them, and they didn't fit together like smells usually do. There was something sweet, like maple syrup, and right there next to it something ghastly. There was something soft and calm and beautiful, but then a pungent undercurrent would shove it over, as if a cat had peed on a lavender bush.

He sat up, rubbed his eyes and looked around. He was sitting on a pile of straw in the corner of a small wooden shack. There was a large rock for a pillow, which explained a terrible stiffness in his neck. In addition to a window and a cracked door, light streamed in through gaps between nearly every wallboard. The floor was dirt, and a single table and chair formed the sum of the shack's furnishings. There was a plate with a crust of bread and a clay cup with a bit of water on the table. Thomas's gear, such as it was, lay piled on the chair.

His head ached. He felt at the spot where his helmet had interceded for the rider's pommel, and his hand came away covered with sticky goo. Instinctively, he brought his hand to his nose and sniffed. In a flash Thomas was on his feet, "Mother of Mercy!" The smells were coming from this stuff on his head. He stared in horror at his hand, shoving it as far from him as anatomy would allow. He'd never in his life wished so hard for longer arms.

He grabbed the clay cup, poured the water on his hand and scrubbed to no avail. The water ran right off the goo, and he succeeded only in spreading it over both hands and up part of his arm. He surveyed the cabin for anything that might help wipe the stuff off. He settled on the straw from his bed. This ended poorly. When an old man entered through the shack's door, Thomas's hands and head were bristling. He looked like a living, breathing scarecrow.

The old man cried out and nearly dropped a whole bowl of the same goo that was on Thomas. This was a fresh batch, ripe and steaming. There must have been some horseradish in the mix. The first wave came like a battering ram and cleared a path straight through the sinuses so the second and subsequent waves could pillage the olfactories at will. The old man wore a clothespin on his nose.

"No, no, no, no, no! You must leave the ointment where I put it!" The old man backed Thomas onto the straw bed and sat him down. Thomas was a sticky, straw-covered mess. "Well, in any case, if it has to come off it's me – that is I – I'll do the... the off-coming and no one else. Unless you want Bane to be the death of you." He unwrapped an oily cloth from around his bowl of goo and set about cleaning up Thomas.

Thomas, still reeling, tried to parse it all. "You're a healer?"

"And lucky for you."

"What's bane? A plague?"

The old man paused. He peered out from behind great, bushy gray eyebrows. His eyes looked like they'd seen all of time come and go, but they sparkled with a youthful mischievousness. "Bane is the boy you met on the road."

Thomas gasped. "*The* Bane? The son of the Baron of Fogbottom... that Bane?"

"There aren't a lot of Bane's in the world I should think," said the healer who seemed to be honestly considering the question.

"But he wasn't wearing his colors... wait, you saw that?" Thomas wasn't sure which to be more embarrassed by: that he'd played a fool to the Baron's son or that it had been witnessed.

"Of course I did, saw the whole thing lucky for you," he said, pointing at Thomas's head and leaning in to wipe a tendril of goo creeping toward Thomas's ear.

"I wouldn't categorize Bane," continued the old man as he rubbed vigorously with the towel, "as a plague so much as an infection perhaps, or an irritation of the skin. If it goes untreated, these things tend to worsen. A person's parts are all connected you see, and if you don't set things straight as soon as possible—"

The old man stood back, inspected Thomas's skull then laid his towel down on the table.

"—a small problem this year can be fatal next. Little chance of getting treatment from the Baron of Fogbottom though. Fortunately for both of us, Bane and his father don't pay much attention to people like you and I. Unless..."

"Unless what?"

The old man seemed to have wandered off mentally.

"Hmmm? Oh. Unless we get in his way. Hold still."

The old man picked up his bowl and a short wooden spoon and began applying fresh goo liberally. Twice Thomas thought he'd faint. When it was done, the old man wrapped a clean cloth around Thomas's head and pronounced him fit for duty. He explained that this was most fortunate for it meant that Thomas would be able to set to work straight away paying off the healer's services and if he was quick about it, could still make Arthur's court in time for the wedding.

"Besides, we'll be helping each other. What good is a knight without a magic sword? How would it look, showing up at Arthur's, lining up with all the other, er, hopefuls, and you with nothing special about you. No real qualifications as it were. I've seen your talent lad. With that and a piece of toast, you'd have trouble serving breakfast. You've got no pedigree, no reputation. What you need is something I've got, and will gladly give if you do this thing for me, and we'll call ourselves square."

"*You* have a magic sword?"

"I sure do. But what use do I have for such a thing? It's good luck you happened along when you did too, I was thinking of taking it to Arthur's tryouts and auctioning it off. Now you owe me sure, but the task I need doing is no easy thing. I'll throw in the sword for the balance and because, well, I saw the kindness you did at the bridge, and you look like you could use a break in life. So, what do you say?"

"But I'm not," stammered Thomas, "that is, the reason I'm going isn't..."

The old man stared at him.

"The thing is – I'm not going to be a knight. I'm going to ask Arthur to pardon my brother." And then Thomas explained his family situation.

The healer listened patiently and when Thomas had finished said simply, "Rubbish."

"Pardon?" said Thomas.

"That's all rubbish. Look around, what do you see?"

"Um," said Thomas. "Well, there's the chair, the pot of goo..."

"Bah. Not in here. Come on." And he pulled him outside. "Here. What do you see?"

Thomas looked, really looked at the forest for the first time. It took him a moment, then he began to see it. The yellowing leaves, the brown and wilted ground cover, the fading wildflowers. Even the stream looked sluggish and cloudy. Directly across the water from the healer's hut was an enormous oak that at one time must have sheltered countless birds and towered as a king among trees. It was now leafless, gray, and splitting.

"The land is dying here too."

"That's right. It's dying everywhere. And let me ask you this: What good will it do if you get Arthur to tell the Baron to let your brother go?"

"Well, he can... He can help us... You know. He can help the family."

"Do what?"

"I don't know. William is quite a guy. He could..."

"I'm sure he is. But will it change the Baron? Will it solve Fogbottom's problems? Will it solve anything in any lasting way?"

The healer was reaching right down into Thomas's heart and tugging at the very thoughts he'd been working to suppress since his father set him on this course.

He frowned. "No, it won't," he said. "It'll make my family feel better, but it won't solve anything. We'll all still be starving."

"That's right. Your brother's confinement is a symptom Thomas. You've got to find the cause of the sickness and set that straight if you really want to fix anything. You've got a dream, Thomas. You have eyes to see the real problem. And you have the heart to want to fix it. Don't abandon that to please someone else."

They both stared at the dying tree for a moment. Thomas could scarcely believe this old man was articulating so clearly what boiled in his heart. If he was going to ask for knighthood – a seat at Arthur's tables – a magic sword sure would help. But William...

"So how about that sword?" asked the healer quietly.

Thomas clenched his jaw. "I'll do it," he said.

❧

As you know, King Arthur established several orders of chivalry in Camelot in addition to the Round one. The Table Round is of course the most famous, and those who sat at it were understood by all to be peers of the court and friends of the king. But there were other tables, some almost as lofty, some not so much. Among those in the not-so-lofty category, the Table of Less Valued Knights was far and away the unloftiest. The Knights of Less Valued Table were the workhorses of the court, performing the inglorious duties that are nevertheless essential to a realm's operation and taking care of any requests that the other orders found... uninteresting. Its first administrator, Sir Tuttle the Authorized, was a quiet man who'd risen to his position mainly by keeping his head down and outliving the more ambitious. The fourth rule in the Table's *Code of Service* read as follows:

Rule IV: Never Promise to do something that hasn't been Spelled out Precisely, in Advance, and preferably in Writing.

Sir Tuttle penned that rule the day Thomas agreed to take the healer's quest. Earlier in the same day, he'd written this one:

Rule II: Know your Limitations.

Sir Tuttle would've shaken his head and frowned at what was taking place by that old oak tree. And then he would have given Thomas a copy of the Code of Service with rules II and IV highlighted.

❧

As night fell, the healer sent Thomas to scrounge some kindling and then built a small fire by a stream outside the shack. They sat on stumps and watched embers float up into an impossibly starry sky while the healer puffed on a pipe and told his tale.

"This stream here is the same that flows under the bridge up yonder where you met Bane. It's old, with a history that makes a man's life look as fleeting as one of these embers." He pointed with his pipe.

"But there are things even older than this, if you can imagine it, and there was a time when the water didn't flow here at all. Giants lived here then, a whole city of them, and they worked and played, got married, had children, and raised families just like we do. They had giant carpenters that could've built one of our ships in a day. It would've been like a toy to them for their giant children who could've smashed that ship in a blink with one giant fist. Their giant masons could have built a man-sized castle a week, but they would've been little more than tourist attractions for them, what with not being able to fit inside and all. They had giant physicians to care for giant wounds, and giant priests too, to deal with giant sins.

"One day, a giantess named Gorgella came to one of the priests to make a giant confession. She'd murdered her boyfriend's other girlfriend. Well, the thing about giants is that they murdered each other left and right. They didn't have any rules about it. You might've noticed that there aren't many giants wandering around today. If someone had introduced them to the right set of precepts early on, maybe things would've turned out different. In any case, murdering her boyfriend's girlfriend wasn't the problem.

"The problem was that Gorgella had tried everything, but her boyfriend – correction: former boyfriend – didn't love her anymore. This was a terrible giant crime, to lose someone's love. Giants were known to bribe their ex-lovers until they were penniless, or even starve themselves to death to try to win back a lost love. Such efforts seldom worked. Of course you and I know the giants had it backwards, it should've been no fault to lose love, but to stop loving, now there's a crime worth confessing. Again, the right set of rules and regulations can make all the difference.

"The giant priest, in light of such a horrible confession, broke his vow of confidentiality and reported Gorgella to the giant constable. Gorgella was sentenced with banishment until and unless her boyfriend wanted her back. She was to climb to a high point on a nearby mountain and wait. Weeping, she left. She didn't bother to pack any bags or say goodbye to any friends. She thought she was a terrible, villainous giantess, because the authorities with the backwards rules told her so. She climbed the mountain, sat down, and waited.

"The boyfriend never called on her. Within five years, the entire giant population save a few stragglers passed away. Murdered each other mostly. There's no such thing as a petty squabble when you're a giant. That shouldn't be surprising; we see it in our own race too. Often times the bigger the man, the more serious he is about how his tea should be served and the more egregious the error if he gets one lump when he wanted two.

"Gorgella followed the rules though, and there she sits to this day, waiting for her boyfriend to call. Her weeping is the source of this very stream."

The healer held out a small glass bottle to Thomas. "Giant tears are wonderful stuff if you can get them straight from the source. By the time they flow down to us here, they've been filtered of the qualities that make them noteworthy. I want you to go find Gorgella and get me a bottle of her tears."

Thomas pursed his lips and took the bottle.

"You want the tears of a giantess," said Thomas, "in this bottle?"

The healer nodded.

"Can I pick you up anything else on the way? A dragon's dimple or... or a dwarf's booger maybe?"

The old man raised his eyebrows.

"Never mind," said Thomas hastily.

و

For two days, Thomas trudged upstream. Early on the second day, the land rose up and started to climb. By mid-day, he was finding it difficult to follow the water directly. When the path grew tricky, the stream was wont to throw up its hands and skip over the details by plummeting straight down, carefree and unencumbered. Never in its life had it stopped to consider the rough time it would have if it needed to go back home for a visit. It flowed in one direction, always, and while this is a proven path to worldly success, it can leave a body feeling sad and lonely and unconnected in spots. As the sun began to set and tinge the world gold, Thomas came upon one of those sad places.

Fed by a trickle on the upstream side, and relieved by a fall on the down, the water collected in a deep, glassy pool. A single, young willow grew by its edge, gripping the mountain. Its longest branches just barely brushed the water's surface. The reflected world was perfect and stunning in every portion, from the way its sky faded between golds and pinks and reds to the gentle twisting motion of the willow's leaves. No particular, big or small, was left unrepresented. It gave the illusion that the entire world was contained in that pool. A person could believe that if you came at it at the right angle, you'd see what was happening anywhere you cared, and if you stepped in, you'd be there.

Thomas got down on one knee and looked at his reflection for some time. Then he cupped his hand and moved to take a drink. When his hand disturbed the surface, the reflection broke and Thomas could see straight through to the bottom. There was an old lady down there, holding her breath and a rock the size of her head. Startled, Thomas jumped back from the pool and nearly slipped over the ledge. The surface calmed, and the perfectly reflected world slid back in, hiding the lady from view.

"She's trying to drown herself," Thomas said, working the thing through. He looked at his reflection who looked right back at him. "She's trying to drown herself!" And he plunged into the pool.

The water was only waist deep. Thomas grabbed the old lady by her shoulders and pulled her upright. Still clutching her rock with one arm, she gasped for breath and beat at Thomas with the other.

"You were trying to kill yourself!"

"And you stopped me!"

"You *want* to die?"

"If I did, I might try lying at the bottom of a pool with something very heavy on my chest."

"You're still hitting me."

"You're still here."

Thomas could see this wouldn't go anywhere if he kept coming at it head on. "I don't think your method's going to work."

"Ooh, an expert! Killed yourself a few times eh? Traveling around giving lectures on the matter are ya?"

"That's not what I—"

"Oh stuff it pipsqueak, and let me go."

"Pipsqueak?" Thomas was of average height and build but stood easily three heads taller than the old woman and twice as broad.

"You heard me. You uppity midgets have given us nothing but trouble all our lives."

"Midgets? But... Given who nothing but trouble?"

"We giants of course!"

Thomas blinked. "Gorgella?"

"Aye, and what's it to ya?"

Things, apparently, weren't what they seemed. They seldom are.

CHAPTER VII

THE HEALER'S GIFT

orgella stood on the shore of the pool wringing her clothes. "I know what you're thinking." She glared at Thomas. "You're thinking what a trophy I'd be, the last of the giants, if you could chain me up and display me outside one of your wee towns."

"That's not quite what I..." But Thomas wasn't sure how to proceed. If this woman really was Gorgella, the Weeping Giantess, the Source of the Healer's Stream, then how was he going to get a bottle of her tears. Here she was: cynical, salty, and suicidal, but clearly not weeping. If she wasn't Gorgella, then who was she and what in God's green earth was she up to? She might be mad. He decided that the wisest course in either case was caution, and the safest move was to play along.

"Madam, know that I am your servant, Thomas of Fogbottom, and I intend nothing of the sort."

"Madam? My servant is it? The boy manhandles me like a hoodlum and then tries to play the gentleman. Well tell me then, good sir," she delivered those words with a theatrical sweep of arm and rolling eyes, "what do you intend?" And then, she shrank, literally, a handbreadth. Thomas was looking right at her when it happened, but it was so quick, and so preposterous, that he couldn't be certain what had just happened. Gorgella stood very still. Her body and face were posed in a perfect image of what they'd been a moment before, but her eyes widened ever so slightly and gave her away.

Thomas broke the silence, "What just happened?"

Gorgella fell to the ground, weeping. "I'm shrinking you great fool! Can't you see? Oh what will become of me?"

Thomas knelt and tried to comfort her. "How long has this been happening?"

"I don't know, but it's speeding up. Yesterday this dress was my left sock." With that, she began to sob with heaves so great that she couldn't get any more intelligible words out. Well, here were the giant tears he needed to collect, but now that he faced it, he realized what a heartless task it had been all along. Gorgella continued to bawl. Just as she'd seem to be winding down a bit, pop! She'd shrink another bit and her sobs would start afresh. Thomas wracked his brain trying to think of anything that could cure or at least forestall such an odd condition, but he came up blank.

Presently, Gorgella stopped crying, and Thomas could see it was fear that had choked her. Her eyes were wide and crazed. She said, "It's not going to stop. I'll shrink right down to the size of a pebble, and an ant will carry me off for dinner. Or I'll keep shrinking and then what? The softest breeze could lift me up and fling me a thousand miles. You have to help me!" She made her way to the rock she'd been clutching when Thomas had found her. She was only as tall as Thomas's knee now. Her clothes, soaked with tears, had become a huge and heavy load. She strained to lift the rock and failed. She flung her hands down at her sides and pleaded in a pathetic voice, "Please, help me Thomas."

Two notions struck Thomas at once. One was that to Gorgella, soon that rock would be a mountain, and the pool a deep ocean. The other was the only hope he could conceive.

"Gorgella, I know someone who might be able to reverse this. Do you like sailing?"

It was boarding time. Thomas had constructed a tiny sailing ship made from leaves and twigs of the willow tree nearby. For ocean water, he'd wrung Gorgella's tears from her old left sock into the healer's bottle. If they had power to heal, perhaps they could help the one who'd shed them. Plus, their saltiness was a nice touch of authenticity for this makeshift ocean voyage, but Thomas kept that thought to himself.

Gorgella, now the size of a thimble, looked both anxious and excited. "You'll carry me gently?"

"I have promised so, and will promise again as many times as will convince you Gorgella. You'll be safest in here where you can't get misplaced on the journey. I've also checked the bottle for ants and breezes. There are none." He winked at her, and she gave a weak but hopeful smile in reply.

Gorgella climbed aboard the ship. "I'm ready," she said. Thomas slid her into the bottle and closed it with the stopper. He carried the bottle carefully and began making his way down the mountain.

It was slow going. The slightest misstep threw what must have seemed like tidal waves at the tiny ship in the bottle. Thomas followed the stream, checking on Gorgella from time to time. For the most part, she clung to the ship's side, looking a little ill. She was still shrinking, and before they'd reached the foothills, Thomas's fear came to fruition. He stood stock-still and scoured the ship for any sign of movement, however small. Failing that, he swallowed and searched the water. There was no sign of Gorgella anywhere. She was now too small to see.

It took three days to get back to the healer's shack near the bridge. He smelled it before he saw it: Cooked cabbage, and something like sour milk. No doubt some new wonderful and hideous balm. Though he'd carried the bottle reverently, he was certain Gorgella was lost.

When he had shown the healer the bottle and told the story of its contents, the healer held it up to the sun and said, "Oh dear, it's worse than I'd imagined."

"Is she... gone?"

"Oh no, she's in there." The healer grinned a warm grin, and his words were tinted with wonder, "Now here's something new eh? A giant in a bottle."

Thomas sighed in relief, "So you can you help her?"

The healer started and looked at Thomas, "Help her do what?"

Thomas couldn't believe his ears. "Help her back to her right size! She can't very well go around being a giant looking like that."

"I will certainly keep her safe. You can be sure of that. As for being what she is, that's Gorgella's affair. Meddling in a matter like this only makes it worse. But I promised you a reward, and you shall have it. Now sit and guard this stump while I fetch it."

The healer disappeared into his shack cradling the bottle. Thomas tried to feel excited about the gift he'd been promised, but he couldn't get past the healer's quick dismissal of Gorgella's dilemma. It'd been the hope of a cure that had kept Gorgella alive and given Thomas the strength to deliver her here in one, albeit tiny, piece.

The healer returned with a long object wrapped in a dark cloth. By now Thomas was so worked up he barely took notice of what the healer carried – the thing that a few days ago had been his best hope of achieving the only dream he'd had in his short life. "You have to help her! You're a healer! Can't you make her herself again?"

The healer paused with one hand ready to pull the veil and reveal the thing beneath. "My dear boy, looking like a thing has little to do with being a thing. Be the thing first, and you will grow to resemble it, if not in this life then when God's trumpets blow at the end of days and all of us are changed. Gorgella started out a giant, but she believed what people told her she was. In her heart, she saw herself diminished and she became so, shrinking bit by bit. Though your mind might be of one conviction and proclaim it with steep vigor, your heart will find a way to betray you. Your heart is who you are, all else follows. Guard your heart, Thomas. Guard your heart."

Then he whipped back the cloth with a flourish and handed Thomas a sword that stank like fine cheese.

Thomas groaned and held the thing at arm's length. "What is this?!"

The healer was positively beaming. "Stunning isn't it? An amazing work of enchantment if I do say so myself."

"You did this?"

"I did! Now, now, it's quite a beauty I know, but if you go on you'll embarrass me. It's my first attempt, a prototype if you will, and I'm sure there will be kinks to be found out and addressed in the next model."

"Kinks?! How can I possibly... Healer, this sword stinks!"

"Why of course! That's its charm! Just be careful where you point it when you really need it to unleash."

"I can't possibly carry this around, I'd look like the greatest fool in Camelot."

"Ah! No, no, the odor you smell will wear off. It's been in storage so long, it's just kind of built up. When you want to unleash its full fury, just hold it aloft and will it."

Thomas was unconvinced, but he pointed the thing straight up and gave it shot.

The healer pinched his nose and said, "You'll want to cover your—"

A nearly visible wave of stench knocked Thomas flat, and everything went black.

CHAPTER VIII

THE BACK OF THE LINE

The queue stretched out of the palace, through the city, beyond the gates, and down the road out of sight.

"Is this the line to receive the king's wedding gifts?" Thomas asked a stranger.

"Aye, and what'll ye be asking for, a bath?" The crowd sniggered, but Thomas kept his mouth shut and headed for the back of the line.

At the end of the line, Thomas found a boy his age, in a get-up of roughly Thomas's quality, who smiled and stuck out his hand. "Philip's my name – oi, what's that smell?"

"Sorry. It's this sword. I'm Thomas."

"You're a cheesewright then? Been using that thing in the shop?"

"No, no. It's a long story," Thomas sighed. "Hold on a second." He pulled a dark cloth out of his saddlebag. "It came wrapped in this, and it seems to stifle it. I was hoping to air it out some is all. If you think it's bad now you should see it in action."

Philip's eyes lit up, "It's a magic sword then? How's it work?"

"Well, you just kind of hold it up–"

Covered in the healer's cloth, the full force of the thing was still strong enough to make everyone within 10 yards groan and back away.

"Sorry!" Thomas yelled. "I've got to stop doing that."

Philip was wiping his eyes but was clearly impressed, "Get on then, that's a piece of work! But it won't do to just hold it up like that." Philip hunched his shoulders, held his nose and lifted his hand in the air pantomiming Thomas. You need to add some flare, you know?"

"Like what?"

"Like a gesture. Yeah, sweep it around in a big arc – no don't do it now!"

"But it doesn't need anything like that."

"Of course not, it's for show. You want to look like you command the thing."

"Frankly, I'd rather look like I had nothing to do with the thing."

"But you do, you do, and that's the trick. It wouldn't be a person's first choice eh? But you've got it, so use it. It's all how you present it see? Sweep it around, bring it up, and say something impressive. Something commanding."

"Like what?"

"Let's see. You probably don't want a whole phrase, because you might want to fire it off quick in a pinch. A word or two is best."

A vendor passed by pushing a cart and selling various bits of meat on sticks.

"Barbeque," sighed Thomas. He was quite hungry and tired of stale bread and old beans.

"Ah no, something made up, or at least less common. Imagine if you actually were going to a barbeque. You'd have to keep firing the thing off just to preserve the illusion. How about 'Fetorflagration!' or 'Dolorous Malodorous!'"

"Maybe something easier to remember," Thomas suggested.

"Well, not to worry. Things like that can work themselves out on the spot. I've seen it happen. Going to ask Arthur to knight you?"

"Um," said Thomas.

"Me too. You have your epithet yet?"

"My what?"

"Epithet. You know, the tag on the end of your name, like Sir Guy the Excruciating or Guillaume le Soi-Disant."

"Le swoy de... Er no, hadn't thought of that. Thomas of Fogbottom, that's the farthest I'd gotten."

"You'll want to replace that Fogbottom part. You want people to remember you for some characteristic, not a scrap of geography."

"What's yours?"

"I'll be 'Sir Philip the Disadvantaged.'"

"The what?"

"It means unlucky."

"Oh."

Philip shook his head, "You wouldn't believe."

"But do you want to advertise a thing like that?"

"Oh sure! People love underdogs. Of course, I wouldn't mind being lucky instead. That'd be something eh? 'Sir Philip the Favored.'" Philip smiled and stared off into space so intently that Thomas actually looked around to see if anything was there.

"Somehow I didn't imagine we gave ourselves our own..."

"Epithet?"

"Yeah."

"Who better? I supposed you could let Merlin assign one, but you're likely to end up with something horrible. And names tend to grow on you, you know? All it takes is a few people consistently calling you 'the Precarious' before you start tripping everywhere you go. Better to pick something you already are, fewer surprises that way.

"Why would Merlin... Wouldn't Arthur be the one... assigning epithets?"

Philip raised an eyebrow. "Wow you do have a lot to learn about this place."

They were both silent for a moment, then Philip continued, "Okay, let's try this... Do you have any outstanding accomplishments?"

"Er, well, I saved a giantess... I think."

Philip raised his eyebrows, "Not bad! By 'saving' do you mean you saved a village *from* her?"

"No, I mean, she was going to kill herself. She was shrinking you see, and I... Well... I put her in a bottle and took her to a healer."

Philip stared for a minute. "Okay, anything else?"

"No, not really."

"Can you tight-rope walk? 'Sir Thomas the Funambulist.'"

"Never tried."

"Hmm. Turn invisible? 'Sir Thomas the Vaporous.'"

"Uh, no, I'm all here all the time. And doesn't vaporous mean, you know, passes gas?"

"Yeah not a great one. Do you like flowers? 'Thomas the Anthophile!'"

"Er, I don't *not* like flowers, I guess."

"Well, we'll have to work on that. It looks like we'll have plenty of time. Guinevere hasn't even arrived yet, and they can't start the wedding gifts until she gets here."

Trumpets blared behind them, and a great and glorious procession came marching over the hill headed for the city. In the center of the train, carried on a litter draped in gossamer white silk, Guinevere waved to a crowd that had gone suddenly still and reverent. Everyone took to his or her knees.

"How about 'Thomas the Not Quite Ready Yet?'"

But Thomas was transfixed. Seven young ladies glided

before Guinevere's litter, plucking petals from white roses and letting them fall. They wore simple gowns of white silk, a redacted version of Guinevere's more complicated ensemble. One maiden in particular moved with a grace with which Thomas had nothing to compare. He'd always thought Solstice, the horse that loved William, was rather light on its feet for its size, but this was different. Snakes, he supposed, kind of moved like this girl – all sort of... flowy. But they didn't have so many parts, all doing their own thing, and still somehow working together in such a magnificent fashion. She caught his eye for a moment, and then she was passed them.

Philip laughed, "I can see 'Sir Thomas the Subtle' is out."

Thomas picked up a fallen petal. "What was it? Antho-something?"

"Anthophile."

"Anthophile. Flowers are nice you know?"

Philip rolled his eyes. "Would you like some of the dirt she trod on too? I think there's a patch right there."

Thomas gave a small chuckle, but he held onto the petal, pressing it to his nose. It was a nice break from the sword.

Guinevere's litter passed, and even the shadow she cast seemed bright. She was followed by six mounted and armored knights arranged in pairs. They wore heavy plate, from head to foot, with white tabards and long white plumes fixed to their helms. Their warhorses were armored too, and draped in white as well. The knights carried lances and shields, each with their own crest.

The first pair passed. "Sir Kay, Arthur's foster brother, and Sir Bedivere," Philip said. Kay was tall, taller than the others by at least a head. "They've been with Arthur forever. They say Kay can turn himself into a tree. Which I think is a rumor Merlin started after Gawain called him 'dumb as a stump.'

"That's Gawain there in the kilt, with his brother Agravain. Their dad is King Lot of Orkney, Arthur's brother-in-law, so these are his nephews. Gawain's all right, gets tired fast though. He fights like three men if you get him in the morning, but all he wants to do in the afternoon is nap. Agravain keeps to himself mostly. Something about him gives me the creeps. Gets it from his mum I guess, Morgan." Philip shivered.

"And there's Pellinore and his son Lamorak. Pellinore is a king himself. Lamorak is the strongest man I've ever seen with a temper to match. Arthur must've ordered those six to personally escort Guinevere."

Behind the knights, an enormous cart pulled by eight horses carried something draped with a giant tarp. An old man in purple robes and a tall pointy hat followed. Golden moons and stars gilded his robes and twinkled in the sun. "Merlin," said Philip. Behind Merlin, a train of what must have been a hundred mounted knights stretched back over the hill. But all eyes were on Merlin and the heavy thing in the big cart. Merlin carried a bone-white staff taller than himself that was gnarled and knotted from top to bottom. He had a great billowy white beard and great billowy white eyebrows that moved like sails. In a gust of wind, they flapped as though the rigging had been abandoned and the ship set adrift.

Philip said, "That must be the Round Table there on the cart. Merlin had it built when Uther was king. Guinevere's dad, King Leo, had it for safekeeping all these years, but now it's coming back to the family. My grandpa saw it once at Uther's court, says it seats thirteen but it's never been full. Supposed to be made of wood from the table Jesus used at the Last Supper. Ask me, I'd have stopped at twelve seats, one for the king and eleven left over. Take a guy who can walk on water, who can raise people from the dead, who can look at you and tell you what you had for breakfast... If a guy like that can't find twelve trustworthy mates, who can? Stop at eleven and call it done, that's the moral of that story."

≈

The queue, finally, began to move. Thomas's stomach lurched. *I'll cross that bridge when I come to it*, he'd told himself, but now he'd come to it, and the bridge looked very high, and very narrow, and constructed of fraying rope and rotting boards. He hadn't decided on an epithet, he wasn't sure if he should mention the healer's sword at all, and he was sure he'd be the only one refused a spot in Arthur's Orders. Obeying his father and just asking Arthur to help William was beginning to make a lot of sense.

"Well, look who we have here."

The voice was terribly familiar. Across Thomas's fraying, rotting, metaphorical bridge, an ogre appeared and started shaking it viciously.

"Hello, Bane." To Thomas's horror, his voice actually cracked as he said it.

Though Bane was no older than Thomas and Philip, the ease with which he bore himself in the saddle, and the way he handled his gear – comfortable, familiar – made him seem much older.

Philip took a step back. "You two know each other?"

"We have a mutual acquaintance," Bane grinned. "But I'm afraid Thomas doesn't like me much. He says I give him a headache. Isn't that right?"

Philip lowered his voice. "Thomas, are there any other unfortunate relational rifts you'd like to tell me about before we become best of friends?"

"Bane's just upset that I got in his way."

"And if you do it again," Bane locked eyes with Thomas and leaned in his saddle toward him. "You'll regret it." Bane shook his reins and rode off toward the palace.

"Not very imaginative is he? 'You'll regret it,'" Philip mocked, but he watched Thomas with a newfound respect. "I'd have said something like 'We'll see how good a scabbard ya make for me sword,' or 'the worms will be wonderin' who their new neighbor is...'"

Thomas laughed. "I don't think having character, of any sort, is something Bane aspires to."

"No argument there. And I suppose he doesn't need an imagination as long as we've got one. I can think of a dozen ways to regret a meeting with him. What did you do to him anyway?"

"He was chasing this wolf... It was an amazing animal. It was hurt. And I thought I heard it... Well, it seemed... It clearly needed help. It ran off, and when Bane showed up I stopped him. Told him to stop hunting it."

Philip looked at Thomas, astonished, "How did that go?"

"Not well. But it sounds like the wolf got away." Thomas grinned, "And I wound up with the Sword of Remarkable Stench."

"The Sword of Remarkable Stench!" Philip slapped him on the back, "Now you're getting the hang of it Thomas."

CHAPTER IX

WEDDING GIFTS

The sun set and rose again before Thomas and Philip gained sight of the palace. They were dead last in the queue which stretched out ahead of them through tall, gilded, and intricately detailed gates. The gates were open, and a soldier not unlike the ones who had escorted the herald in Fogbottom stood in front of them directing traffic. Beyond the gates, Thomas could see the line split in two and head toward different parts of the palace.

"Almost there." Philip was growing more and more excited. He couldn't seem to stand still. Thomas was growing more and more queasy.

"Does it strike you odd," said Thomas with a pained look on his face, "that we're pledging our lives and loyalty to King Arthur, and yet, somehow, it's not our gift to him but the other way 'round?"

Philip stopped fidgeting briefly. "I hadn't really looked at it like that. You're right I guess. Still, it's not like we're not getting something out of it."

"What do we get out of it again?"

"Well... A chance for glory, honor, the love of women, the respect of men, all of that."

Thomas looked doubtful.

"...a chance to make a difference?"

Thomas got the goose bumps. That was hitting a little close to home. He'd never gotten along very well with his father, but he'd never outright disobeyed him either. The thought of letting down his whole family terrified him. He felt tears begin to well up so he quickly looked up and away from Philip. He found himself looking at the blue pennants flying over Camelot's palace. Embroidered gold crowns sparkled on them.

Philip added, "And shiny armor."

"...I do like shiny."

"Focus on that then eh?"

"Shiny?"

"Aye. Shiny."

Thomas's queasiness calmed a bit, Philip went back to fidgeting, and bit by bit the line crept forward.

They had reached the palace gates. The soldier standing there shouted. "Form two queues entering the palace grounds! Knights-to-be on my left. All other requests to my right."

A circle of cobblestones paved the ground just outside the gates. The stone pavement extended through the gates and covered the grounds completely. There were little squares of grassed lawn shaded by ornamental trees, and raised beds filled with blossoming flowers. Bees buzzed between them, hummingbirds darted to and fro, and colorful butterflies danced in the air looking as though they were drunk on pollen.

A big man in front of Philip looked over his shoulder and pointed a thumb at one of the lines. "Knights?" he asked.

Philip nodded pleasantly and raised an eyebrow at Thomas when he'd turned away. Thomas looked longingly at the other queue.

"Honor," said Philip.

"Honor," repeated Thomas.

"Glory," said Philip.

"Glory," repeated Thomas.

"Shiny," said Philip.

"Shiny," said Thomas, and stepped into the queue of knights-to-be with Philip.

❧

Thomas and Philip followed the slow queue through the palace grounds all afternoon. The sun grew hot, Thomas's feet ached, and his back and shoulders had begun to cramp. A palace servant had walked down the line with water, warm bread and cheese, but it had been hours ago and Thomas's stomach was beginning to growl. Finally, they stood before a pair of great bronze doors marking entry into Arthur's throne room. Two soldiers stood guard before the doors and periodically admitted entry to groups of four.

When the group before theirs had entered, Thomas caught a glimpse of the hall before the doors slammed shut again. He'd gotten a quick impression of a long walk between tall pillars and bustling courtiers to a raised dais at the end where Arthur, Merlin and a group of others stood waiting.

"It's time to get your gear ready Thomas." Philip pointed at the oblong bundle of cloth Thomas carried.

Thomas nodded, took a deep breath, and let the cloth fall away from the sword. He opened one eye and looked at Philip. The sword didn't stink.

"It doesn't stink," Philip smiled.

"It doesn't stink!" said Thomas. Elation melted into dread. "What if the magic wore off?"

"Nonsense, the healer told you this would happen right?"

"What if he was wrong? He said this was his first..."

"Well, there's one way to find out."

"Try it?"

"Aye."

"Here?"

"Aye. Hurry."

The soldiers at the doors pulled them open and one of them called, "Last group, inside!"

"Belay that," Philip said.

Thomas gulped and walked inside with Philip and three others. Thomas's sword went with them.

You might think the sword had little choice in the matter, and until recently the sword would have agreed. But something had happened that had started the sword thinking...

The difference between a blessing and a curse is whether or not a person decides to want the thing. The sword, whose real name we'll find out later, had imagined itself a curse its entire short life. Even the healer who'd created and admired it had thought of its quality in terms like terrible, foul, and monstrous. It didn't help that he also made excuses for its construction – calling it a prototype and suspecting it of kinks. Thomas's initial reaction had reinforced its early opinion of itself. But then things began to change.

It started with Philip, who accepted the sword immediately for who it was, kinks and all. When it looked like Thomas himself was starting to recognize the sword's potential, it began to think better of itself. But the kicker came when Thomas declared it not terrible, or shocking, or nightmarish, but rather... remarkable.

Remarkable. Something to talk about, to take note of, something that might be of interest, or might not, depending. Uncommon? Certainly. Extraordinary? Perhaps. Thomas's expression of the sword's potential had been a more effective motivator than if he'd gone all the way and called it grand, or gallant, or glorious. "Remarkable" had a way of putting the sword's destiny in its own control.

The sword had been leaking stink up to this point not because it was newly formed, but because it had been sulking. It didn't want to be a curse, but if that's what people thought it was, why try to be anything else? But now someone believed in it. Now someone was going to give it chance. The sword was determined to make an impression that would last.

The walk down to the throne was long and uncomfortable. Thomas wasn't sure if it was proper to look Arthur in the eye as he approached or not. He caught a few courtiers glancing sideways at him, but most were watching the big man in their group lumber ahead of them. The doors slammed shut behind them, and Thomas gulped.

Arthur stood before his throne looking very regal. Guinevere sat next to him also looking very regal, but in a softer way, a way that still had room for flowers. Merlin stood to Arthur's right in the same astrologically encrusted purple outfit Thomas had seen him in earlier, his staff as gnarled and bleached as ever. There were a dozen or so knights arranged to either side of the thrones. Thomas recognized the tall Sir Kay and Gawain in his kilt. Two ladies-in-waiting waited near Guinevere. One was the girl Thomas had made eye contact with during Guinevere's procession into Camelot. Thomas's stomach lurched.

The hall was draped resplendently in yellows and blues and filled with courtiers who were very good at being decoration. Being decoration was in fact one half of their profession. The other half was flattery, so except for those times when the king called for silence, there was an ever-present admiring hum and a continual polite nodding of heads. Many of those heads wore hats with long, bright feathers affixed, so the nodding was picked up and amplified until it became a sea of swishing color. Here and there a tapestry or banner hung depicting a stylized dragon or a lion or something in between.

Thomas was thinking that if he had to pick two words to describe the place to Elizabeth someday, one would be "polished" and the other would be "marble". The group suddenly stopped.

The last man in the previous group of four was kneeling before Arthur who stood before him with a sword in his hand.

"Excalibur!" Philip whispered.

If Thomas's sword had had a stomach, it would have lurched.

"I dub thee Sir Edgar the Erstwhile," said Arthur and touched the man's shoulders, first the one then the other, with the flat of Excalibur's blade.

Merlin whispered something at this point.

"It means, 'the Former'," said Arthur through the side of his mouth.

"I know what it means," said Merlin, exasperated. "But... Erstwhile what?"

"What do you mean, 'Erstwhile what?' Just Erstwhile," said Arthur.

"But he should be the Erstwhile *Something*," said Merlin. "He can't very well go about not being anything in the present or the future."

"I beg to differ," said King Arthur. "He's been doing everything in the past since he's come in here. For instance, see there, he's no longer kneeling. I distinctly recall him kneeling a moment ago."

"You're very right sire, but you see, now he's standing."

"Ah, I would say he *has been standing.* You see, he can't seem to do anything he hasn't either already done or been doing."

Merlin blinked. "You make an excellent point. I've called the next requestor."

Arthur raised an eyebrow, "No, you haven't."

"Aha! But I'm about to. See, I haven't done it yet."

Arthur sighed. "I didn't say you were erstwhile Merlin. It's Sir Edgar there." Edgar had moved aside to make room for the next person in line.

Merlin looked at Edgar. Edgar shrugged. Merlin opened his mouth to say something, paused, and closed it again. He turned to the four remaining requestors and called, "Next in line!"

A lanky man stepped up. Strangely, instead of aligning himself directly in front of Arthur, he positioned himself about a yard to his right.

"Psst," said Arthur, giving a little jerk with his head. "Over here."

"Oh. Pardon," said the lanky man. He took one big step sideways and smiled pleasantly at Arthur.

Merlin spoke, "For the record, state your name and your request please."

The man said, "I am Dedric of Hammershire, and I request that King Arthur make me one of his knights."

"And so it shall be Dedric of Hammershire," said Arthur. "Do you have any special talents? You understand this is a matter of curiosity and convention, not of requirement."

"Well," started Dedric, then paused. He was twisting his left thumb with his right hand as if he wasn't sure how this next part was going to be received. "I am a diplopian."

Arthur stared.

"He has double-vision," whispered Merlin. "Sees two of everything."

Arthur's eyes widened.

"What a wonderful gift." There was reverence in Arthur's voice.

Dedric visibly relaxed and looked straight at the air between Arthur and Merlin. Merlin's brow creased, he squinted at Arthur and pursed his lips.

Arthur coughed to clear his throat, and Dedric's grinning head snapped to the correct angle.

"What is your current profession?" asked Arthur.

"I'm a farmer sir."

Arthur nodded, then gasped at a sudden realization. "You must be very successful, what with double harvests and all. And half the work too! Sowing two seeds from one, and picking two ears of corn with every pluck." Arthur actually clapped in excitement. "Bravo."

Merlin cleared his throat. "Er, Arthur, I feel I must point out that there aren't, of course, *actually* two things, it's just that he *sees* two. One of the two he sees isn't really there." He waved his hand through the empty space between himself and Arthur. If Merlin's great eyebrows could've spoken they would have said, "See, there's only one of me." Thomas found this ironic because there were in fact two eyebrows.

Arthur rolled his eyes. He addressed the court, "Who is braver? The man who faces an enemy, or the man who faces two? And what if he knew one of his opponents was a phantom, but knew not which? Even braver, I say!"

"But," Merlin started, and Arthur held up a hand.

Arthur turned to Dedric, who hadn't taken his eyes off the real Arthur now that he'd figured out which Arthur that was. "Kneel," commanded Arthur, and when Dedric had knelt, Arthur drew Excalibur and knighted him saying, "I dub thee Sir Dedric the Diplopian, may you slay two foes with every stroke."

Merlin leaned heavily on his staff. "Next in line," he called.

The big bloke that had asked Philip for directions stepped up and bowed. He was tall enough that Arthur on his raised dais still had to look up at him. Despite his impressive size, or perhaps because of it, the man carried himself apologetically.

"For the record," said Merlin, who had brightened at the sight of the current candidate. "State your name and your request please."

"Ox," said the man.

Merlin paused. "I'm sorry, you'll have to clarify, is that your name or your request? If you're asking for livestock, you'll need to report to—"

"Knight!" interrupted the man.

"Ah," said Merlin clearly pleased. This was a sort of soldier they could work with. "Might I suggest—"

But Arthur was a step ahead, having already drawn Excalibur and begun the dubbing. "I dub thee Sir Ox," Arthur paused thoughtfully. "The Monosyllabic."

Merlin sighed. "Perhaps we should take a short break."

"Nonsense, we're nearly finished. Look there, we're down to the last two."

Merlin shrugged and called for the next in line.

Philip grinned and gave Thomas a last reassuring slap on the back, then stepped forward. Thomas's hands began to sweat.

"For the record," said Merlin, sounding like he didn't care one scrap for any kind of written record of the day's proceedings. "State your name and your request please."

"I'm Philip son of Philip, and I request to be knighted."

Arthur nodded, "Any special talents? A matter of curiosity and convention of course, not a requirement."

"I'm terribly disadvantaged your majesty."

"Disadvantaged... as in unlucky?"

Philip nodded, smiling. Merlin looked skeptical.

Arthur looked at Merlin, then whispered something to him. "I'm thinking of a number Philip son of Philip, between one and ten. What is it?"

"Seven," said Philip.

Merlin lifted his great eyebrows and said, "That's the number the king told me he was going to be thinking. That seems pretty lucky to me."

"...On the other hand," said Arthur, intrigued, "if you were going to try to prove yourself unlucky, and you really were unlucky, you'd end up looking peculiarly lucky with each effort."

Merlin sat down on Arthur's throne and ordered some tea. Philip, who'd exuded an anxious kind of confidence before, started to look nervous.

Arthur continued, "If you were instead lucky and wanted to hide it for some reason, you'd show up looking unlucky on every test. The possibility remains that you're of average luck, claiming to be unlucky, and you just got lucky this once."

"We could ask him again," offered Merlin. It was clearly the last thing Merlin wanted to do.

"Yes, let's."

"Why don't we?" mumbled Merlin.

Arthur whispered a number to Merlin who actually brightened a bit then said, "Excellent choice sire. Another number between one and ten please Mister Philip son of Philip."

Philip answered immediately, "Eleven, sir."

"Extraordinary!" said Arthur.

Merlin's face fell. "That's the number," he said.

"Only someone very unlucky could have guessed that. Step forward young Philip."

Arthur drew Excalibur. Philip knelt, and Arthur said, "I dub thee Philip the *Exceptionally* Disadvantaged. May your enemies always doubt the extent of your unluck, and may that doubt, somehow, be their undoing."

Philip half-turned and gave Thomas a thumb's up.

"Next and last in line please!" called Merlin.

Still working through what had just happened, Thomas didn't immediately realize that Merlin was talking to him. Philip motioned with his head, but it wasn't until Arthur cleared his throat that he put it all together and hurried up to stand before the king. Most of the court had had their boredom in the proceedings compounded hourly throughout the day, and they'd managed to express their continued disinterest with refinement. That is to say, their eyes had been on the action, but they weren't really watching. But now evening was falling, and everyone wanted to go home. Having arrived at the last candidate for the day, their attention suddenly manifested and focused itself squarely on Thomas.

Thomas's worry, however, focused on a handful of people that were watching him even more keenly: Arthur, Merlin, Philip and two others. One of these was the girl Thomas had seen in Guinevere's procession. He tried not to make eye contact with her, because any time he did, his insides responded in ways that didn't feel at all secure. He was having enough trouble keeping his insides arranged properly at present, thank you. The other person was one of the attendant knights. Most of the knights yawned, or stared a thousand yards away, or rubbed absent-mindedly at slightly less shiny spots on their armor. This one, though, watched Thomas with a friendly smile. He had riveting pale gray eyes and a shock of silver hair that seemed familiar but out of place somehow; Thomas was sure he'd met him somewhere.

Merlin gave a little cough, "Your name and request please." Merlin seemed excited, but Thomas knew it was just about being finished soon – at least it made him pleasant for the time being.

Thomas cleared his throat and straightened up, trying to appear confident and respectful at the same time. As a result he mainly felt off-balanced.

"My name is Thomas of Fogbottom, and I wish..."

Everyone waited. He could feel the eyes of the courtiers on the back of his head. The oddly-familiar knight's brow furrowed just a bit. Philip cleared his throat. Arthur smiled encouragingly. Merlin raised an eyebrow.

Guinevere pinched the skin between her eyes. The girl from the procession was probably doing something too but Thomas refused to look.

One of the courtiers behind him whispered helpfully, "You wish to be made a knight!"

Thomas closed his eyes and took a breath. This was it; this was the last chance to back out and just do what his parents wanted. When he'd imagined this moment he'd anticipated things like nausea, uncontrollable quivering, and sheer panic, but now that he was in it he felt peculiarly calm. He was very much in control and though he was clearly making the decisions, he felt as though he was watching himself carry them out from somewhere outside himself.

Sorry Father, he said to himself.

"...and I wish to made a knight."

There was a split second that felt to Thomas like freedom, and then he began to wonder what he had done.

"Excellent," said Arthur, then the dreadful question: "And do you have any special talents? Mind, it's not a requirement."

The words "not a requirement" echoed in Thomas's mind. They bounced around a few times in there before they lodged in a spot and formed a plan. The plan that formed went roughly like this: it would be unwise to reveal the Sword of Remarkable Stench unless absolutely necessary, and since it doesn't seem to be necessary, it must be unwise to do so now, so don't.

"Talents? No, not particularly, 'fraid not, um, your majesty" said Thomas and, trying to get past the subject as quickly as possible, gave an awkward little bow.

Arthur frowned. Eyebrows dropped all around. Philip whispered, "What are you doing?"

Arthur turned to Merlin. "Well, this is new. I don't think we've ever had anyone come through completely devoid of talent. What do the rules say?"

Thomas felt a heat spreading inside his chest that he recognized as panic. "Not a requirement?" was all he could get out.

"Oh I know we say that. But now that someone's gone and actually raised the point, I'm not certain we mean it, exactly, as such."

Thomas's heart dropped.

Merlin unfurled a long scroll and scanned it quickly. "Ah, here..." he said to himself, then read with authority, "'General candidates for the position of knight and/or knight errant must furnish their own talent.'" Then he said, "Hmm..." and looked puzzled. He mumbled for a moment, "...thought for sure... not a requirement, per se... Aha! 'If a candidate cannot provide a talent, one may be appointed to him.'"

Arthur looked pleased. "Ah yes, that's it. Good show Merlin. Now, which talent would you like Thomas of Fogbottom?"

"Pardon?" Thomas wasn't following this at all.

Arthur spoke patiently, like a man who'd had lots of practice repeating simple instructions to people who, for reasons unfathomable, continued to find them *un*simple, "You'll have to choose a talent if you want to be a knight. I'm afraid it's a requirement, of sorts."

"You can do that? Make someone good at something... just like that?"

"Well, no, it doesn't exactly work that way. It would be best if you pick something you're already good at."

Thomas paused. Everyone looked at him, waiting for his choice. "But isn't the point...?"

Merlin interrupted, "I don't see that it says the candidate has the liberty of choosing the talent. We could speed this along."

"Splendid idea," said Arthur. "What do you suggest?"

Merlin took a good look at Thomas and stroked his beard. "How about 'able to grow hair of great length?'"

Arthur frowned approvingly. "Not bad at all. Easy to prove, one simply needs to stay clear of the barber." He turned to Thomas. "Thomas of Fogbottom, I–"

"Wait!" said Thomas.

Arthur paused with his mouth open in mid-vowel and raised his eyebrows. He closed his mouth, then opened it again and said, "Yes?"

"I do have this... magic sword."

"Yes!" whispered Philip. Merlin glanced at him, and Philip quickly composed himself, smiling innocently.

Arthur's eyebrows hiked up another notch. "A magic sword?"

Thomas wasn't sure which would be worse, if the sword stank the place up proper or if it failed to do anything at all. Despite his searing panic, Thomas felt morbidly curious about his own ill-made fate – it drove him forward.

Thomas nodded. "Like none that's ever been seen or dreamt of." *Might as well pile it on now*, he thought. *If I'm going to fail, I might as well fail spectacularly.*

"Well why didn't you say so lad? Magic swords are serious business! Right then, we need to go about this properly. First off, where and under what circumstances did the sword come into your possession?"

A buzz of excitement spread across the hall. All the knights were watching now, and the closest courtiers were actually hushing those in the back.

"I... Well," Thomas shot a glance at Philip, who winked. "I found... I mean, I captured... a giantess, named Gorgella, who'd been... Or rather, she was living in the mountains... at the source of a stream that fed our lands."

Arthur had been nodding him on and now he was positively beaming. "Oh good show Thomas," he said. "Poisoning the water and your village's crops no doubt, and you took it upon yourself to rid this plague on hearth and home." He paused. "Captured her though eh? I'd have slain her, but it's a start. What happened next?"

"Well, I took her to an old... to an enchanter... who rewarded me... with this sword of his creation." Thomas patted the hilt.

"Absolutely wonderful. This is the kind of thing I'd been hoping for all day. You knew it didn't you? Waited, last in line, then fooled me with the bit about being talentless. Smart boy. Good show. Alright then, let's have it, shall we? What does it do?"

Thomas basked in Arthur's approval. He smiled, "Hmmm?"

"The sword. What is its power? Show us!" Arthur was still smiling. Thomas imagined he wouldn't be doing that much longer. Thomas sighed. There was simply no way out. He glanced at Philip, and what he saw made his heart leap – hope pierced Thomas like a spear.

Philip was standing there, sporting a smile identical to Arthur's and doing one other absolutely brilliant thing: He was pinching his nose.

Elated, Thomas turned to Arthur, straightened up, cleared his throat, pinched his nose with his left forefinger and thumb and winked at Arthur.

Arthur, intrigued, pinched his own nose. Guinevere and Merlin followed suit pinching theirs. Those of the knights, ladies-in-waiting, and courtiers nearby who were paying attention got the hint and copied. The procession-girl's eyes glinted with curious amusement. Thomas grinned at her and clenched his intestines.

When he saw that the stage was set, he drew a deep breath and the Sword of Remarkable Stench in one smooth motion, swung an arc around his head on the way up, pointed it skyward and commanded in the best, most commanding voice he could muster, "YO HO HO!"

Nothing happened.

Dread washed over Thomas from head to foot.

Wait for it, thought the sword.

The procession-girl's eyebrows drew ever so slightly closer together.

Thomas wanted to crawl under a rock somewhere and never come out.

There was a sound then like none Thomas had ever heard. He imagined it sounded not unlike someone plucking a single string on a lute – if that lute were the size of a small mountain, and that mountain had dragons on it… lots of dragons, and they were all breathing fire right at you. And then the world turned inside out for anything with open nostrils.

The people in Arthur's court who were holding their noses watched as madness unfolded before them. Thomas was simply flabbergasted. Philip looked on amazed. Guinevere and The Girl grimaced. Arthur and Merlin, who'd seen many strange sights – and been personally responsible for more than a handful of them – counted what happened that day as one of the singularly strangest.

The courtiers who weren't initially holding their noses tried desperately to plug them now, but it was simply too late. They swam in memories of places and emotions long repressed. Several courtiers crumpled into fetal positions and called for their mothers. A dozen courtiers leapt through the windows into the courtyard and dashed out of Camelot never to be heard from again. A handful stood staring in the direction they'd been looking, trembled, and quietly wet themselves. One man named Alfonzo ran in circles shouting, "Not the French! Not the French!" A knight who hadn't been paying attention flailed at his nose then gave that up and began punching himself in the face repeatedly. Another knight with watery eyes and a slight tremble calmly removed his helmet, slowly turned it over, and after a moment of heroic resistance, vomited into it with gusto.

"Tahmuss," Arthur said nasally, "cahn you tuhrn thiss ahf?"

"Oh right," said Thomas, and quickly lowered the sword and sheathed it. Immediately, the effect evaporated.

If the sword had had appendages and a face, it would have crossed its arms and grinned.

The courtiers who'd crumpled picked themselves up and dusted themselves off, carefully. Those who needed a change of clothes politely excused themselves and headed for the door. Alfonzo stood slumped, vacuous and drooling. He spent the remainder of his days in the care of a nearby convent, mostly knitting for fundraisers and such. The knight who'd been punching himself was escorted out, holding his face and bleeding profusely. Everyone moved slowly. Each eyed his nose warily, like it was a wild animal crouching in the corner. It didn't seem wise to make any abrupt moves in its presence.

Philip was the first to release the pinch on his nose. When he didn't run screaming, the rest slowly let go of theirs as well and took short experimental sniffs. The air was clear. The court was silent. You could've heard a hummingbird land on a thistle a mile away.

Arthur whistled. "Thomas," he said, "that was something."

Thomas agreed. He was aware of the weight of the sword on his hip in a way he hadn't been before.

"You may kneel now lad," said Arthur.

Thomas knelt, and Arthur drew Excalibur. He touched each of Thomas's shoulders with the flat of the blade and said, "I dub thee Sir Thomas the," he paused. "I confess I'm drawing a complete blank."

"The sword is remarkable," Arthur continued, "but it's not a talent exactly. It's not who you are. Who are you Thomas? Or failing that, who do you want to be?"

Thomas hesitated. "I'm not sure, sir."

"How do I name someone who doesn't even know who he is himself?"

"Well, I'd like to be a knight your majesty."

"That's *what* you want to be, but is it *who* you want to be? Let me tell you a secret Thomas, the first step in becoming something is deciding you are the thing already. The rest is just polishing. But for now..."

He touched Thomas's shoulders again. "I dub thee Sir Thomas the Hesitant. May you find what you're looking for Sir Thomas."

Thomas stood. Arthur smiled and asked, "What do you think?"

"The Hesitant?" Thomas asked. "Well, I'm not certain really."

"Precisely my point," said Arthur. "It's perfect."

CHAPTER X

CAN'T SPELL "TRYOUT" WITHOUT "TROUT"

Each new knight was handed a packet upon exiting the throne room. The contents included a map of Camelot with landmarks noted and connected by a circuitous line labeled 'Camelot, a Walking Tour,' a coupon advertising lunch specials at a pub called The Fine Pickle, and a form letter which read as follows:

Dear new ~~minstrel~~ knight ~~courtier lady-in-waiting~~,

Welcome to Camelot! Your life of ~~fame~~ adventure ~~sycophancy~~ ~~fancy dresses~~ has just begun. You no doubt have many questions which ~~if you didn't you wouldn't be an artist right?~~ will have to wait ~~are largely rhetorical so we won't trouble you with bothersome answers~~ ~~are our pleasure to answer to your satisfaction~~. First things first, as they say.

Please find attached a schedule outlining your first week aboard. Failure to present yourself promptly at any of the appointed times and places will result in ~~your prompt dismissal~~ reassignment to kitchen duty ~~no real consequences whatsoever~~ ~~immediate deployment of emergency personnel~~.

If permanent lodging has not already been arranged, temporary room has been reserved for you at ~~the thick-walled Artist Sanctuary just outside the city gates~~ your own recognizance ~~the Camelot Spa and Relaxorium inside the palace proper~~. During your stay there, please feel free to ~~express yourself~~ remember you represent Camelot, God help us ~~take advantage of palace discounts~~ ~~make yourself at home~~.

We hope you ~~are as good as you think you are, for your own sake~~ know what you're getting yourself into ~~can live with yourself~~ ~~find life at Camelot suitable, we are the vase to your blossoming flower~~. If we can be of any further assistance, don't hesitate to ~~find someone who cares~~ assist yourself, we can't hold your hand forever ~~leave a message with the duty officer, someone will get back to you at their convenience~~ ~~call on us at any hour, we're here to serve~~.

I remain forever your ~~palace ambassador~~ point-of-contact, not your mother ~~patient guide~~ ~~humble servant~~,

Sir Tuttle the Authorized
Chief, Palace Staff
Captain, LVK

Having exited all together, Thomas, Philip, Edgar, Dedric and Ox stood in the hall examining their letters. Edgar finished first. Dedric read his twice. Ox was at least going through the motions. None of them got anything out of it because not a one of them could read.

Thomas read his out loud, then read the letter with alternate phrases selected.

"This Tuttle's got all his vegetables in one pot don't he?" said Dedric when Thomas had finished.

They all looked at him.

"Er, sorry. Farming metaphor."

"No need to explain," said Thomas who had been trying to recall the last time he'd had a vegetable to put in a pot. "And yeah, he does. What's 'LVK'?"

"It's what we'll be most likely," said Edgar.

"Table of Less Valued Knights," said Philip.

"They actually call them that?"

"Well, sure, I mean, at least it's honest right?" said Philip.

"But it's kind of, I don't know, demeaning isn't it?"

"What? You didn't think you'd sit right down at the Round Table did you?"

"Well, no, but, aren't there other, you know, more valued tables?"

"Of course," said Philip, "there's the Knights of the Watch, but we've got a long way to go before *we're* considered for that kind of duty. Bane maybe. But not people like us. Then there's the Queen's Knights and the Errant Companions, but those are more like special assignments."

"Huh," said Thomas. "So how do we know which, you know, order we're in? For sure I mean."

"I'm telling you, we're Less Valued. That's just the way it is."

"Fight!" said Ox.

"Whoa," said Philip. "Let's all take a deep breath, eh?"

Ox shook his head and pointed at the wall, "We fight!" He grinned, "See?"

A big white sign with simple black letters and a picture of two knights fighting hung on the wall where Ox indicated. It read:

Table Tryouts
– Monday, Dawn –
South Field

They took it all in.

"We fight?" said Thomas.

"We fight," said Philip.

"We fight!" agreed Ox grinning broadly.

"That's tomorrow," said Dedric.

"Every day is another day's yesterday," said Edgar the Erstwhile. They all looked at him. "I'm just sayin'," he apologized.

Thomas and Philip spent the night in a grove of trees outside the city walls. A stretch of lush green grass ran down from the city walls to a clear stream flowing between hills flowered yellow and, further out, forested with thick old oaks and maples. Butterflies flitted about haphazardly and birds sang to each other merrily about things like cats and where to find the best worms and who had the best nest. The evening was comfortably cool and required no fire. A magnificent expanse of stars spread out overhead as night deepened, and every so often a shooting star arced across the heavens. Lying on his back amidst it all, the sum of all this wondrous natural beauty had absolutely no effect on Thomas whatsoever.

"Knights," sighed Philip. "We're knights, Thomas!"

"I know. It's hard to forget with you continually reminding me." A ray of light that had left its home on a nearby star and traveled eight years to reach him found Thomas's eye and twinkled in it happily. Thomas pointedly ignored it.

Philip propped himself up on one arm. "Don't worry about tomorrow, Thomas. Like my dad always says, 'Tomorrow will take care of itself.'"

"Yeah? My dad always said, 'Thomas, tomorrow is a three-legged dog. It doesn't have to lift its leg, so you never know if it's going to pee or roll over.'"

Philip mulled that over.

Thomas said, "He meant you can't count on things going well or things going poorly, just that they will, inevitably, go."

Philip said, "That's depressing."

Thomas shrugged, "It's practical."

Philip said, "It's practically morose is what it is. You won't get anywhere thinking like that. The world isn't entirely out of your control."

"Isn't it?"

"No, it isn't," Philip insisted. "Just look at the way you played that room with your sword. Yo ho ho! Ha! That was great."

"That did work out alright there didn't it?" A smile visited Thomas briefly, then faded again. "But *The Hesitant*? What kind of epi...?"

"Epithet," said Philip.

Thomas rolled his eyes. "What kind of title is that?"

"Seriously, it's not that bad. You were about to be Sir Thomas the Magnificently Mulletted," Philip chuckled. "Or worse. My dad told me of a guy once – Sir Ulfus the Unwilling. For honor's sake, he was only able to do things that he didn't want to do. 'Want to shine our armor for us Ulfus? Want to get us some sandwiches Ulfus? Want to take on those thirty bandits by yourself Ulfus?' they'd ask him. 'Not really,' he'd say and off he was obliged to go, shining armor or making sandwiches or fighting bandits. Finally one day he snapped. He went down to the Fine Pickle and just started eating ice cream. His wife, whom he detested and who had been the last person he'd wanted to marry, found him and started yelling at him, making a big scene right there saying they'd throw him out of court, revoke his knighthood. He told her they could take his knighthood and stuff it somewhere. He didn't want it anymore. Which, of course, just made him all the more Unwilling. The more he rebelled, the more everyone loved him. It got so he couldn't even enjoy the things he once liked."

Philip stopped. "I think I've lost my point," he said.

Thomas waited a minute, wrestling with himself. Philip was cheering him up and he wasn't sure he wanted to be. He sighed. "You were saying things could be worse."

"Oh right," Philip resumed. "Take me for example. I'm likely to have something quite dreadful happen tomorrow, being so unlucky and all. But I'm looking forward to it. Know why?"

"No," said Thomas. "Why?"

There was a glint in Philip's eye. "Because when we walk out on the field tomorrow, with Gawain and Pellinore and all the rest, we're all *knights* Thomas! They might be the superstars, but we're all part of the team. And we can all make a difference."

They were both quiet for a while.

"I wonder how Bane did," said Thomas.

"Oh, I'm sure he did just fine."

"I didn't see him in queue at all."

"Well, really, the whole point of being a person of privilege is to, you know, have privileges."

"Must be nice."

"Mmm."

Another flaming rock committed suicide by velocity in the night sky.

"Wonder what epithet he got," Philip pondered.

"Bane the Privileged," suggested Thomas.

"Bane the Obnoxious is more like it," said Philip.

"Bane the Appropriately Named."

They laughed. "There you go," said Philip.

Time passed and Thomas's thoughts drifted to his family in the cottage back in Fogbottom and his brother locked away in the Baron's keep. He hoped he was following the right path, but from where he sat now, he didn't see how being a member of the Table of Less Valued Knights was going to help anyone. If Philip was right, there was little chance of becoming much more unless something absolutely spectacular happened tomorrow. If he'd made the wrong choice, if he'd just asked for William's pardon like his father had wanted...

He rolled on his side to tell Philip how he came to be in Camelot in the first place, but Philip was fast asleep. Thomas rolled onto his back again to stare at the sky.

Some time later, he drifted off watching meteorites incinerate themselves gloriously to the shimmering applause of incomprehensibly well-traveled starlight. On a neighboring hill, a pair of unblinking, pale grey eyes watched him sleep.

᷅

Trumpets blared. Crowds cheered. Banners flapped in a steady breeze. Thomas and Philip stood in a group of newly minted knights at the edge of Camelot's South Field. Arthur and Guinevere had just arrived and made their way to a specially constructed covered section among the bleachers. With them was the usual entourage of Kay, Bedivere, and Guinevere's Ladies including The Girl.

"I've got to find out her name," muttered Thomas.

Shortly after they were settled, three more figures entered and were seated with them. One appeared to be a king, though older and not quite as richly ornamented as Arthur, and with him, a young knight. Several people greeted this other king warmly, but the object of the crowd's main concern was the woman with them. Tall and imposing, she swished around in long, heavy black robes. Only her face and hands were exposed. Her porcelain white skin and her long, deep black hair formed a disturbing kind of beautiful. An intricate, bone white crown finished the picture. She moved with an unnatural grace and exuded the kind of seductive charm that inspires tragic fairy tales. Thomas found himself thinking of a Venus flytrap he'd had in his room as a child.

"Morgan," said Philip. "She's Arthur's half-sister." Philip pointed to the old man with Morgan. "King Uriens is okay, and their son Owain. Owain is probably trying out with us today. But stay away from Morgan if you can."

He shivered.

"Owain is trying out with us?" Thomas swallowed. "You mean we have to fight real knights?"

"You are a real knight, Thomas. Look, what have they got that you haven't?"

There was unmasked panic in Thomas's voice now, "Well, there's armor for one. Good armor. And training. And long, sharp blades, Philip, with *points* on the ends..."

"Right. Good point, er, so to speak. Well, I'm sure they'll be handicapped somehow. Wouldn't be fair otherwise eh?"

Arthur stood, and the crowd quieted. Someone handed him a megaphone.

"Welcome Ladies and Gentleman of every rank and flavor!"

Guinevere giggled, and the crowd followed suit. Morgan looked severe.

"In preparation for our forthcoming wedding, we've prepared a festival to determine the position and placement of Camelot's new knights!"

One of Guinevere's ladies whispered something to The Girl who glanced briefly at Thomas, blushed and giggled behind her hand. Thomas suddenly felt very conspicuous.

Arthur continued, "As you all know, Guinevere's father King Leo..."

The crowd applauded, and an elderly King seated near Arthur's pavilion waved with both hands.

"King Leo has graciously supplied us with the Round Table. The same table given to him by my father Uther Pendragon for safe-keeping. The table originally constructed by Merlin from sections of our Lord's table at his Last Supper."

Merlin bowed.

"Twelve of the kingdom's best knights will sit at this table with me as peers of the court!"

The crowd erupted, and several of the more favored knights shifted their weight from foot to foot affecting self-conscious acceptance of the praise which they assumed, rightly, was for them. Gawain raised both arms above his head to wave at the crowd. The movement hiked his kilt up half an inch. The ladies cheered.

"Sir Kay will lead that order, but it won't be filled today I'm afraid. Positions of such high honor must be granted only with the greatest care and consideration and shan't be settled with a simple contest. But there are two other orders we will fill by the end of the tournament: The Knights of the Watch, whose duties include, but are not limited to, observing and reporting on the states of all sorts of important things. And the Table of Less Valued Knights, who handle the various details that the others don't.

"Sir Marrok, of course, leads the Watch..."

The familiar-looking knight that Thomas had seen in Arthur's court stepped forward, gave a subtle bow of his head and stepped back. The crowd applauded. Arthur beamed.

"And Sir Tuttle continues his competent work with the Less Valued."

A small, thin knight pushed his way to the front and bowed. He was easily the most kempt man on the field. His armor was meticulously polished and blemish-free. He executed a perfect about-face and marched back into the nowhere from which he'd come.

"Sirs Kay, Marrok, and Gawain—"

The crowd exploded. Gawain was a favorite of favorites. It was impossible to say his name without setting the packs of girls who followed him into fits of giggles and hand-fluttering.

When the crowd died down, Arthur continued, "Sirs Kay, Marrok, and Gawain will choose teams for the tournament and lead them through the events. In the end, each knight will be assigned to an order based on his team's performance and his personal contribution in said events."

Even from where he stood, Thomas could see the crowd's eyes glazing over. Merlin, leaning against a bleacher to Arthur's left, actually snored.

"Enough said," Arthur concluded and gave Merlin a swift kick. "Let the games begin!"

Kay, Marrok, and Gawain took positions in the middle of the field. All three held rolled parchment that they unfurled dramatically. Marrok was the first to speak. He held up his scroll and read the first name, "I choose..." He looked straight at Thomas. "Sir Thomas the Hesitant."

Somewhere in the crowd, Thomas heard Bane snicker.

The knights were split into three teams that then huddled in different corners of the field. Thomas, Philip, and Ox all landed on Marrok's team. Gawain chose, among others, his brother Agravain and his cousin Owain. Thomas thought he saw Dedric the Diplopian there too. Sir Kay chose some ringers like Bedivere and Pellinore, but for the most part, the teams looked like reasonably balanced mixes of veterans and rookies.

When they'd gathered at their corners, each team was outfitted with colored tabards. Marrok's was green.

"Philip," said Thomas, "I think I've figured out what they're using for a handicap."

"What's that?"

"Us."

A half an hour later, Ox had an egg strapped on top of his head with a scarf, and Thomas was sitting on his shoulders wielding a trout.

The idea, basically, was to slay the dragon, storm the castle and rescue the fair maiden, armed, of course, with the fish. If the egg that was strapped to your base's head got smashed, you were both out.

Marrok yelled, "For Camelot!" and led his team's charge toward a mass of encircled knights in red tabards, Gawain's team.

The dragon, as it was, consisted of egg-headed, trout-wielding knights holding on to each other's shoulders and forming a protective circle around the dragon's head. The dragon's head was another knight rolling a wheelbarrow filled with small bundles of flour wrapped in cheesecloth. To be hit by one of these parcels that he periodically pitched meant instant elimination.

Marrok's and Gawain's teams collided. Fish were flailed, eggs splattered, and when the flour settled, all of Thomas's team was covered in dust, dripping with goo, or both. The dragon roared with victory.

"Two points to Gawain!" shouted Arthur through his megaphone. The crowd was on its feet cheering. "Alas, the damsel remains distressed." A young lady atop a pole in a barricaded square surrounded by evil trout-brandishing knights waved. She appeared to not be in the least bit distressed.

Thomas had decided to keep his immediate goals small, measurable, and achievable. Having found himself to be alive and unharmed, he considered the round a success.

In the second round, Marrok's dragon put up a valiant effort, but Kay's team in their blue tabards eventually tore it apart. They took a systematic approach of knocking out knights on the dragon's perimeter one by one. They'd feign an attack on one side to draw the dragon's "fire", then rush the other. In the end, Bedivere chased down the last two dragon guards and the dragon head itself single-handedly. With their surgical precision, Kay lost not a single man to the dragon that day.

Storming the castle was a different story. Gawain's team hurled great sacks of flour from their battlements that smote several of Kay's knights with each blast. Inside the barricade, dressed as the evil wizard of the keep, Gawain shouted, "Ye canna beat us, ye grrreat overgrown apes!" The ground, slick with smashed egg, gave no grip, and Kay's team was slaughtered to the man.

"Two more points to Gawain," called Arthur. "Will no one save the fair maid Marie?"

Lying on the field with the rest of the dragon carcass, Thomas took a closer look at the girl on the pole.

"That's her," he said, poking Philip.

"Who's her?" said Philip, "What?"

"The girl on the pole, Philip. That's the girl form the procession." Thomas let his head fall back on the gooey lawn. "Marie..." he said and sighed.

Philip picked himself up. "Well, let's keep her there then eh? It's our turn in the castle."

A familiar voice said, "And it looks like it's time for you to choke and for me to rescue your girlfriend."

Thomas was on his feet in a second, but Bane in his bright red tabard had already rejoined Gawain's team at midfield.

"Of course he gets picked for Gawain's team," grumbled Philip.

"Well, he's not going to be a hero today if I can help it," said Thomas.

Gawain's team divided itself, flanked Kay's dragon, and smashed it to pieces in one concussive strike. Gawain lost several men, but the dragon was out before the audience had even stopped applauding the start of the round.

Gawain guffawed, "Ye didnae expect such a fearrrsome opponent didya Kay, ye enahrrrmuss stump?"

Inside the barricade, Thomas had been nominated to play the role of the evil wizard. If Gawain's team broke through the defenses, all they needed to do was smash the egg strapped to Thomas's head and Marrok's whole team would be out. Thomas stood near Marie's tower, fumbling absent-mindedly with his own bucket of eggs. These had been dyed red and had "FIREBALL!" painted on several. He watched Gawain do a victory dance over the dead dragon, but his mind was focused some fifteen feet above his left shoulder.

"He'll save me, you know."

She spoke. Thomas was reasonably certain she was talking to him – he was the only one within earshot.

It's a funny thing, Thomas would later tell Philip, *but once you've had eggs smashed on you all day, and flour puffed at you, and then you've been stuffed in an old robe to pretend to be a wizard, and then let the egg dry so your skin is tight in patches and your hair is as stiff as a meringue, your worry about your self-image kind of bottoms out and you find yourself rather uninhibited.*

"Who?" said Thomas, "the man in the dress?" indicating Gawain who was now doing a jig of sorts around Kay's prone team.

"That's a skirt," said Marie, "*you're* the one in the dress." And she giggled.

Thomas thought it was the most wonderful sound he'd ever heard. If sounds were dreams, this one would be about someplace warm and sunny with nothing to do all day but to kick your feet in clear blue water.

Thomas threw a fireball at her and she ducked just in time. It lobbed through the air and came down right on the head of Philip. Philip picked a fragment of red eggshell off his face then turned around slowly to glare at Thomas. Marie burst out laughing, then stopped when a fireball shattered against the side of her head, dripping goo down onto her shoulder.

Then she laughed again and slipped right off the pole.

CHAPTER XI

THE BLACK KNIGHT

"You look fine," said Philip for the dozenth time. "Are you sure?"

"Yes, Thomas. Quit worrying. Oh look, here she comes."

Thomas panicked. Philip slapped him on the back and faded into the shadows. Thomas caught his breath and stepped into the light cast through a window of the Fine Pickle. Marie spotted him and waved.

Thomas gave what he hoped was an obviously theatrical bow and was rewarded with a laugh and a curtsey of equal caliber. He offered his arm, and she took it.

"You look much better when you're not all covered in flour and egg," she said.

"That's funny," he said, "I was just thinking I rather preferred you as a pancake."

Marie affected offense and punched him lightly on the shoulder, but she held onto his arm, her eyes sparkling with something that wasn't just the reflected light of the Pickle.

"C'mon," said Thomas when he'd managed to pull himself out of her eyes, "I hear this place has great cheesecake."

❧

He'd just begun to hope that the topic wouldn't come up. They were sitting in a warm booth in a quiet corner, sharing a slice of *White Chocolate Heaven*. A single candle flickered gently on the table. The walls of the Fine Pickle were decorated with tapestries of knights in various predicaments. The one above their table depicted a knight in pitched battle with apparently no one. The caption read, *Sir Balin Defeats The Invisible Knight*.

"I thought you showed mummum," Marie said, chewing. They had both agreed the cheesecake was too good for manners.

"Muht?" asked Thomas.

She held her fork hand to her mouth and indicated it would be a minute. Swallowing, she said, "Gumption. And a certain big-picture awareness." She took another bite.

Thomas decided the thing that was sparkling in her eyes was mischievousness.

"Really?" Thomas asked and frowned doubtfully. "Tell me, was the impressive part where I dropped my bucket of fireballs to catch you and smashed them all, or was it the part where I ran around like a mad rooster trying to keep the egg on my head intact?"

"Both!" she said. She paused to dislodge stuck bits of chocolate from her molars with her tongue. To Thomas, even this was mesmerizing. He caught himself staring, and jerked his focus back to the cheesecake.

"But you didn't give up," she continued, "it kept your team in the game long enough for them to whittle each other down. Everyone thought when it was just you and Bane left that you were a goner. What you did was really clever."

In the face of these unexpected compliments, the room was quickly growing uncomfortably warm for Thomas.

"Well, that was more about being stubborn than clever. I've had run-ins with that guy before, and I'll be sacked if I was going to let him beat me..." He almost said "again", but stopped himself in the nick of time.

Marie laughed, remembering. "No one knew what Arthur was going to do. The look on Bane when you took the egg off your head and smashed him in the face with it... Priceless." She shook her head and sighed.

"You know him?"

"Know him? Ha." She rolled her eyes. "He's always coming around the palace acting like he's God's gift to lasses." She paused then added, "You made a lot of friends today Thomas."

They just looked at each other for a moment. Thomas decided the sparkle in her eye might not be mischievousness, or at least, not *just* mischievousness.

"Well, I'll grant you the gumption, but I don't see how it helps the big picture. Arthur ruled it a draw, and now we have to decide the contest tomorrow. We're right back where we started."

Marie rolled her eyes. "Would you forget about your silly contest for a minute?"

The first thought that popped into Thomas's head was that *she* had brought it up. He wisely left the thought unarticulated.

She rolled her eyes again. "The *big* picture," is all she said.

His mind raced. She was watching him carefully. He had the overwhelming feeling that it was very important he figure this out on his own. What could be bigger than the tournament?

She split the last small bit of cheesecake in two and took one piece, leaving him the last. Thomas marveled. Watching someone eat had never been so enthralling. He gave himself a mental smack in the head.

"Oh, *that* big picture," he said. "Well, I'd trade a bucket of fireballs for you any day."

She smiled. "That's all a girl really wants."

"That'll be two pence, Sir."

It was the serving girl.

Thomas stared at her for a moment. He was still caught up in the joy of having passed the unexpected test.

The girl raised an eyebrow.

"Oh!" said Thomas and fumbled around in his pocket.

He pulled out a penny and stared at it. "I could've sworn I had two." The thought of not being able to pay the bill made Thomas's face grow hot and his throat start to close.

The girl tapped her foot.

Thomas searched his other pocket and found a slip of parchment.

He pulled it out and read the over-sized calligraphy. It was the coupon from their welcome packet. Thomas's heart started beating again.

"Here you go, Miss."

"Yer a knight?" said the girl.

"Of course he's a knight," said Marie.

The girl shrugged, picked up their dishes and walked away.

"Let's get out of here," said Thomas.

"Let's," said Marie.

They made their way back to the palace grounds talking about all sorts of things: where they grew up, their families, their favorite animals, the things they liked to do, the things they didn't like to do. Thomas didn't want the night to end, but end it did.

He said good night at the steps to the palace proper. Marie curtsied, and Thomas bowed. After the guard closed the doors behind her, Thomas simply stood staring at them.

After a while, the guard cleared his throat and said, "You're gonna have to move along, mate."

Thomas felt like he floated back to his barracks. He fell asleep certain that all was right with the world and everything would surely work itself out.

"We're... jousting?" Thomas's brain let go of his jaw.

"Looks like it." Even Philip looked rattled.

The field had been converted from the previous day's mock dragon-slaying, castle-storming, princess-saving extravaganza to a very official looking jousting field. Colored banners flapped with snaps and swooshes. A long fence ran down the middle of the field paralleling the bleachers and separating the tracks down which opposing jousters were apparently meant to careen. At either end, racks held dozens of polished lances pointing skyward.

Except for their impending deaths, the day seemed to be shaping up marvelously. Tall green grass waved in happy breezes on distant hills. Great forests stood beyond as if to say, "There's no rush, we'll be here." The sun climbed gracefully through a robin egg blue sky dotted with the kinds of clouds that make you think there's a reason for everything.

It was the kind of day you decide to go apologize to someone for something, and without hesitation, they forgive you and admit they weren't entirely guiltless themselves.

"Um..." said Thomas.

"You can say that again," said Philip.

Thomas's mind struggled to reconcile the beauty on the surface of the day with the horror just beneath it.

The stands were filling up. Everyone looked radiant. The excitement was contagious, and it swam around Thomas mixing with something cold and hard in his stomach that was undoubtedly pure, distilled dread. The juxtaposition made everything seem surreal. Colors were more colorful. Breezes were more breeze-like. He was unusually aware of the ground, as if it and his feet were just casual acquaintances who were meeting again unexpectedly and whose future relationship was uncertain. He had an overwhelming urge to pick up a handful of dirt and feel it. He felt like he could catch a fly by its wing with his forefinger and thumb. He felt like he was going to throw up.

Thomas looked at Philip to see if there was any sign that he was experiencing the same. Philip was staring at a fly he'd caught by its wing with his forefinger and thumb. He looked green.

※

Arthur lifted his megaphone.

"Welcome again, Gents and Gentry, Ladies and Laudables. As you well know, yesterday's contest ended undecided. No team managed to rescue the fair maiden..."

Marie stood and curtseyed. The crowd applauded sadly.

"...and the day ended in a draw between Marrok's team and Gawain's when the evil wizard, Thomas the Hesitant..."

The crowd gave a short, but enthusiastic cheer. Thomas, surprised, gave a surprised little wave.

"...destroyed himself and his army to bring down Gawain's last man, Bane the Appropriately Named."

Thomas and Philip shot looks at each other.

"No way," said Philip, and they laughed.

The crowd applauded sympathetically.

Bane bowed deeply, then looked at Thomas and drew his finger across his throat. Thomas, aware now of the crowd's attention, blew Bane a kiss. Laughter rolled from various spots in the audience, and Bane turned away steaming.

Philip said, "You really need to learn how to play nice with the other kids."

"Evil wizards," Thomas replied, "aren't fancied for their neighborly dispositions."

"We had an evil wizard for a neighbor once." Philip nodded in response to Thomas's disbelief. "Pyralis the Prestidigitatious. He was rather pleasant on a personal level. He'd bring over the best biscuits. There was the occasional slightly-too-maniacal cackle, but overall he was really rather endearing. My mum used to say, 'Now there's a man that knows what he's about.' That always made Dad a bit testy. 'Knows what he's about?' he'd say. 'Everyone knows what he's about! Wants to rule the world or turn us all to slugs. Or both! Great biscuits though. What d'ya think he puts in 'em Maud?' Mum would say, 'I'll tell ya whut he puts in 'em Phil–'' Philip put one hand on his hip and punctuated each syllable by poking at Thomas: "Am – bi – tion.'"

"Today," megaphoned Arthur, "nothing will be undecided!" The crowd failed to respond. He fumbled with his collar. "That is to say, everything that's been decided will stay that way. Whereas, things that haven't been decided... won't!"

Merlin whispered something.

Arthur continued, "Let's joust!"

The crowd, having found a footing, used it to stomp their approval.

Leagues away, the healer woke up in his small, homey shack by the stream. He stood and stretched and tried to recall what he'd been up to the day before and if there was anything worth following up on today. He scratched. He rearranged. He straightened his beard and felt around his teeth with his tongue. He'd made a career change years ago, and since then he'd slept the kind of sleep that most people don't even dream of. The kind that goes uninterrupted. The kind that clears and refreshes the mind. The kind that you couldn't disturb if you fired a canon over his bed.

He grabbed a biscuit from a bowl on the table and munched, staring at the open door of his shack while he chewed. His eyes dropped to a wet footprint on the threshold while his jaw worked contentedly. His gaze followed a line of footprints to its origin near a shelf while he swallowed and took another bite. Chewing lazily, he stared at a mess of shattered glass beneath the shelf.

He stopped.

A tiny, crude ship made, apparently, from leaves and sticks was lying on its side amidst the shards of glass and haphazard puddles of water.

He resumed chewing, a bit faster this time.

Later that morning, he set off with his walking staff and a pack full of sundries to find Gorgella. He felt somewhat responsible. And she wasn't the only thing missing.

The jousters who live the longest, joust the least. In a friendly contest, where the two combatants know each other and genuinely like each other, there's an unspoken agreement to charge short of deadly speeds. There's no guarantee, of course, and if you didn't know who your enemies were before the tournament, you learn about halfway down the runway when you notice the guy coming at you is giving it a bit more gusto than is sociable.

For these reasons and more, it's an advantage to the participants in a tournament to know with whom they'll be competing. For the same reasons, it's to the tournament organizer's benefit to keep this information confidential, even to the extent of encouraging select knights to compete incognito. Take a favored and popular knight, dress him up with a black tabard, a helmet that hides his face, a shield with an unfamiliar crest and voila. Where before you had a contest that no one believed would be an honest go, now you've got something to talk about.

Occasionally, the most-skilled knights would disguise themselves just for the fun of it.

And finally, there was the rare but not unheard of event where a mysterious knight from unknown lands and of questionable allegiances would show up who really, in fact, was a mysterious knight from unknown lands and questionable allegiances.

That is why, when the black knight appeared, everyone looked around to see if anyone they knew was missing.

❧

"Where's Arthur?"

"Over there," Philip pointed, "in the popcorn line."

Thomas scanned the field. "Gawain?"

"Talking to the cheerleaders."

They were both quiet for a moment.

"Where's Bane?" asked Philip.

"I saw him rubbing down his horse by the stables." Thomas shook his head. "Anyway, Bane doesn't have to pretend to be bad news."

Philip conceded the point.

"I don't see anyone missing," he said.

"Nor do I," said Thomas, "nor do I."

❧

The black knight was unstoppable. In a long succession of imploded shields and cracked lances he unhorsed everyone who rode against him. Gawain was first, landing squarely on his rear behind his surprised steed. When they carried him from the field clearly rattled, he was heard to say, "I canna feel me rrrump. I didna leave it behind did I? That wouldna do at all. Who was tha' anyway?"

Kay and Bedivere fared somewhat worse. They both shattered their lances and left the field unconscious. At first, the field rallied against the knight, seeking to avenge their fallen comrades. Pellinore, Agravain, Owain, and Marrok all went down. Lamorak landed a square blow and split the black knight's shield, but failed to unhorse him.

The knight was given a new shield and, in a second run, launched Lamorak so high off his saddle that he had time to wonder if he'd been knocked clean out of his body and was just going to keep ascending. Gravity eventually re-asserted itself and brought him home with vigor.

"Find it funny do you Bane?"

Bane was smirking, and Philip was livid.

"Why don't you give it a go then, eh? I'd like to see you land on your rear like all the others."

Bane didn't seem at all perturbed. "I've got a better idea," he said as cold as ice. "Why doesn't Thomas give it a run? And if he wins..."

He looked square at Thomas.

"If he wins, I'll tell my father to pardon his brother."

Thomas felt all the blood drain away from his face.

The black knight had ridden up and was standing alone, facing the king's pavilion.

"What's he talking about, Thomas?" asked Philip

Arthur addressed the knight, "It would appear there are none left to challenge your supremacy on the field today stranger-knight. You have fought magnificently. Better than any that have ever competed on this field. Unmask yourself and claim your victory!"

The crowd cheered expectantly.

Philip looked from Thomas to Bane to the black knight and back again.

"Thomas," hissed Philip, "what's he talking about?!"

"Wait!" shouted Thomas.

The crowd went silent.

"I challenge him," Thomas said and stepped forward.

CHAPTER XII

THE GAUNTLET OF SMASHING SUCCESS

"I really don't think this is a good idea," said Philip.
"Nonsense, I'll be fine," replied Thomas though he didn't believe it himself.

"You're insane," said Philip as he suited Thomas up.

"I have to do this," said Thomas.

"It doesn't change the fact that you're insane."

Thomas had explained, briefly, the situation. As unlikely as it was that Thomas would best the black knight when all others had failed, he had to try to make this work.

"There's got to be a better way," said Philip. "This guy's going to kill you. Have you ever jousted before?"

Thomas just looked at him.

"You haven't, have you? You could appeal to Arthur! You could–"

He was interrupted by the sudden appearance of a very old, very out of breath man.

"Oh, good. I made it," he said. "Where's the glove, do you have it?"

"Healer?" said Thomas.

"Pyralis!" said Philip.

"Riders ready!" shouted the joustmaster.

"Oh dear," said the old man.

ॐ

"Well," said Pyralis, "for one thing, if I were still evil I wouldn't be here trying to stop it, would I?"

"I don't know," said Philip. "That's the sort of thing an evil wizard might say in order to get us to let our guards down. I'm just pointing this out Pyralis. I don't mean anything by it of course. Boy, it's good to see you. Still baking?"

Pyralis visibly relaxed.

"Oh yes," he said. "I should have brought something. In fact, just yesterday..." but that brought him back round to the problem at hand and he visibly tensed again. He gave himself a little shake.

"Just yesterday," he continued, "I was telling Gorgella about some of my favorite pieces that I'd kept from the old days, you know, for sentimental reasons."

He gave the sort of sheepish, worried, and guilty grin that people give when they've done something foolish that hasn't been worked all the way out yet.

"Wait, what?" Thomas interjected, "You were talking to Gorgella? Is she... Is she..."

"Aye," Pyralis nodded. "She's grown."

Joy slid down Thomas's face through his eyes and landed on his chin with a wide smile.

"Well, that's..." Thomas shook his head. "That's fantastic. How did you do it? I mean, when I left I thought she was, you know..." Thomas didn't want to admit to Pyralis or himself that he hadn't really held much hope for her in Pyralis's care.

Pyralis fixed Thomas with a look that was not very like an evil wizard at all and said, "You did it Thomas. You tried to help her, and when you did so, you made her think she might be worth helping. Now I think she wants to return the favor."

"What do you mean?"

Pyralis shrugged. "She wants to help you."

"But, how?"

"She stole something from me, a piece of armor. It's very powerful and very dangerous. It's called the Gauntlet of Smashing Success, and it's cursed. It makes the wearer invincible as long as he fights, but as soon as he retreats, shrinks from a fight, or even pulls a punch, he's toast."

They stared at him blankly.

"Kaput. Wormsville. Cadaver City."

They continued to stare at him blankly.

"Dead?" said Philip.

"That." Pyralis frowned.

"Fine bit of work for its purpose if I say so myself. My, em, former employer commissioned it for his champion. He'd gotten tired of training people then having them use the experience he'd supplied to find other jobs. Of course, this was right when I was making my own career-shift, and I never actually delivered the piece.

"It was some of my best work," Pyralis said quietly. "Er, you know, back in the day," he added.

Philip, still suspicious, interrupted, "Hold on. You can craft a gauntlet that makes the wearer invincible, and you give Thomas a sword that just... stinks?"

Pyralis looked hurt. "Now hold on. Ambrosia is a very fine sword."

"*Ambrosia*?" said Thomas.

"The perfume of the gods?" asked Marie. "Are we talking about the same sword?"

"Where did you come from?" said Thomas, startled.

"I'm not talking to you. You're insane," she said.

"It's not easy, you know," Pyralis blistered. "I made cursed weapons and armor for so long, and no run of the mill stuff either. I was good at it, you see. It's a gift... of sorts. It's hard to work that stuff completely out no matter how much your heart changes. I can't seem to get entirely rid of the cursing part, so I work on ways to turn a thing's curse into its blessing. Anyway, if the gods made a perfume, what would it be like eh? Would it smell the same to everybody? Surely they'd be more clever than that."

Pyralis stopped and seemed embroiled in an internal struggle between his mouth, which wanted to say more, and his brain, which wanted him to put a cork in it.

"You're telling me that the sword," said Thomas, "that Ambrosia... can change how it smells?"

"Maybe," said Pyralis guardedly. "But the glove," he sighed in a way that was a little unnerving, "that was pure evil. I'm afraid when I was showing Gorgella the piece I never got around to actually mentioning the, you know, the evil bit."

Philip glared at him.

"Alright," said Thomas trying to work all this through. "What do the gauntlet, Gorgella, and the black knight have to do with each other?"

"Well, first I thought Gorgella had stolen the glove to bring it to you, not knowing about the cursed part. But seeing as how you don't have the glove – now I think..."

"What?"

"I think," said Pyralis, pointing at the black knight, "I think Gorgella *is* the black knight."

Pyralis and Thomas stared at the black knight.

"Pardon," said Philip. "The theory here is that Gorgella..." He said the name carefully, and raised his eyebrows at Thomas.

"Uh huh," agreed Thomas still staring at the knight, eyes wide and worrying.

"Gorgella," continued Philip, "is the black knight?"

"Right," said Pyralis.

"And this Gorgella," said Philip, "is a giantess? That is, a female of the Giant species, characterized by, oh let's call it 'excessive anatomy'?"

"That is correct," said Pyralis.

"Have you noticed," said Philip in an I'm-trying-very-hard-to-stay-calm sort of way, "that the black knight is rather – how should I put this – short?"

Thomas broke his wide, worried stare to look at Philip. Pyralis blinked.

"I'm just saying," Philip tried to continue patiently and failed. Instead he stomped, pointed and said, "Oh, come on. How can that be Gorgella? The black knight is shorter than me, and Gorgella is a giantess... You know..." He threw his arms and eyes wide. "...big!"

Thomas and Pyralis both said, "Oh!"

"Gorgella–" said Thomas.

"Has self-esteem issues," finished Pyralis.

Thomas added, "Try to be sensitive, Philip."

Philip let his hands fall to his sides, cocked his head sideways, and looked utterly exhausted. They all looked back at Gorgella.

Philip said, "I suppose next you're going to tell me that Ox is really a dwarf with delusions of grandeur?"

Thomas looked sharply at Ox who was busy trying to swat something on the back of his neck.

Pyralis shook his head. "Dwarves are far too practical to believe in the illusions that could change them. Giants, though, are dreamers."

Philip considered this. He mumbled to himself, "You could certainly say they've got their heads in the clouds."

"What?" said Thomas.

"Nothing," said Philip. "Come on. We'd better do something about this if you don't want your giant friend to get hurt."

He didn't move. Thomas and Pyralis looked at him. Thomas coughed.

"You have a plan?" said Pyralis, looking at Philip.

"Er, no. Not exactly. Was hoping one of you two did?"

Thomas shook his head. Pyralis shrugged.

"She's your friend?" asked Marie.

Thomas nodded.

"Then you have to forfeit."

Thomas grimaced. She was right of course.

"If there was just some way to tell Gorgella..."

"Tell Gorgella what?" said Gorgella from behind them. She was munching popcorn. All four of them jerked around so hard that they nearly fell over.

"Gorgella!" cried Thomas and hugged her. She smiled, hugged him back with one arm and protected her popcorn with the other. He stepped back. "But if you're..." He pointed at the black knight. "...and if that's not—"

"Kindly hand over the gauntlet Gorgella," said Pyralis.

"The gauntlet?"

"Yes."

"The black one you showed me yesterday?"

"Yes."

"The Gauntlet of Smashing Success? The one you neglected to tell me was cursed?"

"Yes. Er, how did you...?"

"I don't have it."

"You don't have it? Then who—"

"Beats me," Gorgella shrugged. "It was gone when I got up this morning. Maybe he's got it." She nodded in the direction of the black knight.

"Last call!" shouted the joustmaster. "Jousters ready!"

"I'm so confused," said Philip.

Thomas grinned. "Everything's okay. Gorgella is not the black knight, she's not wearing the gauntlet, and she's not going to die trying to make me look good. Now, all I have to do to free my brother is beat a knight who's beaten every other knight we've ever admired and who is possibly enchanted and invincible."

Thomas saddled up and rode away.

"I think he might be in trouble," said Philip.

"I think he's insane," said Marie.

"Sanity is overrated," said Pyralis.

Trumpets blew. The crowd roared. Thomas and the black knight started to charge.

❧

It's not the kind of story that anyone likes to tell. Sometimes the bad guy plays the game better, or the good guy makes a mistake, and against all hope, the thing people fear will happen happens.

When you get knocked down, the good guys will say, the important thing to do is to get back up again. Thomas got knocked down a lot. First he got knocked off his horse. Then the black knight dismounted, and they went at it with swords and shields. That's where the real knocking-downs started coming. He kept getting up, which everyone applauded for a while until even the crowd was hoping Thomas would just stay down.

You want a hard slog like that to end with the bad guy losing. Through some last minute opportunity, or some deep fault of the villain, or even just sheer stubborn grit on the part of the hero, you want the good guy to stand alone in the end, battered but victorious.

It didn't end like that.

Thomas got knocked down a last time, and didn't get up. The black knight mounted and rode back to the jousting line as if to say, "Next!"

A group of knights carried Thomas off to a nearby pavilion where some nuns set about seeing if they could keep him alive. They shooed Philip and Marie away and wouldn't let Pyralis anywhere near their equipment. Apparently they recognized him.

To everyone's astonishment, there was one more challenger that day. He too was beaten by the black knight who, afterwards, simply mounted up and rode away without a word.

For a long while, the crowd wasn't sure what to do. They kept waiting for the twist at the end that would make everything work out right. It didn't come.

CHAPTER XIII

AFTER ALL THAT

"Well, hello there."

It was Marie's voice. Thomas opened his eyes to a blurry mess of mostly white and various shades of gray.

"Can you move anything?"

The last thing Thomas wanted to do was to try moving something, but he gave it a shot. It hurt, but it worked.

"It seems you're back in the land of the living." Marie's face resolved out of the white and gray fuzziness, more beautiful than ever and very close. Thomas's heart tried to leap, but then everything came rushing back at him. He'd blown two chances now to help William, and he had no guarantee there would be a third.

"I thought you weren't talking to me."

Marie frowned exquisitely. "I was hoping the tossing you got might've knocked some sense into you." Her eyes sparkled with tears ready to spill.

Thomas sighed and laid back.

"I'm sorry," he said. "It's just – I had to try. And now, ugh, I don't know where to begin.

"What a mess this has all become."

"He's alive!"

Philip was walking down the row of gurneys carrying a giant basket of flowers. Gorgella and Pyralis followed.

Thomas smiled, waved, and immediately regretted it. One time when they were younger, William had convinced Thomas to climb into a barrel and roll down a hill in it. He felt like he had after that ride – if there'd been several large rocks in the barrel too, and instead of a sloping grassy hill it had been a tall scraggy cliff, and if at the end when the barrel smashed to pieces, an armored knight had picked him up and punched him repeatedly.

Pyralis rushed to his side and began prodding, pinching, and bending various bits of Thomas's person.

"I'm *fine*, Pyralis!"

"I'll be the judge of that. How many fingers am I holding up?"

"Er, none?"

"Good. Who sits on the throne in Camelot?"

"...the king?" Thomas said smiling.

Everyone but Pyralis laughed. Pyralis raised an eyebrow.

"Oh, come on." Thomas waited for Pyralis's stare to break, but it wouldn't. Thomas rolled his eyes. "Arthur. Arthur sits on the throne. I'm fine!"

Pyralis frowned, but seemed at least momentarily satisfied.

"Everyone must think I'm a fool," said Thomas.

"Well, yes." They were all nodding.

"But a brave one. And not as big a fool as Bane," said Philip. "At least you had a good reason."

Thomas gave a puzzled look.

"After you rode up against the black knight, Bane took a whack too."

"You're kidding."

"Nope. He rode right up to the challenging line acting for all the world like he had the contest in the bag. I've never seen someone look so pompous."

"What happened?"

"Well, same as everyone else basically. He got destroyed. Then the black knight rode off and that was that."

Thomas mulled this over.

"That doesn't make any sense. Why would Bane..." Thomas trailed off shaking his head, but stopped because it felt more like he was shaking a bag of bricks.

"Who knows," said Marie, still sounding a bit perturbed by the whole affair. "But you can ask him yourself at the commissioning ceremony tomorrow."

"Ugh," Thomas groaned.

"It won't be that bad," said Philip. "No one faults you for trying. We'll get assigned to our table, *you* can stop fretting about it, and then we can all think of some way to help your brother."

"It's not that," said Thomas, "though that all sounds great."

He scooted himself into a better sitting position and grimaced. "It's just – I imagine – the ceremony's going to require things like..."

"Standing?"

"Yeah, that," said Thomas.

"Leave that to me," said Pyralis who pulled something foul from his satchel and began to grind it in a pestle.

Thomas and Philip shared a horrified glance.

Marie patted Thomas lightly on the arm. "I'll get the nuns," she whispered.

&

The hall had been divided into two sections. The back half was packed with seats for what Thomas estimated was roughly a hundred knights. The tables and devices here were nondescript. The uninterrupted ordinariness of this

107

back section of the hall pushed the eye toward the front section, which wasn't ordinary at all.

Three tables dominated the front of the hall, one table a bit larger than the other two. The two smaller tables flanked the larger table, one to each side. The flanking tables were ornate, richly varnished, and polished so that they reflected the dancing torches on the walls. One could imagine that the tables burned with some inner fire that failed to consume them. They looked important. Their chairs looked important. Clearly, the twelve knights who would sit at each of these tables would also be important. But these two tables were to the third like barren moons to a blazing sun. From its position between the flanking tables, the Round Table asserted its presence. Everything else orbited this one thing that among all seemed singularly confident and securely fixed. Ringing the Round Table were thirteen of what an unimaginative person might call seats. These majesties of carpentry were for sitting the way an ocean is for getting wet. In other words, they looked like they'd be very, very good for it, and then some.

Arthur stood beside one. Merlin stood beside Arthur. The knights were assembled in lines on either side of the hall, and the courtiers mingled behind them. Guinevere and her ladies sat on a balcony above it all.

Arthur motioned for quiet, and quiet went to work straight away. Thomas thought this was probably one of the most critical abilities a leader could possess, the ability to get people to settle down and pay attention. He wondered if the ability had gotten Arthur the job or if the job had gotten him the ability, or if they came hand in hand like chickens and eggs.

"Two sieges," said Arthur.

"Two what?" whispered Thomas.

"Sieges," said Philip.

"Sieges?" said Thomas.

"Aye, well, you can't really call those things seats, can you?"

Thomas said, "Ah, right. Good point."

"Two sieges," said Arthur, "have been revealed."

An excited murmur wafted through the crowd like a nervous breeze.

"Did he say 'revealed?'" said someone.

"Aye," said another.

"Does he mean 'announced'?" said the same someone.

"Shhh," said a third.

Merlin stepped forward, raised his staff and said in a very serious tone, "Two names have appeared on the table.

"Mysteriously," he added and casually brushed something from the table that looked to Thomas like wood shavings.

"Magically," he added, "these names have appeared, and therefore pre-ordained are the eponymous to claim their sieges and sit with the king as his peers."

"I can never understand a word he says," said someone.

"Aye," said another.

"Shhh," said a third.

Arthur put his hand on Merlin's shoulder, smiled and said, "Sir Kay and Sir Bedivere, come take your seats."

The assembly cheered, stomped and applauded. Kay and Bedivere came forward, bowed to Arthur and folded themselves into their chairs like one might fold oneself into the sea for a bath.

Merlin cleared his throat and said something in Latin. Latin always made Thomas a little edgy. It was the domain of wizards and priests and he always felt a bit nervous about what might come of it: lightning shooting from fingertips, or statues weeping, or the sudden inexplicable need to go to Confession.

Apparently, the rest of the assembly shared his opinion. Silence descended on the hall with an almost audible 'fwump.'

"He's going to prophesy," someone wanted to say and thought better of it.

"Aye," another would have replied.

"Shhh," said a third because he could see what the other two were thinking.

"Thirteen seats," said Merlin into the absolute lack of hubbub.

"Thirteen seats at a table that hasn't been full since our Lord's betrayal in Jerusalem. But I tell you today, these seats will be filled in this generation. And when they are..."

He paused so long that people began to glance left and right to see how others were handling it. Most everyone was pretending not to be uncomfortable, which oddly enough, Thomas found rather comforting.

"And when they are," Merlin continued, startling everyone who'd forgotten he'd been speaking, "a miracle will be visited upon it. A stunning manifestation will betide those present that day, invigorating the virtuous and ensnaring the vainglorious.

"But this gift comes not without cost. For the thirteenth siege," he said and stepped up behind it.

"The thirteenth siege is perilous. Only one of greatest virtue, of noblest heart – only the one who will achieve the vision that shall come to pass may sit at this, the Siege Perilous, and live."

Some of the knights looked at each other. The courtiers blinked. No one moved a muscle.

"Right then," said Arthur, "we won't be filling that one any time soon, eh?"

Gawain, his brother Agravain and his cousin Owain, along with Pellinore and his son Lamorak were inducted into the Knights of the Watch. Sir Marrok, the Watch's captain, welcomed them to the table to the left of the Round. Colorful, paper table-tents illustrated with their titles and crests marked their spots. They also received a lovely stationery set.

The other table, it was explained, was the Table of Errant Companions. It was set aside for those knights of any order who had left on extended quests. Thomas wondered aloud to Philip what use was a set of seats reserved for people who were certain not to be there. Philip replied that he thought the main point of the empty seats was to remind everyone else that they weren't allowed to sit in them.

All the knights who were left, numbering just over one hundred, were inducted into the Table of Less Valued Knights which for obvious logistical reasons was seated not at one but at all of the tables in the back of the hall. Each knight received a handshake from Sir Tuttle, the table's Captain, and a manual penned by him, *The Code of Service of the Table of Less Valued Knights*.

Philip shook Tuttle's hand with vigor. Dedric the Diplopian asked why he was only getting one manual when everyone else had gotten two. Ox the Monosyllabic said, "Thanks," and in his enthusiasm accidentally cracked several small bones in Tuttle's shaking hand. Marrok, who'd been helping hand out manuals, offered his hand to Thomas while Tuttle recovered from Ox's handshake.

Marrok had a curiously proud glint in his eye that made Thomas smile but look away. He looked down at their hands instead and noticed a jagged scar around Marrok's forearm where his sleeve had pulled up. The scar looked terribly familiar. He glanced back at Marrok's eyes as they let their hands go, and that's when it hit him. He'd seen those eyes before, and he'd seen the wound that made that scar. But the last time he'd seen them, they'd been on a majestic silver wolf.

A thousand questions competed to get out of Thomas's mouth, but none of them made it. They must have played across his face though, because Marrok smiled, winked, and then turned to the next in line leaving Thomas awkwardly alone and flabbergasted. He moved to stand next to Philip.

"You look like you've seen a ghost."

Thomas shook his head. "Not a ghost," he said. "I think Marrok's a..."

But it was Bane's turn in line, and the sight drove all other thought from Thomas's mind. Bane was visibly furious. He looked like the kind of volcano you don't want to build your tranquil fishing village beneath.

"I think someone is a wee bit upset," said Thomas nodding toward Bane.

When Marrok handed Bane his manual and shook his hand, Bane held his grip longer than was appropriate and gave Marrok a look that would've reminded tranquil fishermen of molten lava and caused them to politely excuse themselves and flee for their lives.

Through clenched teeth Bane hissed, "I don't belong here."

Marrok dropped his grip and his smile but held his gaze. With a firmness that a mountain would admire, he replied, "No, you don't."

As Marrok and a recovering Sir Tuttle moved on to congratulate other less volcanic inductees, Philip said, "I'm liking that guy more and more. You were saying, you think he's a..."

"Oh," said Thomas. "Yes, um. I think Marrok's a fine fellow."

Thomas felt odd. As he watched Bane stomp out of the hall, his brain spun trying to resolve what his gut felt. There were puzzle pieces here that wanted assembling.

Arthur tried to conclude the evening with some final words before he went off to do the things a king does the week of his wedding, but Merlin had one last go at upsetting everyone's equilibrium when he announced that a strange and troublesome event would befall the wedding reception. The result, of course, would be the glory of some and the doom of others including, possibly, Merlin himself.

To which Arthur, who hadn't completely been paying attention replied, "Splendid. Let's get on with it, shall we?"

And that was that.

≈

Later, Thomas remarked to Philip that the final assignments were not surprising. That is, he felt he could have predicted at least who would be sitting in the front half of the room and who'd be sitting in the back without all the fuss and bother of the tournament.

Philip replied by pointing out a section in *The Code* under the heading, *Duties and Responsibilities*. It read:

Whenever, and being in all places and circumstances, it is the duty of the foresworn Less Valued to make his betters look better even be it a tarnish to himself and his own reputation. In all things, the character and manner of appearance of the higher Orders must be preserved.

"You're missing the point of the tournament I think," said Philip. "We're here to make the heroes look good."

After a moment, Thomas sighed, "It's not surprising. It's just... I guess I'd hoped for more. It doesn't quite seem fair, in this day and age, for there to be this impenetrable order of things, you know? And it makes me angry that they made us believe we had a chance at one of the other tables when all along we were just..."

He sputtered and searched for the word, "We were just the *entertainment*."

"Did you think you did well enough to make it to another table?" asked Philip.

"Well, no, but–"

"Did you think *anyone* did well enough to make it to another table?" asked Philip.

"Well, no, but—"

"Did you think that smashing an egg on Bane's head was going to land you a seat on the Round Table?"

"No," said Thomas, laughing at the unexpected memory, "but it's worth something isn't it?"

After another quiet moment, Thomas said, "I just hate to be strung along, you know?"

Philip flipped to a section of *The Code* titled "The Twelve Basic Rules" and pointed to number six which read:

𝕽ule VI: 𝕰xpect to be trifled with, caboodled, shucked, and/or generally 𝕾trung 𝕬long – oftentimes 𝕼uite severely.

Thomas opened his mouth to reply, but just then the door of the barracks slammed open and a lanky boy with a pockmarked face lumbered in carrying a heavy bag. "Mail call," he yelled, his voice cracking.

Thomas's heart sank. He was sure if there was anything in that bag for him, it wouldn't be pleasant. Halfway through the bag, the post-boy called his name "To: Thomas Farmer, of the Fogbottom Farmers; From: His Mother." Several of the other LVK sniggered. Thomas made his way dutifully to the boy and accepted the letter like a man accepting a sentence. He imagined that was exactly what was inside.

Thomas sat on his bunk, sighed, and opened the letter.

Dear Thomas,

We expected to have you home by now. Have you spoken with King Arthur? I'm sure he's a very busy man. I imagine the palace is wonderful.

114

All is well here. We've run out of meat and grain, but I've managed to make a kind of paste out of roots from the cellar. Your father complains, but that's nothing unusual. William, of course, still languishes in prison. The warden is gracious and has allowed him to write to us nearly every day. I've told William not to worry — that you're in Camelot petitioning for us. When can we expect news from you?

Grandma is her old self, but Elizabeth is taking all of this rather poorly. She spends most of her time in the loft with that old stuffed rabbit. I have half a mind to toss it just to snap her out of it.

You remember Ackerly and Royden — two of William's chums. They came around shortly after you left looking for William. Apparently he didn't tell them what he was up to either. Your brother is so noble. I don't know where he gets it. Anyway, when they heard what had happened and that you were off to Camelot and what with your Father's gimp, they were distraught for us and have been coming around to help with your and William's chores and anything else that needs doing. They helped your Father mend the roof yesterday. I gave them some root paste, and they were so grateful. I don't know what their mum's been feeding them, and they said they didn't want to talk about it.

How are things in Camelot? Write soon.

Luv,
Mum

Thomas folded the paper, hung his head and sighed again.

"Letter from home?" asked Philip.

Thomas nodded.

"I know how those go." Philip was holding a flowery lavender flyer from a place called Madame Rhapsody's Dance Emporium. "Say, are you going to be dancing with Marie at the wedding reception?"

He held the flyer out to Thomas who took it, groaned, and collapsed on his bunk. On top of it all, here was a whole new world of worries to explore.

CHAPTER XIV

DOUBT & REDOUBT

Madame Rhapsody's Dance Emporium was the sort of place to which few men went willingly. The oil lamps had sparkly things dangling from them. The chairs were flowery and plush. The air had a tinkling sound in it, and it smelled nice. There was even a cat who lived on the premises. His name was Sir Cuddlington. Madame Rhapsody called him Sir, or Cuddles, and he rubbed his cheek a lot on her chin. Thomas was about to turn around and make a fast escape when she came around the corner and spotted him.

"Well, hello!" she crooned. "Classes begin at half past eleven. You're welcome to wait." She smiled. She was the kind of large woman who knows it and isn't afraid of it.

"I, um," said Thomas, his body still half turned toward the corridor. He sighed and turned back toward Madame R. "I'm here for a, er, I'm a knight you see." He started ruffling through his pockets for his identification.

"Oh I could've told you that, honey. You move like one." She winked and sauntered back around the corner.

Thomas grimaced, sat down, and waited.

Sir Cuddles decided Thomas was his new best friend and planted himself on Thomas's lap, purring like a toneless bagpipe.

Once things had gotten going, it wasn't nearly as bad as Thomas had dreaded it would be. Dedric and Ox had shown up, among others. There were no girls in the class, so they took turns leading and being led around the studio floor while Madame Rhapsody corrected their feet, hands, hips, heads, shoulders, and alarmingly, buttocks. She had a skinny, wrinkled old man for an assistant. His name was Hedley, and he played the harpsichord. Thomas had found the music actually rather pleasant and tried to focus on it rather than what would otherwise have been a grossly inappropriate lack of distance between himself and his partner, Ox.

The lesson was just ending, and Thomas's spirit was just beginning to rise when Madame Rhapsody thanked them for coming and told them she'd see them all again on the morrow.

"Again tomorrow?" asked Sir Edgar the Erstwhile, looking as distraught as Thomas felt.

Madame Rhapsody laughed, and her whole body participated. "You didn't think we were through here, did you? You've all got a long way to go before you're ready to dance publicly let alone at an affair like the King's wedding! You represent Camelot! We've got less than a week, and I've got to get you looking like you've danced all your lives."

She put her hands on her hips and shook her head at them. "An impossible task, some might say. But those people wouldn't be Madame Rhapsody! Mm-mm. I make princes out of frogs, mountains out of mole hills, and I can make you all into *dancers*." She said the word "dancers" with a flare, a gleam in her eye, and an especially breathy voice, even for Madame R.

"You just get here tomorrow, and let Madame Rhapsody do the rest."

Thomas was pretty sure it wouldn't work out just as she described it, but he resigned himself to returning. He didn't want to embarrass Camelot, Marie, or himself – not necessarily in that order anyway.

Steeling himself for the days ahead, he began the walk to the barracks where the LVK slept, ate, washed, and did just about everything really. On the way, he decided to take a street he hadn't yet explored and came upon the post office, closed for Sunday. A jolt of guilt struck him like a spear. He surprised himself by feeling suddenly rather homesick as well. He saw his whole family in his mind's eye, waiting on word from him, their hope. Thomas... his family's hope.

Well that's something new, thought Thomas.

When he got back to the barracks, he found a quill and some clean parchment and tried to figure out what to say. An hour later when Philip burst in, the page was still blank.

"We're going to be late," blurted Philip. "What are you doing? You smell like–" Philip took a whiff. "Ugh, you smell like flowers."

Thomas bolted to his feet and splashed his face with water from a bowl near the window. He took a last look at the blank parchment on his bunk.

"Let's go," he said. And they went, arriving just in time at St. Stephen's cathedral for the inaugural Orientation & Briefing of the Table of Less Valued Knights.

St. Stephen's was huge. All one hundred – plus or minus – of the LVK sat comfortably in the sanctuary's transept. Enormous, stained-glass windows lined the walls and decorated the floor with colored sunlight, contrasting the rich, earthy hues of the stone tile floor and wooden pews.   The apse of the cathedral, behind the altar, shimmered. A countless array of tiny golden discs were affixed to the wall in a way that let them wiggle when the air was disturbed.   With preparations underway for Arthur's wedding and all the workers coming and going, they were wiggling incessantly. It looked like someone had managed to mount a golden pond vertically on the wall. A crucifix hung in front of the shimmer. St. Stephen's Jesus was easily three times Thomas's height.

The wedding workers hauled in piles and piles of decorations and other accoutrements, passing them up to more workers on scaffoldings. They showed no sign of letting up as Sir Tuttle stepped up into the chancel and disappeared behind the ornate mahogany pulpit. A few seconds later, his head appeared over the speaker's stand. He pulled a cord attached to a shutter high above, and a beam of light illuminated the stand.

"Welcome, Less Valued Knights," said Tuttle. "We have a full agenda, so let's get started."

They started with a roll call. Two knights were absent: Sir Mendhel the Misfortunately Placed – who'd been missing from the beginning – and Sir Remi the Imperturbable.

"I couldn't wake him up, sir," said Dedric, who bunked next to Remi.

When it was Bane's turn to sound off, Thomas could tell from his tone of voice that "Here" was the last place Bane wanted to be.

Tuttle began by outlining general rules and regulations for palace employees. Thomas's mind kept drifting to the blank parchment on his bunk. It needed to become a letter to his parents.

While Tuttle droned on, Thomas found himself staring at an ornate stained glass window. It depicted Pontius Pilate enthroned before a recently arrested Jesus. The question, "Are you the King of the Jews?" was worked into the window near the bottom of the scene. Thomas knew it to be the first of the fourteen Stations of the Cross. The chapel in Fogbottom had the same stations, though Fogbottom's weren't stained glass; the Parson had carved tiny figures and set up mini-dioramas in niches around the sanctuary. Every Easter for as long as Thomas could remember, he and his family had dutifully walked the stations, meditating on Jesus's death.

Somewhere off to his left, a Less Valued Knight stood at Tuttle's behest and recited an article from the Code of Service. Maybe it was the sunlight ebbing and flowing through the stained glass as clouds passed by, or maybe it was just the sheer overwhelming size of the windows compared to those tiny scenes in Fogbottom – Whatever the case here in St. Stephen's, Thomas found himself caught up in the artistry.

Philip elbowed him in the ribs. Tuttle had stopped talking. Tuttle was, in fact, staring directly at Thomas. He raised his eyebrows and said, "I say again, the Ninth Article if you would please Sir Thomas."

Thomas stood and cleared his throat. Somewhere behind him Bane sniggered. Thomas glanced at Philip looking for help.

Philip, eyes wide, shrugged.

Panicked, Thomas shot a look back at Tuttle who was now glaring at him and tapping his quill against the lectern. At the edge of his vision, the image of Pontius Pilate interrogating Jesus brightened with a surge of color and pressed on Thomas's mind.

Memory stirred, and with it, a wash of relief. He cleared his throat and began, "The Ninth Article of the Code of Service of the Order of Less Valued Knights..."

Tuttle stopped tapping, lifted his chin and frowned.

"It's not about you," said Thomas.

Tuttle lowered his head in a nod of approval.

121

Encouraged, Thomas continued, "It's never about you."

Behind him, Bane snorted.

"Except, of course," finished Thomas, "when it would be better for your superiors that whatever it is be not about them."

Tuttle said, "Excellent." And Thomas sat down.

Philip looked stunned. "Where'd you pull that from?" he whispered. In answer, Thomas simply pointed at the stained glass.

While Tuttle worked his way through more of the Less Valued and the rest of the Code, Thomas stared at the windows. He returned again and again to two in particular: one of Jesus taking up his cross and another of a Roman soldier striking him on the cheek. The second was inscribed, *Præbe illi et alteram* – "Offer him the other".

Someone was reciting Rule X – "Choose your battles wisely." – when the thought struck Thomas.

"Philip," he whispered. "Do you think..." started Thomas, then sat, mouth open, staring intently at the stations.

"You're kind of freaking me out Thomas."

"Do you think Jesus," he nodded at the stations. He started over. "Philip, I think Jesus was a kind of Less Valued Knight."

"That's ridiculous Thomas, the order's only just begun."

"I don't mean he *was* a Less Valued Knight," said Thomas, frustrated but excited. Behind them, Bane stood up and moved to the other end of his pew and sat down again. Tuttle paused, frowned at him, and continued.

"I mean, our Code is rather like what he was trying to say don't you think?"

Tuttle was growing increasingly agitated at the noise coming from the vicinity of Thomas and Philip.

"Philip," said Thomas, "if this is what we are. If our lot is cast..." Thomas looked again at the glass depicting

122

Jesus taking up his cross on the road to Golgotha. "I'm going to be the best Less Valued Knight I can be."

"SIR THOMAS OF FOGBOTTOM," roared Tuttle. "Would you please stop your incessant chattering, or is there something you'd like to share with the rest of us?"

And at that moment, Bane the Appropriately Named stood up, turned his back on Tuttle, and started walking.

"Who is that?" said Sir Tuttle. "Is that Bane? Bane! Halt! Halt, I say, and return to your post – your seat I mean – this instant."

Bane slammed the door shut behind him.

Tuttle was furious. He shuffled his parchments and rocked from one foot to the other, muttering well-I-nevers and in-all-my-days. Finally, he picked up a quill and spoke the words through clenched teeth as he wrote them:

Rule XIII: Sit when it is Time to sit. Stand when it is Time to stand. And above All, Leave when it is Time to go.

The meeting only lasted another five minutes. Tuttle was apoplectic, and it was all he could do to simply hand out wedding assignments. Thomas and Philip drew ushering detail. Ox got a special assignment: Find and sit in front of Arthur's half-sister Morgan.

"Won't that rather block her view of the proceedings Sir?" asked Dedric.

Tuttle fixed him with a cold stare that said, among other things, 'That's pretty much the point.'

"Oh," said Dedric.

A thought struck Thomas.

"I've got to find out where Bane went," he said as he and Philip made their way out of the cathedral.

"What makes you think he was going anywhere other than away from here, where I'm sure, we'd all liked to have been?"

"Bane's a lot of things, but purposeless isn't one of them. He's up to something. Did you see when he changed seats in the middle of the meeting?"

"I did notice – odd that, eh?"

Thomas stopped walking and pointed at one of the laborers carrying wedding props into the cathedral.

"Bane moved because the wedding decorators had blocked his view of the clock. He moved to a spot where he could see it better, and he kept his eyes on it."

"As if he had somewhere else to be?"

"As if he had somewhere else to be," said Thomas nodding. "Now come on, let's find him."

Neither of them moved.

"Er," said Philip, "how exactly do we do that?"

"I haven't got a clue," said Thomas.

CHAPTER XV

MACHINATIONS

T homas the Hesitant and Philip the Disadvantaged of the Table of Less Valued Knights scanned the crowd for any sign of their fellow Less Valued Knight, Bane the Appropriately Named. With King Arthur's wedding to Lady Guinevere fast approaching, it seemed the whole world had flocked to the streets and shops of Camelot. Shoppers needed gifts, and those gifts needed pretty packaging, and the shopping and the packaging took time, and the shoppers grew hungry and tired. So, food and drink were sold, and places to sit were provided, and when there's food and drink and places to sit, talking happens. When talking happens amidst all the shopping and packaging and eating and drinking, a hubbub brews. Amidst the hubbub, people get excited and start to feel good and look at their gifts and their pretty packaging and think to themselves, 'Why shouldn't I buy something for myself?' And they think, 'While I'm at it, why don't I pick up something for Aunt Sarah?' And the well-fed and mostly rested shoppers get back on their feet and do more shopping, and so it goes.

The net result for Thomas and Philip was that in all the hubbub – which from any high vantage point would look like it was mainly constructed of fancy hats – there was little hope of spotting Bane. They were also being jostled quite a bit, because standing still in a hubbub is rather asking for it.

Someone slammed into Thomas, nearly knocking him over.

"Oh *excuse* me sir, I didn't see you there."

"It's alright m'Lady," began Thomas in a way that he hoped conveyed that it wasn't entirely alright. "It's my fault for standing so close to this wall and out of the – Marie!"

Marie peeked out from under a giant hat fitted with several large birds-worth of blue feathers and topped with a tiny palace made to look like it was resting on a fluffy white cloud. She giggled, and she handed Thomas three packages she was apparently tired of holding.

"How are the dancing lessons going?" she asked.

Two girls behind Marie giggled.

Thomas straightened up. "They're going just fine. Madame Rhapsody says I'm a natural."

"A natural what, exactly?" said Philip.

Marie's friends giggled some more, and Philip blushed.

"Oh, where are my manners," said Marie. "Sir Thomas, Sir Philip, may I please introduce Lady Chastity and Lady Virtue. They serve with me in Lady Guinevere's entourage."

"Pleased to meet you," said Thomas and Philip simultaneously.

"Charmed," smiled Chastity.

"The pleasure is ours," said Virtue, and gave a little curtsey.

"So what are two of Camelot's finest up to this afternoon? Shopping?"

"In this madness?" said Thomas. "No, we're trying to find Bane. Have you seen him?"

Marie shook her head. Thomas frowned and scanned the crowd again.

"What's this about?" said Marie.

"He's up to something," said Thomas, "and I need to find out what it is."

"So you're going to do what? Spy on him?"

Thomas looked at her. "Er, something like that, yes... Why?"

"Well, Sir Thomas of Fogbottom, I never thought a knight of your noble stature would stoop to such shenanigans. Next you'll tell me you're off to consult with that allegedly-former evil wizard friend of yours to see if he could, somehow, locate your quarry.

"I'm sorry, sir, but I just can't be a party to such devilry, especially when you should be practicing your waltz. Come on girls."

She winked at Thomas and marched off.

"Hmpf," said Virtue, tossed her hair and marched away, then returned to drag away Chastity who was still giggling and batting her eyelashes at Philip.

"Where are we going?" said Philip, who was himself being dragged now through the crowd by his arm.

"Didn't you hear any of that? We're going to find Pyralis."

"What do we need him for?"

Thomas stopped and looked Philip in the eye.

"Oh!" said Philip. "Right. Well then, what are we waiting for?"

Pyralis had leased an apartment at the top of a very long set of rickety stairs overlooking the cemetery behind St. Stephens. He'd told Thomas that he'd finished his experiments of the more pungent persuasion, and now that his work would draw less attention, was moving into town to "keep an eye on things."

Thomas knocked hard on the door at the top of the stairs. On the third knock, an explosion from inside the apartment shook the building. Black smoke poured out of the windows and between cracks in the walls. The door burst open and a coughing Pyralis stepped out of a dark, sulfurous billow.

"Oh! Hello, there."

He wiped his hands on his apron, which seemed to do little more than smear the already soot-covered garment with more soot. His hair looked like it had been caught and frozen in the act of trying to escape his head.

Someone banged on a pot from down below, and a woman screamed, "That's it! I'm calling the guard!" A stooped old woman rounded the corner beneath them and spotted Thomas and Philip. Thomas had grabbed Pyralis's shoulder to steady him on the swaying platform. The sight of two knights, such as they were, laying hands on Pyralis brightened her up immediately.

"Good show! Arrest that fool. Myrtle was just saying the other day 'Where's a knight when you need one?' and here's two!"

"Um, right, we've got it under control ma'am," said Thomas in a deeper than normal voice. "We're just going to, er..."

"Check the premises," said Philip.

"Right. In you go then," said Thomas, and they followed Pyralis into the apartment.

Inside, Pyralis gave Thomas a sheepish grin.

"What happened to lying low? Sticking to work that drew less attention?" asked Thomas.

"What? Widow Haypenny? She's harmless. Nothing a nice batch of turnovers won't fix."

Smoke was still pouring out of something on a table in the corner and wafting across the floor. Pyralis clamped a lid on it and leaned on the table.

"So, what brings you here, boys?"

"We need to find someone," said Thomas, "fast."

❧

"It's a compass," said Pyralis.

"I can see that. What's it do?" said Thomas.

"The needle spins as you move and tells you what direction it thinks you're heading."

Thomas laughed. "I know how a compass works Pyralis. What's this one do?"

Pyralis raised his eyebrows. "The needle spins as you move and—"

"—tells me what direction I'm heading, I get that—"

"No, no. It tells you what direction it *thinks* you're heading."

Thomas stared at Pyralis blankly. Philip furrowed his brow.

"Here, look at the markings," said Pyralis.

Where there should have been indicators for the cardinal directions, there were tiny phrases. Where *North* should have been, the compass read *Right*. At *South*, it read *Wrong*. Instead of *West*, the compass had *Early* and at *East*, *Late*. The needle was pointed southeast.

"Wrong," said Thomas.

"And Late," said Philip.

Thomas shot up and moved around the room. The needle danced and spun. Thomas froze when it pointed toward Right. He shifted carefully sideways so he could see out the window. He was facing the palace.

"Before you go rushing off, you should know—" started Pyralis.

"It still says Late," said Thomas in a panic. He grabbed Philip by his arm and pulled him out the door. "Come on!"

"It's not exactly a moral compass," shouted Pyralis after them.

"What do you think he meant by that?" said Philip to Thomas between breaths as they raced up the alley toward the palace.

"Well," said Thomas, "there's right, I guess, and then there's Right. I suppose you can be one without being the other. But it's all moot if we miss the thing to be right or wrong about altogether."

"Good point," said Philip in a way that made it clear he had no idea what Thomas was talking about, but ran harder anyway.

Every important building has someone whose job it is to make sure people stay out of where they shouldn't be. In Camelot, at the palace, that someone was Horace Felrigger. Horace was known simply as the Watchman.

Horace was having a bad night.

"I really don't think this is a good idea," said Philip.

"Nonsense," said Thomas eyeing the compass. "We'll be fine."

"I've heard that before..." said Philip.

"Seriously, what can go wrong?" said Thomas waving the compass at him.

The compass needle was pointing solidly in the Right direction. Thomas was standing at the top of a narrow set of dark stairs that spiraled down underneath the palace.

"What can go wrong? What can go *wrong*? Thomas..." Philip blustered, but the question was apparently too preposterous to answer.

"I think we're even on time," said Thomas.

"What do you suppose we're on time for, exactly?"

"Stop worrying," said Thomas. He stepped around a sign reading "Authorized Personnel Only." "We're knights of the court, investigating reports of unauthorized personnel in unauthorized places. Tuttle would be proud."

They began climbing down into the darkness.

"You do remember my epithet?" said Philip.

"Sir Philip the Disadvantaged."

"And, you remember what it means?"
"Unlucky?"
"Just checking."
Darkness closed in around them.

CHAPTER XVI

THE UNDERCROFT

"What does the compass say?"

"I don't know, I can't see it."

Thomas made his way along the narrow corridor by holding his hand out and feeling the damp, rough wall. At one point, he'd stopped and Philip had kept going, smacking right into him. Since then, Philip had kept his hand on Thomas's shoulder. Passages branched frequently, and Thomas had decided to follow each right hand branch reasoning that if they had to go back they could just keep making lefts until they were back where they started. Their footsteps crunched on the corridor's floor and echoed louder than footsteps had a right to.

"Another door. You know," said Thomas, "these things are better armored than most of the LVK."

"Doesn't take much," said Philip.

They'd passed several doors. All of them massive constructions of heavy wood with iron plates and bars riveted into them, and all of them locked. They'd heard a scuttling behind one, and since then had passed them all by as quickly and quietly as possible.

"There's a light up ahead," said Philip.

"Good, we can check the compass."

A thin line of something so dull it could only be called light because it was something other than complete black suggested the shape of something that might be another passageway up ahead.

"I think for Christmas I'm going to get you a compass that says 'wrong way' in every direction so there's nothing to do but stay put somewhere safe."

They passed another armored portal, and Thomas heard something metallic and heavy slide along something else similar. He stopped. Philip took a sudden step to the right to avoid bumping into Thomas and smacked his temple hard on a torch sconce mounted on the wall.

"Ow," he said in a normal tone of voice. It was probably the loudest thing that had happened in this part of the castle in a hundred years.

"Oh I think I'm bleeding."

Thomas sucked his breath in. "Shh," he said as quietly as he could, but it was too late.

The heavy, metallic sound happened again, only quicker. This time it sounded clearly like some piece of the door being operated on the other side. Then a light flared from underneath. Compared to the pitch black they'd been in, the hall seemed to blaze. Thomas could see Philip clearly: he stood frozen with a terrified expression on his face and his hand on his head where he'd knocked it against the sconce.

The door flew open, faster and more quietly than something that size should, and two large, muscled, and tattooed arms grabbed Thomas and Philip and pulled them into the room.

Thomas caught a fleeting look at the compass as he was hurled into the light and the door slammed shut behind him. It seemed to think they were in the right place, right on time.

❧

Horace Felrigger wasn't tall, but he was thick. He had thick arms, a thick neck, and a thick trunk all stacked on top of a pair of thick legs. He was the most solid person Thomas had ever seen.

He picked up a pair of rickety wooden chairs from a pile of haphazardly piled furniture and sat Thomas and Philip down on them. A single torch burned near the door and glinted off a set of manacles dangling from an iron hook in the wall. The walls and floor were just as Thomas had imagined when they'd been creeping down the dark corridor: big, old, cut stone, dry, and crumbling in some spots, wet and slimy in others.

Horace grabbed a third chair, set it pointing away from Thomas and Philip, and sat it in backwards. He crossed his arms and leaned over the top.

"My name's Horace. What's yours?" His voice was gravelly and, like the rest of him, thick. A tattoo of a snake coiled around his forearm and seemed to stare at them. In the dancing torchlight, Thomas could almost imagine the tattoo flicking its tongue at them.

"Ph – Ph – Ph..." said Philip.

"I'm Sir Thomas the Hesitant, and this is Sir Philip the Disadvantaged."

"I'll say," said Horace, glancing at Philip and chuckling at his own joke. Philip gave a little experimental laugh and Horace's face fell immediately. Philip shut his mouth tight, and Horace growled, "...and what brings you to the Undercroft this fine evening?"

There was something alarming about the way Horace said the word "fine".

"We were..." Thomas trailed off. He'd found it much easier to be brave when Horace had been looking at Philip.

"Investigating–" said Philip.

"A disturbance–" said Thomas.

"There were some reports..." said Philip.

Horace raised an eyebrow. Philip swallowed. He looked pale.

"Investigatin' reports?"

They nodded.

"Of a disturbance, is it?"

They nodded a bit less certainly.

"Well, that's interesting, ya see, 'cause I'm what ya might call the Chief Disturbance Investigator down here. I've been investigating some disturbances myself, and all I've found is the three of you."

Thomas blinked.

Philip looked around the room, puzzled.

"The three," said Thomas, "of us?"

Horace cocked his head. "Shh!" he said.

Thomas and Philip exchanged a look.

"I told that boy to stay put," said Horace. He stood up, kicked his chair aside and pointed his finger at them. "Don't move," he said. "I'll be back, and we're going to have a little chat about disturbances and investigations."

He left the room and slammed the door shut behind him. Thomas and Philip looked at each other. The silence of the Undercroft deepened around them as Horace's footsteps faded. In the quiet, they began to make out the faintest of sounds – voices drifting in from... somewhere.

Philip looked around the room, but couldn't spot the source.

"Do you hear..." said Philip.

Thomas was nodding and staring at the wall where a ventilation shaft opened onto the room near the ceiling. He got up, stood beneath the shaft, and checked the compass. The needle pointed straight in the Right direction, but slowly began to drift toward Late.

"You've got to boost me up," said Thomas.

"You're joking."

Thomas brandished the compass at him.

Philip rolled his eyes then stooped down and cupped his hands. Thomas put a foot into them, and Philip heaved. Thomas slid right into the opening. It wasn't uncomfortably tight, but there was no chance of Thomas turning around.

"Right. Have fun then," said Philip. He didn't sound too happy.

"Here," said Thomas. "Take the compass and get out of here." He tossed the compass down.

"It thinks I should go out the door," said Philip.

"Go. I'll be fine," said Thomas.

"Um," said Philip, "You mind if I take the..."

Thomas knew without looking what he was talking about. "Go ahead," he said.

He heard Philip lift the torch out of the sconce and saw the shadows dance on the walls of the shaft.

The door opened.

"Be careful," said Philip. Then the door shut, the room went black, and Thomas crawled forward through the darkness, following the voices.

"I gave him to Morgan," said an aged, but not old voice.

Thomas had shimmied straight ahead for what felt like a mile but was probably more like a hundred feet, then taken a right hand branch. The voices were directly above him now. There was a dull light coming down through a grate above, and he lay on his back listening. He'd even caught sight of a swoosh of velvety robe at one point. It had given him a fright, and he'd inched backward so in case anyone looked down, they wouldn't see him looking up.

"The most skilled fighter in all of Britain and you *gave* him to Morgan."

It was Bane's voice. *But who's he talking to?* thought Thomas.

"It's an investment, son."

"The Baron," hissed Thomas, and then clamped his hands over his mouth.

"What was that?" said the Baron.

"It was the sound of my future collapsing," said Bane. He was clearly angry. "The investment was supposed to be in me, Father. The black knight beats everyone else, I beat the black knight, Arthur commissions me to an Order, and our little borough of Fogbottom is finally on the map."

"But you *are* in an Order," the Baron sniggered.

Bane blew up. "It's your name too Father! How can you be so dim-sighted?"

"Don't tell me about my name boy." The Baron's voice was ice cold. "While I walk the earth, Fogbottom is mine to do with as I see fit. Or perhaps you'd prefer to spend some time in my basement with that Farmer boy?"

"William," whispered Thomas. He had a sudden and completely irrational urge to fly up the shaft, burst through the grate and strangle them both.

There was no audible reply from Bane.

"Good," said the Baron. "Anyway, honestly, who would believe *you* could beat Accolon? It was a foolish plan, and when I realized it, I changed it."

"You should have warned me. I looked like a fool," said Bane.

"We all make sacrifices," said the Baron in a tone dripping with mockery. "The peasants of Fogbottom, for instance. Speaking of which, the shipment is almost ready."

Shipment? mouthed Thomas to himself, in the dark.

A door opened.

"I thought I told you – oh sorry, m'Lord, I didn't see you there."

It was Horace's voice. There was a pause. Thomas imagined the Baron glaring at Horace.

"I'll just be on my way then," said Horace, and the door closed again.

"I had to put up with that idiot while you were busy being late," said Bane.

"My affairs are my affairs. The sooner you learn that, boy, the sooner we'll both get what we want. Now come along and tend to your duties. We can't have the country falling apart on the Less Valued's watch." The Baron sniggered again.

Thomas heard the door open and close, and then all was quiet. Thomas started hoisting himself up the shaft toward the floor grate. As he climbed, so did his anger: Anger at being manipulated into participating in their ruse with the Black Knight, anger at the sheer audacity of their attempt to hoodwink Arthur, anger at himself for putting off dealing directly with his brother's situation for so long.

He shoved the grate over and climbed out of the shaft. He aimed a mad kick at a convenient piece of furniture, then remembered Horace and stopped. Thomas opened the door as quietly as possible and peered down the hall. He recognized this part of the palace from their swearing in. He didn't want to bump into Horace again, but he didn't feel much like creeping about anymore either.

Thomas picked his head up, acted like he belonged where he was, marched down the hall and, ultimately, out of the palace.

Back at the barracks, he took the blank parchment out of his footlocker, penned something quickly, sealed the letter and shoved it all back where he'd got it. He'd take the letter to the post office in the morning.

He dropped onto his bunk and fumed. It was a good half hour before it dawned on him that Philip's bunk was empty.

❧

The mistake most people made with Pyralis's Moral Compass was believing that the thing in any way, shape or form reflected their own sense of right and wrong. A device that decides for the wielder what he should and shouldn't do, and when, is bad enough. Pyralis's diabolical pre-career-shift innovation had been to make the compass fairly clever. With clever came bored, and with bored came mischievous and with mischievous came – well, luckily, that's as far as the compass ever really got.

The compass was smart enough to know that it needed to deliver, in the end, the thing the wielder was after. And it never lied, technically. But it had learned to have fun with people's readiness to believe that there was just one right way in all matters.

It would examine a number of ways to have the thing the wielder wanted come about, then pick the way that was the most fun for itself. There were lots of ways, for instance, that Thomas could have wound up overhearing Bane and the Baron, but the compass had particularly enjoyed scaring him with Horace.

It had decided to have some more fun with Philip.

The door to the barracks opened and there, lit by the moon, was a sopping wet, leaf-covered, mud-encrusted Philip. He was holding a shiny gold compass out in front of him like it was a wild animal that could strike out at him any second. There were branches stuck to him and sticking out at odd angles.

His lips moved, but his jaw stayed clenched. "Take... this... back," he said.

Thomas thought he could even see a seashell stuck in Philip's hair.

He tossed the compass at Thomas, turned, and sloshed back out the door, presumably to – somehow – clean up.

Thomas hurried after him.

"It led me right up out of the Undercroft, no problem," said Philip. "But I think it decided to have some sport with me in the palace."

"*It* decided..."

"Yes, *it* decided," said Philip. He stopped wringing out his shirt, and the look he gave Thomas made it clear this point was not up for discussion.

"Please continue," said Thomas.

"I was out the door and on the palace grounds when I started to think about how the compass worked, and if there were more than one, you know, right place to be at any given moment. So I tried it out. I started thinking of different things to test it."

Philip gave up on his shirt for the time being and began picking leaves off of himself.

"I stood still and thought how nice it would be to have a hot sandwich and a cold drink just then and wham! The compass needle went nuts until I started heading toward the Pickle. So, then I thought to myself, 'Forget the sandwich, how about some of Mum's Shrewsbery cakes–"

"Your Mum's what?"

Philip was aghast. "You can't possibly have never had Shrewsbery cakes."

"Er, my mother doesn't really... That is, in the kitchen, she kind of does her own thing."

"Ah," said Philip, scraping clumps of mud off his arm. "Well, you'll have to come over sometime. They're these delicate nutmeg and rosewater cakes... more like a thick cookie really. If you dunk them in warm cream..."

Philip looked up to see Thomas staring back with one raised eyebrow.

"Anyway, as I was saying, I thought of Mum's Shrewsbery cakes and wham! There goes the needle again until I start heading home at which time, of course, it tells me I'm heading in the right direction.

"So," said Philip. "That's when I decided to really give it a go, and the compass was more than happy to oblige," he finished with clenched teeth.

Philip looked himself over. He was still a mess. He gave his shirt some consideration, seemed to come to an internal conclusion, picked it up and started toweling himself off with it.

"And..." said Thomas.

Philip tried to ignore him, toweling even more furiously.

"And so you thought..." said Thomas.

Philip stopped and looked at the sky. "I thought it would be nice to, you know, bump into Chastity again."

Thomas grinned. "I see," he said and had to work hard to stifle a laugh. He bounced on his toes instead.

Philip went back to scrubbing.

Thomas tried to keep a straight face. "And how did that go?"

In answer, Philip quickly spread his arms, shook his head, raised his eyebrows and glared at him. Thomas was having a really hard time holding it in.

"The compass," said Philip, "led me right back into the palace, upstairs, and eventually through a window out onto a ledge."

"You *didn't*," said Thomas, surprised, impressed and aghast all at once.

"Oh I most certainly did," said Philip.

"You went climbing around on the balconies outside of Guinevere's chambers?!"

"I didn't say anything about a balcony, did I? No, the compass had me stick strictly to footing of a much more questionable variety. Someone should see what the court architect has been up to, because I can tell him the stonework up there leaves something to be desired."

"Still, I can't believe you followed the compass up there!"

"Well, you reach a certain point, you know, and you're committed."

"Or you should be," said Thomas.

Philip ignored that. "Anyway," he said, and began to laugh at himself. "I came round to where I could see the windows of their suite. I was just starting to think this wasn't such a good idea—"

"Just starting?" said Thomas.

Philip ignored that too. "I heard a cracking under my foot, and that quick, I was off the ledge and in the moat."

Thomas finally let himself laugh. It felt wonderful after all the stewing in self-doubt and anger he'd been doing. "Nicely done," he said.

Philip had cleaned up as best he could. They headed back toward the barracks.

"So the compass lied," said Thomas.

"Hmm?" said Philip.

"You never got to see Chastity."

"Oh no. No, I saw her. And Virtue. And Marie. They all popped their heads out the windows – I must've made quite a racket thrashing around in the water."

"Were they upset?"

"Oh no. Well, startled of course. I told them it was me and I was," he coughed, "investigating a disturbance."

Thomas laughed again and patted him on the back. "There you go. Did they buy it?"

"Well, Marie said she was pretty sure I was the disturbance—"

"She's a smart girl."

"—and Chastity wanted to know if I was working for Horace."

"They know Horace?"

"Apparently they *love* Horace."

"You've got to be kidding."

Philip shook his head. "I think girls like mean and creepy as long as it's a mostly safe kind of mean and creepy and the mean part is pointed at somebody else."

Thomas thought about that. "Hmm," he said. He thought about it some more. "Nope, that doesn't make sense. Because if my dance lessons are any indication, they prefer genteel and embarrassing. Because honestly, even if a guy dances well, it's still a bit embarrassing for everyone involved."

"But," said Philip, "if one of them could convince someone like Horace to dress up and go dancing... she'd be the stuff of girl legend."

"That doesn't make sense."

"It doesn't have to Thomas; they're *girls*."

"Good point."

"And we're in their world next week's end. Weddings are..." He shook his head. "Weddings are the kinds of things you get when you put girls in charge."

Later, as they lay in their bunks on the edge of sleep, Philip gave a start and whispered, "Oh! What happened? Did you find him?"

Thomas sighed and said, "Aye."

When he didn't continue, Philip rolled to his side and said, "And...?"

"He was with the Baron, and they're up to no good."

"Well, there's news," said Philip, but Thomas didn't laugh, and Philip had to prompt him again. "What sort of no good, precisely?"

"I don't know. There was something to do with the Black Knight – he was in the service of the Baron, and Bane was to beat him and earn a promotion."

"No," gasped Philip. "That scoundrel. We have to tell Arthur."

"Tell Arthur what? That the Baron of Fogbottom put on the best show Camelot can remember?"

"Right," said Philip. "Yeah that's a rub, isn't it." After a pause, "Wait you said he *was* the Baron's?"

"He's a knight named Accolon. And apparently the Baron's given him to Morgan."

"To Morgan?" Philip gasped again. "The Baron's in business with Arthur's sister?"

Thomas decided to treat all of Philip's questions as rhetorical until further notice.

"And there's a new plan. Something to do with a shipment. He said it was 'almost ready.'"

Philip sat up. "Now we've got to tell Arthur."

Thomas sighed. "Again, tell him what? The Baron is... shipping... something. Arthur will like that." Thomas shook his head.

"But it can't be good, Thomas. Just listen to the way it sounds: The Baron gives a champion knight to Arthur's evil sister, and is now preparing..." he lowered his voice. "A shipment." Philip opened his eyes wide and spread his hands.

"'A shipment of what?' Arthur will say," said Thomas.

"'A shipment of no good,' is what we – is what *you'll* say," said Philip.

"And when they go investigate the shipment of no good and find out it's tea services for Morgan's staff..."

"You tell them to investigate the tea services because they're obviously befouled."

Thomas laughed. "And when they turn out to be just plain, old, normal, tea services?"

"We point the other way and run," said Philip.

They both laughed.

"I see your point," said Philip. "We need more information."

"Aye," said Thomas.

After a while, when Thomas was nearly asleep, Philip asked one more question.

"Thomas," he said quietly.

"Yes," Thomas replied.

"Why don't you just go ask Arthur to help your brother and Fogbottom?"

"The Baron *is* Fogbottom Philip."

"You know what I mean."

Thomas was quiet for a while, then said, "Honestly Philip? I don't think Arthur *can* help. I mean, you've heard what the Round Table is talking about. They think the cure for the land is found in some magic cup."

"The Grail," said Philip.

"The Grail," said Thomas. "The cup from Jesus's Last Supper. Imagine it. The night he uses the grail, he makes a point of washing his friends' feet and tells them, '*This* is how you can be great.' And then he dies and people scheme, plot, and kill each other to get their hands on some stupid cup."

"It is a bit ironic when you put it that way," said Philip.

"It's ridiculous is what it is," said Thomas.

"So... We can't tell anyone about Accolon. We can't do anything about the shipment until we know what it is. And not even Arthur can fix Fogbottom. What *do* we do Thomas?"

"We do the best we can."

"I hope it's enough."

"I hope so too, Philip. I hope so too."

Thomas fell asleep that night staring at the words he'd etched on his bed frame.

Somnia, Salvebis.

Nonsense, you'll be fine.

CHAPTER XVII

A DAY IN THE LIFE

Day two at Madame Rhapsody's was not unlike day one. The lamps were just as sparkly, and the air was just as flowery. If anything, Thomas felt he was getting worse at dancing rather than better. There were too many things to pay attention to all at once: the bend of his wrist, the angle of his elbow, the position of his feet, where he was looking, where the other dancers were, and in Thomas's defense, the rather unsteady rhythm of Hedley's harpsichord-ing.

Thomas's neck ached from looking up at Ox, and he tripped twice over Sir Cuddlington who Madame Rhapsody eventually shooed out the window. "I've never seen him take to a young man so swiftly. You must be a special one," she said to Thomas with an appraising look Thomas found unnerving. In an effort to change the subject, he made the mistake of asking about the bend of his knees to which Madame Rhapsody replied, "Oh honey, it's not your knees you need to worry about," and strolled away chuckling.

Ox gave him a smirk and a wink, and it was all Thomas could do to not bolt out the window after Sir Cuddlington.

In time, the lesson ended, Madame Rhapsody gave her until-tomorrows and the bedraggled Less Valued shuffled out the door.

A woman older than Grandma Farmer stood on the corner. Carriages and horses raced by in both directions. Thomas watched her glance around the intersection, trying to time her attempt to cross while plotting a navigable route through the great piles of manure and churned mud.

"Take my arm," said Thomas.

"Oh," said the woman, and in a moment they were across the street together. Dedric and Edgar followed, while Ox stopped three drivers with a single raised hand.

"Thank you dearie," she said.

"My pleasure," said Thomas and gave a bow.

The LVK headed off to cut through Isolde Park on their way back to the palace grounds.

No one noticed the woman frown at the store fronts and then make her way to stand at her new corner.

"That was nice," said Dedric.

"Always wanted to do that," said Edgar.

Ox grinned and slapped Thomas on the back, knocking him forward.

Isolde Park paled only in comparison to the meticulously cared for palace gardens. Even now with most of her trees dropping their last leaves, there were still some blooms here and there. Variegated bushes and groomed wild grasses added variety and a bit of color. The paths were covered with raked gravel and bordered with cut stone. A stream meandered from one corner of the park to the other, crossed by a small stone bridge arching from one side to the other with no support other than its own keystones. It reminded Thomas of another bridge that seemed so far away and so long ago now.

With the chill in the air, there were fewer people in the park than usual. A few families picnicked, a pair of small boys – orphans by the look of them – played with sticks at the stream's edge, and a trio of young women sat on a bench under a willow.

"Isn't that–" said Dedric.

"Marie," said Thomas.

Ox elbowed Thomas. Edgar said, "We'll see you later Sir Hesitant," and they headed across the bridge to the other side of the park and the exit.

The girls spotted Thomas heading their way. Chastity and Virtue whispered something to each other and giggled.

"Good day ladies," said Thomas, bowing enough to be proper, but not enough, he hoped, to be a rube.

He must have succeeded. Marie's friends excused themselves and pranced off, still giggling and throwing the occasional fleeting look back at them.

Thomas sat down next to Marie and took in the park.

"You smell lovely," she said.

"Ugh," said Thomas. He affected Madame Rhapsody's throaty voice: "Madame Rhapsody's Dance Emporium. Where Knights become Men..."

He rolled his eyes, "Or something like that." Marie laughed.

"Well, I'm sure you're doing wonderfully," she said. "At both tasks," she added, grinning.

Thomas blushed, and then embarrassed for blushing, blushed some more.

Marie gasped suddenly. "Philip told me what you overheard in the Undercroft," she blurted.

"He did?"

She nodded and put her hand on his leg. "What are you going to do?" she said, eyes wide and breath held.

Thomas honestly couldn't think of anything other than her hand. And her eyes looking so intently into his. ...and her hand.

He shook himself mentally.

"Um," he said. And then told her the same thing he'd told Philip.

"We've got to find out what they're up to before we can do anything about it. And in the meantime, we've got to just, you know, do what we can."

He shrugged.

She frowned.

"But what do you think it could be – the shipment?" Her hand was no longer on his leg, but Thomas still found it difficult to focus.

He shrugged again. "It could be anything. Gold, weapons... biscuits."

They laughed, but something tugged at Thomas's thoughts. Something about biscuits.

Marie noticed the look on his face. "What is it?" she said.

"I don't know," said Thomas.

They were quiet for a while, watching a sord of ducks paddle around an eddy in the stream.

"How's your brother?" asked Marie.

"How'd you get from biscuits to my brother?"

It was Marie's turn to shrug. "I imagine he's not eating all that well."

"The whole town's not eating all that well," said Thomas.

Marie frowned.

"I haven't heard from him, but I did get a letter from Mum." Thomas looked down at his hands. "They're hanging in there," he said. "I'm sure William is okay." But he wasn't sure at all.

Thankfully Marie didn't press him. Thomas offered his hand and said, "Escort you back to the Palace m'Lady?"

"It would be my pleasure," she said, smiling up at him, and they headed for the exit. The pair of orphans at the water's edge had decided it was time to go as well and shoved out the gate just in front of Thomas and Marie.

One of the boys bumped into an older man on the street in a way that startled the man and made him stoop a bit. The boy apologized and tipped a non-existent hat to him while the second boy brushed past the other side of the man and back-tracked toward Thomas and Marie.

Thomas caught him by the collar. "Whoa there little nipper."

"Thomas!" gasped Marie.

The first boy shot a look at Thomas, then turned and ran.

"Hey!" said the second boy, struggling against Thomas's grip. "Lemmego!"

"Sir!" called Thomas to the man. "I think this boy has something to say to you."

The boy gave Thomas a vicious look while the man walked over.

"What's this about?" said the man.

"Hand it over," said Thomas.

"Dunno what yer talkin' about mister."

"Are you missing anything?" Thomas asked the old man.

"Don't think so..." said the man, patting himself down. He froze. "Why that little sneak thief. He's got my coin!"

The boy struggled, but when he couldn't free himself to run, he changed tactics. He slumped and began crying pitifully.

"Puh puh puh please, sir. I wouldn't steal it if I didn't need it. Me mum's in a bad way and... And we ain't got no bread. And she ain't had her apothecaries in days."

The man's face melted.

Thomas called the boy's bluff. "Right then, let's go see your mum shall we?"

In the midst of his performance, the boy shot Thomas another vicious look.

"You don't want to go doin' that sirs. Doctor thinks maybe she's got the plague. She's got these big buboes..."

The boy held his hands up to his neck and made a sick face.

The man grimaced and took a step back, shooting a look at Thomas.

"If I could just help her be comfortable here in her final days."

Thomas rolled his eyes and shook the boy.

"Hand it over," he said.

Furious, the boy produced a shiny, silver coin and held it out to the man.

The man gave Thomas a questioning look.

"Lies," said Thomas.

The man knit his brows, but took the coin, thanked Thomas and strolled away. He was still holding the coin at arm's length when he rounded the corner up the street.

Thomas looked down at the boy. "What's your name?" Thomas asked.

The boy seemed startled by the question.

"Um, Ollie", he said.

"The road you're traveling leads to no good, 'Um Ollie,'" said Thomas. "What do you want to do with your life?"

In answer, the boy stomped on Thomas's foot hard.

"Ow!" said Thomas, and let go.

In a flash, the boy was gone. Thomas took a step after him, but Marie grabbed his arm.

"How did you know...?" she started.

Thomas shook his head. "That's how William and I made our living one summer."

"Sir Thomas the Hesitant was a *pickpocket*? A common thief?"

"And a lousy one at that."

"You got caught?"

"No. We just... stopped."

"Why?"

Thomas thought for a moment. "I don't know. I think Old Lady Applebutter was the real winner – all we did with our plunder was buy her tarts. Then one day William just said we needed to stop. So we did."

Thomas offered his arm.

Marie put one hand on her throat. "I don't know if it would be proper for one of Guinevere's Ladies in Waiting to be seen consorting with a ne'er-do-well, Sir Thomas."

"How about a rehabilitated ne'er-do-well?"

"Oh, I suppose *that* would be alright." She fluttered her lashes, took his arm, and they made their way toward the palace. They parted ways awkwardly when their paths diverged. Marie headed toward the palace proper, and Thomas veered off in the direction of the barracks. When they were almost but not quite out of earshot, Marie turned and yelled, "Will you come back through the park again tomorrow?"

"I will," said Thomas, "if you'll be there!"

She smiled, turned, and hurried into the palace, curtseying to the liveried soldier who opened the door for her.

Thomas stared at the closed door long enough that the soldier shot him a look and gave a sort of shrug that clearly meant, *Can I help you?* Thomas grinned, saluted and walked away humming.

Remi the Imperturbable slept on his bunk near the back, but besides him, the barracks were empty. There was something on Thomas's bed.

"I thought I put that parchment away," Thomas mumbled to himself. Halfway to his bunk he realized it wasn't his parchment. It was another letter. Bracing himself, he picked it up, sat down, took a breath, and read.

From: William Farmer, Prisoner
Dungeon I, Fogbottom Keep, Fogbottom

Dear Thomas,
    Salutations. I hear little from the
outside these days, but word has it from
Mum that you're in Camelot. I pray you can
enjoy it with all that's going on – you know,

the land dying, Mum as she is, me locked up in
here and all that.

I must say though, prison is quite fasci-
nating. I'm fed every day at least once; twice for
good behavior. Bread and water mostly, which
is alright by me. Wendsley says there might be
sourdough today. You remember Wendsley Hunter?
A Baron's guard now, not a bad fellow. He tells
me every day that I'm wasting away, and alas,
I have to agree. I'm sure I've lost at least a
stone. No worries though, who do I have to impress?
Sure wouldn't mind a bit of cheese now and then or
meat. Sorry, I trailed off there a bit. With the
other cells empty, I got my pick of the lot. I'm
right next to the one that used to sport a window.
End to end, it's the biggest by a meter. When they
loosen the manacles, I can really stretch out.

Ages it's been since that window was bricked.
This dungeon wasn't always a dungeon I suspect. Time
ebbs. Things are what they are now; that's what matters
right?

Which brings us to it. Thomas, I don't want
you to worry about me. I'm here because I chose to
be. If, in some great plan of the Almighty this works
out to help the people of Fogbottom, what is my suffering in the face of it. And what suffering? I
have a roof, food and, look, I even get to write.

As if this weren't enough, I've befriended a large,
brown rat who I've named Cartwright the Pluck. He's
a bit skittish, but he's warming up.

Be well, Thomas.

Your loving brother,
William

Thomas stared at the letter, slumped. His brother's encouragement somehow made Thomas feel his small efforts for Right that day were... well, the word "ridiculous" came to mind. Here he was helping old ladies cross the street while his brother sat in prison for trying to save a whole town.

As he mulled over William's letter, his eyes drifted across the page, and suddenly he saw it.

"Oh!" he said, and shot to his feet, eyes still locked on the parchment. He took two steps in one direction, said "Oh!" again, turned on his heel and took two steps in the other.

"Philip!" he said to himself and headed for the door. He found him with a small group of other Less Valued at the notice board across the Commons from their barracks. Philip spotted him coming and called him over, "Thomas! Take a look at this!"

Philip pointed to a new announcement. "The armory's supplying us with... well... armor!"

"That's nice," said Thomas and dragged Philip away from the group. When they were out of earshot, he thrust the letter into Philip's hands and told him, "Read this."

It took Philip a moment to realize what it was. "Oh Thomas," he started, but Thomas stopped him. "Read it," he said again.

Philip frowned and read. Halfway through Philip stopped and said, "Thomas you mustn't feel guilty."

Thomas put his hand on Philip's shoulder. "Read," he said, "it."

Philip read. When he was done he looked to the sky and said, "Oh, Thomas."

Thomas waited.

"He's befriended... a rat," said Philip.

"No, no, no." Thomas grabbed the letter and pointed. "Here," he said and ran his finger down the first letter of each line.

Philip read, "S–o–m–e–t..."

Thomas groaned. "Put them together, lug."

Philip's brow knitted as he puzzled it out. "So met hing is ami smores later wyb of habab," he said, slowly.

Thomas shook his head and pointed. "*Something is amiss*," he read. "*More later.*"

Philip looked. "Oh!" he said.

"That's what I said!" said Thomas.

"Who's 'Wyb of Habab?'"

"I've no idea," Thomas shook his head again. "I've never heard of Habab."

"Sounds Turkish maybe."

They both stared at the letter in silence.

"What do we do?" said Philip.

Thomas threw his hands up and let them fall and smack against his legs. "I've no idea."

"But this is proof!"

"Of what? Proof my brother is barking mad? You read it, he's named a rat... What was it?" Thomas read from the letter, "Cartwright the Pluck."

"It's proof that... It's proof that, well, something's amiss. And we know about the shipment. And... Saint Stephen's sandals," Philip conceded. "It's proof of nothing," he sighed.

They walked toward the barracks.

"Cartwright the Pluck," said Philip for no reason in particular.

"I wonder if he could take Sir Cuddlington in a fight," said Thomas.

"Who?" said Philip.

"Never mind," said Thomas.

CHAPTER XVIII

THE SLOPPY PANTS GANG

Thomas had a terrible time focusing on his dance lesson the next day; he was too excited about meeting Marie in Isolde Park after. "Dance from the hips," Madame Rhapsody exhorted for neither the first nor, Thomas was sure, the last time. Thomas had never really thought about his hips, but he was fairly certain moving his from side to side and tilting them was against their design. The only exciting part of the day's lesson was when Madame Rhapsody startled Sir Prescott the Pococurante out of a daydream causing him to back into Sir Cuddlington who hissed and darted straight at Hedley. Hedley deftly blocked the feline missile with his hammered dulcimer. Cuddles bounced off the strings, snapping three, and shot out the window.

"Hedley!" barked Madame Rhapsody. Hedley, apparently, was somehow at fault for the whole affair.

Hedley said, "Sorry Mum," and that, for all intents and purposes, was the end of the day's lesson.

There were no elderly citizens to help cross the street, so Thomas tried to satisfy himself with picking up a stray sack and depositing it in a nearby trash receptacle. The act felt hollow though, and for some reason brought William to mind – adding to Thomas's empty feeling.

He was staring at the trash can and thinking that he should set up a similar sanitation system in Fogbottom when the hairs on the nape of his neck prickled. He felt as though he was being watched. He glanced around and spotted a pair of orphans across the street, occupying themselves with a game on the ground involving several small stones.

They seemed to be ignoring the world around them completely until one of the boys looked up, straight at Thomas, and then went back to his stones.

Thomas, unsettled, walked down the street to the corner and made toward Isolde Park. Near the entrance he encountered another pair of boys, similarly unkempt and equally self-engrossed. Again, one made eye contact, and this time the other punched him in the arm for it.

Thomas picked up his pace. There were three more pairs of boys scattered about the park. One set was harassing the ducks, the second set was lounging in the branches of a tree near the exit and the third was talking to Marie. Marie was no slouch; she carried herself with the posture of a dancer under normal circumstances, but at the moment, she sat particularly upright. She looked as alarmed as Thomas felt.

"Oh, hello, *Sir* Thomas," she said as he approached and gave a very formal curtsey. Thomas hesitated, then returned the formal greeting with a bow and a "Lady Marie." Glancing at the boys he added, "Of the Queen-to-be's Ladies."

"Hello Gov'ner," said one of the boys much too casually. The other boy just grinned. Neither stood taller than Thomas's elbow, but they were somehow all the more frightening for it.

"Right then, let's be off shall we?" said Thomas, taking Marie's arm.

The boys followed them. "Where ye goin' in such a hurry Misser Thomas?" said one.

"Aye," said the other, "we was just tellin' the Lady here how you inspired our friend *Ollie* yesterday." The second boy snickered at the name "Ollie," and the first elbowed him.

As they neared the exit, the boys in the tree dropped to the ground.

"There's Ollie now."

Sure enough, one of the boys from the tree was the boy Thomas had collared the day before.

Thomas and Marie stopped.

"Thomas," whispered Marie. "I don't have a very good feeling about this."

"Nonsense," said Thomas. "We'll be fine." But he didn't feel fine at all.

The boys from the tree approached. The two boys at the stream were making their way up to join the rest, and at the entrance to the park, the four Thomas had spotted on the way in appeared.

"Good day, Ollie," said Thomas in a voice he hoped sounded very firm and authoritative.

Ollie gave a full bow. "Good day, Sir Thomas."

Marie tightened her grip on Thomas's arm.

"I've been telling my friends what you did for me yesterday," said Ollie.

"Oh?" said Thomas.

"How inspiring it was. I mean, usually people like you and the Lady here just ignore us."

Marie's grip loosened, and an audible "Aw" actually escaped her lips. Thomas shot her a warning look.

"We were wondering, sir..."

They were completely encircled by the boys now. Thomas didn't like it at all.

"...how we could... well... if it were possible to..."

"Go on," encouraged Marie, smiling.

Thomas couldn't believe her. "Marie!" he hissed.

"...We were wondering how we could become knights... like you," Ollie blurted. Thomas gaped. Ollie looked terrified of how Thomas might react. Thomas glanced at the other boys. They too seemed to be waiting anxiously on Thomas's response.

Disarmed, and frankly stunned, Thomas stammered a bit. He'd never been the object of anyone's admiration before; that had always been William's job. He wasn't quite sure how to handle it. Marie was beaming at him.

"Well, I..." said Thomas. "The thing is..." he tried again.

"Would you mind coming and meeting me mum?" interjected Ollie.

"He really does have a mum," said Thomas to himself.

"Oh let's do," said Marie to Thomas.

"It would be an honor," said Thomas to Ollie.

Ollie's face lit up. He couldn't stand still. He grabbed Thomas's elbow, then seemed to think better of it and let go. "Follow me then, eh?" And he was off.

If it weren't for the crowd of boys also tracking Ollie, it would've been impossible to keep up with him as he weaved in and out of traffic. The convoy drew more than one curious stare from the people they passed. Eventually, the group took a turn down an alley in an area of Camelot Thomas had never been. He was surprised a region so depressed could exist right around the corner from the luxury of Camelot's more showy parts.

The boys dodged piles of festering garbage and rusting heaps of junk. A scrawny cat hissed at them and darted into a culvert reeking of things on which Thomas didn't care to dwell. Laundry hung on lines above them looking more forgotten than clean.

The boys stopped at a door at the end of the alley and waited for Thomas and Marie. The door's paint was peeling and it hung from one hinge, but it served to separate the alley from what Thomas assumed was Ollie's home. Nicking a coin here and there was starting to seem to Thomas like a smaller and smaller crime.

Ollie grinned as Thomas and Marie caught up. After they'd caught their breath, Thomas nodded, and Ollie rapped hard on the door.

"Mum! It's me, Ollie! Can you come out here? I've got someone I want you to meet."

There was a clatter inside, and the sounds of a body moving. Ollie's grin grew even larger. The rest of the boys shuffled around, spreading out.

It was how the boys fanned out that set off half a dozen alarms in Thomas's gut.

"Marie," he said. "Get out of here."

"What?" she said.

"Get—"

The door slammed open, and an enormous boy squeezed through into the alley. He stood a head taller than Thomas, and twice as wide. His gut was enormous, his head was too large, and his hands were the size of small hams. One eye was larger than the other and twitched constantly. His lower lip hung loose and exposed far fewer teeth than there ought to have been.

"Who's calling me 'Mum' again? I told you not to call me 'Mum'!"

"Sloppy, this is Thomas, the bloke I was telling you about."

Sloppy peered down at Thomas.

"Thought you said he was a knight? Where's his shiny armor?"

Sloppy grabbed Thomas's shoulder and half-turned him to look at his hip. "Where's his sword?"

"He's a Less Valued Knight" said Ollie, still grinning. "I guess they don't rate that stuff."

"It's being issued tomorrow," said Thomas shaking off Sloppy's hand.

"Tomorrow?" said Sloppy. "Tomorrow ain't your problem mate. It's today that's your problem."

"Where's Ambrosia?" whispered Marie. There was more anger in her voice than terror.

"I'm off-duty," Thomas shot back in defense. "I was meeting my girlfriend in the park – who needs a magic sword to go meet their girlfriend in the park?"

"Did you say 'girlfriend'?" said Marie.

"I – what?"

"Anyway," hissed Marie, "*apparently* meeting your girlfriend in the park is precisely the kind of time when you want to have a magic sword around."

He knew he was being scolded, but he didn't care. "Now you said it," he said.

"Said what?" she fumed.

"Girlfriend," said Thomas and grinned.

"Oh," she said and gave a tiny, embarrassed smile. "I guess I did."

"I hate to break this up," said Sloppy who clearly didn't. "But I believe you owe young Ollie here a shilling."

"Now see here–" snapped Marie.

Thomas grabbed her arm. "Let her go first."

Sloppy looked hurt. "We'd never harm a lady, would we boys?" He gave a theatrical bow and winked. "Never let it be said that Sir Sloppy ain't a gentleman."

One of the boys guffawed, "Sir now is it?"

"Shut up you," snapped Sloppy. All humor drained from his face, and he said to Marie, "You'd best be off now miss."

Without taking her eyes off Sloppy, Marie took a step back. "Thomas?" she said quietly.

"Go," he said. Thomas breathed a sigh of relief when she turned and sprinted off. When she rounded the corner, Sloppy turned his attention to Thomas.

Thomas held up his hands. "Now, Sloppy–"

"Sir Sloppy," retorted the overgrown ringleader.

"That title is for knights, Sloppy."

Sloppy looked him up and down. "Seems to me I'm as much a knight as you," he said and poked him hard in the chest with one big, fat sausage of a finger. "Now about that shilling."

"The armor doesn't make the knight," shot Thomas. The boys shifted around him. Thomas scanned the alley for a weapon. One boy kicked an old rolling pin out of his path. It rolled up against another boy's foot who grinned and picked it up.

"Oh it don't? What's it then? Your honor? Helping old ladies cross the street?" Sloppy sniggered at Thomas's surprise. "Your blessed Code?"

The Code. *There's got to be something in there for situations like this*, thought Thomas. His mind began rifling through what he'd memorized.

Article II. Know your limitations. Too late for that. III. Don't burn bridges. Right. Um, V. Always leave yourself a clear path of retreat. Thomas didn't have to look to know he'd blown that one too. He looked anyway. The six or seven boys behind him smiled. *X. Choose your battles wisely.*

Thomas laughed at himself. *That one's right out.*

Sloppy's face went red with anger. "Think it's funny? You and your kind cavorting with princesses, dining on crumpets and tea, walking about all day in... in... freshly laundered garments."

Ollie shot Sloppy a curious look. Sloppy ignored it.

"...while we're forced to wallow 'round here in our own muck and filth."

Sloppy advanced, spitting as he ranted. Thomas stepped back and bumped into the boys behind him.

"And when one of the least of these, one of the innocents, ventures out into your world to earn an honest shilling, you snatch it right out of his hand."

"An honest... Now hold on–" said Thomas. But anything else he was planning on saying was quickly forgotten when Sloppy's balled up fist flew out of the air and hammered into his jaw.

Thomas spun completely around once, and fell over.

The boys cheered. Thomas expected to be piled onto, but it didn't happen. He peered up. Sloppy had backed up a step or two and stood there, fists clenching and unclenching.

"Get up and fight," he said with a grin. "It's time to earn that shilling."

Getting up was the last thing Thomas wanted to do. Thomas's vision swam with color. Shapes shifted and blurred. Overhead, the sun slipped passed a cloud, and the alley lit up briefly. In that moment, Thomas was reminded of the stained glass in St. Stephen's – Jesus wearing a crown of thorns, the solider striking him. *Offer him the other.*

Thomas blinked and shook his head. His vision cleared.

Thomas stood up slowly. "Sloppy, all I had to do to become a knight," he said, dusting himself off, "was ask."

Thomas expected this to surprise or at least confuse Sloppy. Instead, Sloppy seemed to grow more enraged. Thomas ran the sentence back over in his mind.

"Oh, that didn't come out right at all. I meant—"

And there was Sloppy's fist again hurtling through the air. This time Thomas wasn't as off guard and was able to absorb most of the blow by turning his head. The punch still left him stunned and positioned perfectly to watch Sloppy's other fist swing around from the opposite direction and smash straight into his nose and mouth.

Thomas was actually lifted off his feet for a moment before he crashed to the ground, battering his elbow and wrist in the fall.

The boys erupted in hoots, hollers, and cheers.

"Get up," said Sloppy.

Thomas laid there for a moment looking at the sky framed by the dilapidated roofs and lines of old laundry.

"I just meant," said Thomas, "that you're never going to be anything more..." Thomas pushed himself up.

Everything hurt – it was becoming an all too familiar feeling. Standing and wobbling slightly, Thomas finished, "...than what you can imagine yourself to be."

Sloppy stepped in and threw his fist at Thomas's head again. Just before it connected, Thomas thought he heard a horse whinny.

The world spun around Thomas. All sound had drained away. Eventually his field of view settled on the same square of sky he'd pondered before. This time though, the clouds danced and cavorted with the laundry in ways Thomas was fairly certain weren't usual.

He was vaguely aware of the boys around him scattering. They climbed over heaps of garbage and fought each other to duck through cracks in the alley's walls and under a small fence separating this alley from the next. Sloppy was pulling at several boys, including Ollie, who'd jammed up at the one door in the alley wall.

Sound flooded back into Thomas's world. He pushed himself up on one elbow, staring at Sloppy and trying to puzzle out what was going on. Even with the alley still tilting and shifting, he could tell Sloppy was scared of something. Thomas wondered if he should be scared too.

There was another whinny and the sound of hoofs behind him. Thomas twisted around, and there, framed in the light spilling into the alley from the more presentable parts of Camelot, was a knight. A real knight. His polished armor shot beams of reflected sunlight in all directions. His white steed, dressed in bright red quilted armor, stomped and snorted menacingly. The knight carried a shield that matched his horse's armor in color, and bore a five-pointed star. That alone was enough to identify him to Thomas and, Thomas imagined, Sloppy's gang. But the knight also wore a kilt, and that clinched it.

"Gawain," said Thomas.

"Ye cannae rrrun, and ye cannae hide Mister Sloppy Pants," roared Gawain. "Yer rrreign of terror is at its end.

"Thanks m'lady," he added to a figure behind him on the saddle. "I'll take it from here." He helped her slip off the horse, and she stepped aside.

"And Marie..." sighed Thomas, letting himself flop back onto the ground.

There was clatter and the sounds of a brief struggle. Thomas didn't bother looking up. While Gawain apprehended Sloppy, Ollie, and most of the older members of the Sloppy Pants Gang, Thomas laid on the ground, testing his jaw and other bits of his face to see if anything was broken, and reciting Article IX to himself: *It's not about you. It's never about you. Except, of course, when it would be better for your superiors that whatever it is be not about them.*

When the scuffle died down, a gauntleted hand grabbed him by his shirt and hauled him to his feet. Gawain gave him a vigorous slap on the back and caught him when he stumbled forward from it.

"Timothy, isn't it?" said Gawain.

"Er, Thomas, sir," said Thomas.

Gawain dismissed the correction with a wave of his hand. "Good show lad." Gawain had his hands on his hips, surveying his work. The boys that hadn't managed to squeeze out of the alley early had their hands tied and were bound to each other with one long rope.

Thomas rubbed his jaw. "I didn't really do anything," he said.

Gawain slapped him again on the back. "Ha!" he boomed. "That's the spirrrit."

Gawain swung up onto his stallion and trotted out of the alley, towing the Sloppy Pants Gang behind him.

As he passed, Sloppy spat at Thomas, "All this over a lousy shilling. Hope you feel good about yourself."

"But I didn't... Hey!... *You* were the one who..." As Thomas spluttered, Ollie passed by. He didn't look up, and Thomas felt an overwhelming sense of sadness move with him. Thomas watched him shamble along with the rest of the gang out of the alley and around the corner.

Marie's hand settled lightly on Thomas's shoulder. "Are you okay?" she asked, peering up at him.

She smelled as wonderfully as she always did. It made him realize how much he smelled like the floor of the alley with which he'd recently made acquaintance.

He nodded.

"You were very brave," she said quietly as she led him out of the alley. "Or very stupid. But for now I'm sticking with brave." She grinned.

Thomas laughed and then moaned from the pain that invoked. While Sloppy had focused on Thomas's skull, gravity and the alley had done a number apparently on the rest of Thomas.

"Thanks for getting help," said Thomas.

She smiled, "Thanks for being my hero."

"Is that what I was?"

She looked puzzled.

"Gawain looked pretty good there in the end."

"Oh him," she said. "He's just a big show-off."

Thomas smiled. "Well, we wouldn't have needed him if I hadn't messed with that boy, Ollie, yesterday."

"Exactly," said Marie. "That's why *you're* my hero."

Thomas assured Marie that his injuries didn't warrant a trip to the infirmary, and they parted ways on the palace grounds: Marie once again heading for the palace proper and Thomas making for the barracks. All Thomas wanted to do was to lie down and sleep. It was midday and he dared to hope that the barracks would be empty with the rest of the LVK off doing duty or drilling or simply not being in the barracks when they didn't have to be. Sure enough, the place was as still and silent as a tomb.

Thomas made his way to his bunk and was welcomed

by another letter – this one again addressed from Mother Farmer.

Dear Thomas,

I put an inquiry in at the post office and they assured me that my first letter was delivered – that you're alive in Camelot and are receiving room and board from none other than Arthur himself! I'm so happy for you. Do please send news when you can. I assume you're working for your keep, and if you're working for the king, it must be good and honest labor. I do hope it helps to convince Arthur to help William.

Speaking of William, between you and me, the sooner we get him out of there the better – and not just for his poor mother's sake. Something is addling his brain in that moldy dungeon. I don't know why, he's eating better than all of us! Well, except probably for you there at the king's own table!

As for us... As creative as I can be in the kitchen, I must admit there's only so much a person can do with root paste and only so much of it a person can take. We're all rather grumpy, some more than others. But we manage. Every day is a gift.

William's friends Ackerly and Royden have stopped coming to visit us. When they were here last, they were talking of sailing to France to seek their fortune. Your father threw them out of the house – you know how he is about the French. Speaking of your father, he's been spending most of his time with Smitty and old Abraham Chisel. Abraham has a grandson your age you probably know. Anyway, with Smitty practically out of work, those three are bound to get themselves in trouble sooner than later. You'd think they'd get tired of talking about the war. I know the rest of us get tired of hearing them!

Elizabeth is begging to write. I'll sit down with her this evening and help her and we'll send off her letter on the morrow. I do help all is well.

Love,
Mum

"Jiminy Chisel," muttered Thomas to himself and shook his head. He collapsed on his bed and drifted off to sleep in a sea of memories from another life.

CHAPTER XIX

A SONG & TWO LETTERS

"Wake up!"

Thomas groaned. Half of him ached while the other half felt alarmingly numb. He felt worse than he had after meeting Accolon's lance and the jousting field's turf in rapid succession. He vaguely recalled the sun being on the other side of the barracks when he'd closed his eyes.

Thomas rolled over, slowly.

"Oi, what happened to you?" It was Philip's voice.

Thomas yawned. It was a bad idea. His jaw didn't feel right at all. He made to rub his eyes, but stopped short. He could tell by the heaviness on one side of his face and the way the world was all swimmy on that side that at least one eye wasn't right either.

"I was walking Marie back to the palace. A bunch of orphans wanted us to meet their mum except their mum wasn't their mum it was this big... kid. Sloppy."

"Whoa. Sloppy... As in, The Sloppy? As in, the Sloppy Pants Gang Sloppy?"

Thomas nodded.

"They're singing about him."

Thomas blinked, or rather, winked – his second eye refused to participate in such shenanigans after all it'd been through.

"Who's... What?"

"The bards. They're all over town singing about how Gawain took down Sloppy."

Thomas frowned. "A knight of the Round Table taking down an overgrown orphan... That's something to sing about?"

Philip laughed. "C'mon," he said, and dragged Thomas out of the barracks. They headed to the palace steps where a crowd had gathered.

A minstrel sat at the top of the steps. His shoes were green, far too long, and curled. They matched his pants which were short and puffier than pants ought to be. Between his shoes and his pants, he wore canary yellow tights. The same green, puffy theme was duplicated on his epaulets. His vest matched his pants and shoes. Something white and frilly was spilling up his neck from underneath the vest – 'ascot' wasn't quite the word for it, and 'shirt' was way off. Whatever the thing was, and whatever it was doing, it was doing it at his wrists too.

He was mustached and bearded. The sides of his mustache were grown out, waxed, and twirled. His beard was braided. His nose was too big for his face. His eyes twinkled. And on top of it all sailed a great, green, three-pointed hat complete with a long yellow feather.

He strummed a lute expertly, smiled at the crowd amiably, and sang superbly:

> Listen oh, Camelot! Harken, hear tell.
> How virtue triumphed. How a ne'er-do-well fell.
> Camelot's cry and a fair maiden's plea
> Demanded a hero or two. Maybe three!

To undo a great villain at Innocence' behest
A single knight pledged himself to the quest
Like sun on his armor, his bravery shown
Into the dark labyrinth, he rode alone

Oh who is the subject of my refrain?
The glorious, the noble, the dear Gawain
Gawain, Gawain, Gawain, Gawain

The thieves' den held forty; two score and more.
But numbers are nothing when righteousness roars
Wild brigands, fierce bandits, Gawain bested them all
Then Sloppy himself met our champion's call

In the villain's dark fortress, the two titans fought
In the end it was Sloppy who ought to have not
Fear not dear Camelotians! Take courage, rejoice!
Today hope has a fist, today virtue has voice.

Oh who is the subject of my refrain?
The glorious, the noble, the dear Gawain
Gawain, Gawain, Gawain, Gawain

The minstrel repeated the chorus four more times after executing a stunning bridge. The tones were lilting, the melody pure. A yellow finch landed on his shoulder during the final refrain. He smiled at it, and it chirped at him. When he'd strummed the final cord, he stood and gave a sweeping bow. Ox wiped a tear from his eye and gave the first loud clap. The audience erupted in applause. The bird fluttered off, and the minstrel moved about the crowd accepting donations in his upturned, oversized hat.

As the crowd began to disperse, he announced he'd be playing at several locations throughout Camelot that day including the Fine Pickle, Isolde Park, and outside the Post Office. When the contributions dried up, he gave a final sweeping bow and headed for the gate.

When it was just him and Philip, Thomas burst.

"You've got to be kidding me. A labyrinth? Sloppy's dark fortress? *Forty* brigands? It was an alley! And there were like a dozen eight-year-olds."

Philip replied, "You seem surprised."

Thomas stammered. "Well, yeah, I... Wouldn't you be?"

"Who'd want to hear a song about a knight arresting a bunch of kids?"

Thomas gaped. "Well, apparently... everyone," he said sweeping his hand at where the crowd had been.

"C'mon Philip. 'Hope has a fist?' 'Virtue has voice?' Because we broke up a pick-pocketing ring?"

Philip shrugged. "Wait... We?"

"Yes," growled Thomas. "We."

"Ooooh," said Philip, comprehension dawning. "Oh my. You were there."

Thomas widened his eyes and nodded, "That's what I've been trying to tell you."

Philip gasped and pointed at Thomas's swollen eye, "You fought Sloppy!"

The conversation had barreled right through terrain Thomas wanted to talk about straight into areas he didn't want to try to explain. He gave a shrug and tried to divert it, "Well, I... That is—"

Philip gasped again and actually put his hands on his cheeks. "It wasn't Gawain! It was you!"

Thomas shook his head frantically. "No, no, that's not what I..."

"Thomas! This is terrible! You've got to tell someone. You've got to tell Tuttle, or the bards, or... or Arthur! Was Gawain even there at all?"

"Well, yes. He was... I mean he did all those things... er, not *all* those things, like I said. But yes, I mean no – he wasn't *alone* anyway."

The alarm slipped off Philip's face and was replaced by wonder. "You and Gawain fought *together*? You and Gawain? Gawain and you? Against all those brigands?"

"Philip!" shouted Thomas. "There weren't any brigands. They were kids! Orphans! Sloppy himself is just a big, tough kid!"

Philip looked confused. He shook his head. "It took two of you to take down a bunch of kids?"

"Well, no. I mean, it was just Gawain – he's the one who fought the kids."

Philip frowned. "Hold on. Let's start from the beginning."

Thomas sighed. "Yes. Please. Let's."

"There was an alley," said Philip.

"Yes," said Thomas.

"And a dozen or so small children."

"Well, not so small I guess."

"Orphans anyway."

"Yes."

"And they were a pick-pocketing ring, and one of them was Sloppy, and Gawain fought them all and arrested Sloppy and broke up the ring for good."

"Yes."

"And you were somehow involved in the fight," said Philip, pointing again at Thomas's eye.

Thomas conceded, "Well, yes and no."

"See this is where I get confused. You were there. You got hurt. But you didn't fight the kids."

Thomas took a breath. "I turned the other cheek," he mumbled.

Philip blinked at him. "Come again?"

Thomas gritted his teeth, looked Philip in the eye and said, "I turned the other cheek. Because that's what Jesus did and Sloppy beat the tar out of me and Gawain showed up and arrested them all."

Philip chewed on this.

"Huh," he said finally. "I don't think that's in the Code."

"Well no, not exactly," Thomas admitted. "But you've got to admit there are parallels."

"Aye yeah, I'll give you that. In any case, you've got no right to be jealous if the guy saved your butt."

"Who, Jesus?"

"No," said Philip and rolled his eyes. "Gawain."

Thomas sighed. "I guess not. But I mean, c'mon... *Titans*?"

"It's just a song Thomas."

"I guess so," said Thomas, glaring at the steps where the minstrel had played.

"You're an odd sort of knight," said Philip after a moment.

Thomas snorted, "Tell me about it."

It was their last dance lesson, and Madame Rhapsody was a blubbering mess. "You've all come so far," she kept saying. "I'm so proud," she repeated. "To see you become men before my very eyes," she sighed.

"Madame Rhapsody's concept of a man scares me a little," said Edgar.

Even Sir Cuddlington seemed proud of Madame's students. He sat on a high shelf watching contentedly as the dancers moved about the floor. The curses and trips of a week ago were replaced with only the occasional grunts of pain as the Less Valued stepped on each other's feet. In short, they were a picture of patient tolerance and inherent un-talent.

"You've come so far," said Madame Rhapsody, sighing.

When Hedley had played the last note of the final dance, Madame Rhapsody lined them up and gave each a bracing hug.

"I send you off," she said, "into a new world. A world where music moves, where life has a rhythm, where hearts come together and spin apart in a beautiful calypso of love.

"I send you," she said in her best breathy voice, "to dance."

Thomas, Edgar, Dedric, and Ox agreed to never discuss the experience with anyone.

∿

Exiting Madam Rhapsody's, Edgar glanced at the clock on Winchester Mercantile and panicked.

"Isn't today the day we get outfitted? We should have been at the armory already."

With Ox leading the way through traffic, they raced to the palace grounds. Thomas noted a distinct lack of pairs of small boys torturing ducks as they cut through Isolde Park. He wasn't sure if he felt better or worse because of it, but was pretty sure the ducks were better off.

They dashed up a side street, through the palace gates and around the barracks. A small, squat building next to an open forge served as the Less Valued's armory. The good stuff, of course – the gear belonging to the other orders – was kept elsewhere in armories specifically outfitted for the care and maintenance of higher quality materials.

The Less Valued's armory was a different story. It leaned to the right, and pitched just a little forward. It looked like it had picked a fight with a larger, more athletic building and lost. But it also looked like the kind of building that wouldn't think twice about picking the same fight again. It looked scrappy.

A blacksmith stood at the forge next to it. He leaned to the right and a little forward as well.

"Yerrrr," he yelled at them, "late!"

He glared.

"And," he sniffed, "ye smell like flawrs."

"Like what?" whispered Dedric.

"Flowers," said Thomas.

The smith bellowed, "Enough chit chat, girls. Line up!"

One by one, he called them forward – they were all named 'you' or 'next' as far as the smith was concerned – and measured the circumference of their heads with a string. He notched a pole with each measurement and had the head's owner make a distinguishing mark next to the tick on the pole.

When one of the knights questioned why this was the only measurement needed, the smith replied, "Thahr's two reasons yer skull's th'most impahrtan' pard o' yer head, butterscotch. One: It keeps yer brains in, an' two: it keeps yer nose outta my business. Next!"

Night was falling, and Thomas sat with his knees tucked up and his back against the wall at the head of his bunk.

Philip laid on his side on his bunk, flipping aimlessly through a stack of playing cards.

"I thought we'd actually be getting some gear today," said Thomas.

Philip shrugged. "One of Arthur's smiths is custom crafting a piece of armor for us. I'm not gonna say no to that."

The color of the sky through the barracks' windows was slowly changing color from the bottom up.

"Wonder what Marie and the rest of them are doing," said Thomas.

"The night before the biggest wedding *ever*?"

Thomas looked at Philip, thought about it, and nodded. "Yeah."

Philip stared back at Thomas for a moment. "All I know is it's best to stay away."

Philip pointed to two letters lying beside Thomas. "Are you going to open those?"

"Nope," Thomas said and shook his head.

Philip laughed. "Oh come on, how bad can they be?"

Thomas looked at him and raised an eyebrow.

"Aren't you curious?" goaded Philip. "I am!" he added and reached for the letters.

Thomas snatched them up. "Fine," he said, and then sat staring at the addresses. One was from Farmer, William; Prisoner, Dungeon at Fogbottom Keep. The other was written in the obnoxiously cute handwriting of a little girl: Farmer, 'Lizbeth, Cottage at the End of the Road, Fogbottom.

Thomas rolled his eyes. "This can't go well," he said.

"Nonsense," said Philip with a sardonic grin. "You'll be fine."

"Oh stuff it," said Thomas and ripped open the letter from his baby sister.

Dear Thomas,

It's too bad you had to go to Camelot to save William. If you were here we could play together more. I made a picture for you. It has bunnies but I'm not going to tell you what it is so I can show you when you come home. Are you coming home soon?

Dad is grumpy and Mum is sad a lot. I tell Mum root paste is good stuff to make her feel better but then she just cries more so I changed the subjects. Grandma is sleeping so I have to be quiet.

You're the best second biggest brother ever. I love you Thomas. Bye!

'Lizbeth Farmer

P.S. If you see a princess in Camelot try to remember what her dress is like so you can tell me. And her crown. If it has jewels and what kinds and how many. Write it down so you don't forget. Okay thanks! Bye!

Thomas let the hand holding the letter flop down onto the bed, closed his eyes, and banged his head against the wall behind him repeatedly.

"Lemee see," said Philip and took the letter.

Thomas didn't move or open his eyes while Philip read.

"She sounds awesome."

"She is," said Thomas.

He pulled his head off the wall, took a breath, and opened the letter from William.

From: William Farmer, Prisoner of Fogbottom
Dungeon I, Fogbottom Keep, Fogbottom

Dear Thomas,

You will recall in my last letter, no doubt, how I'd befriended a lovely fellow by the name of Cartwright the Pluck. I regret to announce his passing yesterday morn. I'd been feeding him portions of my rations for some time, as he seemed ill of health from the beginning, but it was all for naught. My cell seems so much larger emptier without him.

The other day, Wendsley took me to the courtyard to help load bundles of something or other onto a cart bound for I don't know where. The sun was delicious. I have to say, the novelty of the dungeon experience is beginning to wear thin. Speaking of wearing thin — I can grasp my bicep and touch the tips of my thumb and middle finger. I loaded three sacks of what felt suspiciously like grain onto the cart and promptly fainted from the exertion. I woke up back here in the cell, and there was Cartwright, no longer pluck.

Oh, and I've discovered the guards who examine my letters can't read, so here it is: There's a shipment of some sort due to leave the keep. I suspect it is most, if not all, of the grain from the storehouses. I don't know when, but if there was ever a time to act – that time is now.

God's speed little brother,
William

Thomas moved to the edge of his bunk and handed the letter to Philip.

Philip took the letter without a word, read it, and said, "What do we do?"

Thomas shook his head. "We've got the wedding tomorrow. We can't very well just disappear."

"You're talking about going to Fogbottom and...?"

Thomas shrugged. "And I don't know what."

"You've got to talk to Arthur, Thomas. You've got to tell him how poorly the people of Fogbottom are fairing and how the Baron has it in his power to alleviate that suffering and, even if there isn't some conspiracy going on, how he's not living up to the responsibilities of his title."

Thomas gritted his teeth, then nodded.

"I'll talk to Arthur. Tomorrow. At the wedding."

Philip gripped Thomas's shoulder in silent encouragement.

Thomas smiled and took a deep breath. "I'm going to turn in. G'night Philip."

Philip nodded. "Me too. G'night Thomas."

Thomas found himself staring once again at the words he'd etched on his bunk, and fell asleep worrying about how to approach the King on his very wedding day.

CHAPTER XX

THE WEDDING OF KING ARTHUR &
PRINCESS GUINEVERE

It was the kind of affair that gets pages and pages of fancy prose written about it in storybooks. Words like fairytale and gossamer and the names of half a dozen subtle variations of the color white flapped from onlooker to onlooker like doves. The doves themselves cooed romantically at each other, and did their best to make everyone feel as if everything important in the world was right here.

It was held outdoors next to St. Stephen's under a flawless sky. A woman in the congregation remarked that there was no cathedral on Earth that was large enough to contain Arthur's love for Guinevere. Her husband replied that he could relate to the sentiment, and indicating a wine glass that looked very small and dainty in his hand, excused himself to go look for a larger, sturdier variety.

Stringed instruments comprised the majority of the orchestra. They played the kind of music that makes people walk on their toes and turn more dramatically than would otherwise be appropriate. Aside from two brief interludes during the homily and the vows, the orchestra played continuously. The priest spoke of the importance of honest communication, supportive friends, and separate bedchambers for a long and lasting marriage. Arthur's vows were enthusiastic and incoherent. Guinevere's were poetic, enchanting, and pointedly non-specific.

Everything seemed to be made of flowers.

The reception that followed continued the floral theme. There were chocolate flowers that tasted of orange, flowers made of icing that confused and delighted passing bumblebees, and flowers that tasted remarkably like flowers, which people all seemed to agree was wonderful and not something they were terribly interested in at the same time. The flowers were contrasted by a scattering of amazingly detailed, remarkably accurate, and wholly inedible reproductions of fruit. The wedding planners concocted all of this on the theory that there is no better way to get people socializing than to upend their understanding of what's safe to put in their mouths.

"Everyone's talking about Merlin's prophecy," said Philip.

Thomas was staring at a woman whose hair had been done up so that it was piled straight up, easily doubling her height, and crowned with a model frigate. She was carrying a cane which she used periodically to push and poke at the ship when the whole thing started to lean the wrong way.

"Which prophecy?" said Thomas.

"The one that happens here," said Philip.

Thomas tilted his head as the ship began to slip, then straightened up again as the woman set it aright without missing a beat in her conversation.

"The one where Merlin dies," said Philip.

Thomas jerked and looked at Philip. "The one where he does what?"

"They say he said he's going to die."

"I don't remember him saying that. I think 'doom' was the word he used. There are all sorts of doom."

"Really? For instance?" said Philip

"Well, for instance," said Thomas, "there's the sort of doom where you have to try to explain to a king on his wedding day that one of his trusted lords is probably, actually, quite untrustworthy and his people are suffering for it and, in fact, one of his knight's own brothers is in dire straits for the simple crime of petitioning said lord for some sufferance."

Philip frowned. "Well, yes I guess there's that sort."

"And then," continued Thomas, "there's the sort of doom where if you fail to convince the king that one of his lords is a scoundrel – on his wedding day, at his reception – your entire village along with your dear mother, your war-hero father, your doting grandmother, your kid sister, and your loving and frustratingly noble brother will probably all starve to death in the coming winter."

Philip blinked and tried to change the subject. "Is that Dedric? Hello, Dedric!"

"AND," continued Thomas, "then there's the sort of doom where you do, in fact, convince the king that some conspiracy is afoot, and he rallies his troops, and he sends them to your village to roust out the despot, and it turns out you were wrong about everything."

Philip swallowed and picked at his fingernail.

Thomas bowed his head and took a breath. In a quieter voice he said, "And then there's the sort of doom where you convince the king, and it turns out you were right, and everyone wants to know why you didn't say something sooner. Why you didn't help out the suffering people in your village the moment you had a chance. Why you let your mother, and your father, and your grandmother, and your kid sister, and your loving and frustratingly noble brother suffer as long as they did while you lived it up like a prodigal son in the land of plenty. Why when you had the chance to be a hero..."

"Stop," said Philip, and put a hand on Thomas's shoulder. "Whatever happens, happens. And whatever choices you made, you made for reasons that seemed right at the time."

"I fear that Hell is filled with people who made choices that seemed right at the time," said Thomas.

"That may be true, but Heaven is full of people who made lousy choices and know they don't deserve to be there. And in any case," Philip grinned and continued, "we're not dead just yet, depending of course on the particular sort of doom Merlin was talking about."

Thomas smiled and wiped the palms of his hands on his trousers. "What's keeping them anyway? I want to get this over with."

"I think they're having their portraits drawn," said Philip.

Philip said something else, but Thomas didn't catch it. Bane had just arrived with his father. They immediately began making their way from group to group, the Baron often forgetting – or purposefully neglecting – to introduce his son. Bane looked like he'd rather be anywhere else.

"How are you going to do it?" asked Philip.

"Do what?" said Thomas. "Oh," he added when Philip raised an eyebrow.

Philip offered, "If it were me, I'd march straight up to him and lay it all out at once. Arthur's a reasonable man, and a good king."

He popped a flower into his mouth and chewed.

"Philip," said Thomas. "Did you see the roast pig they have done up like a dragon?"

Philip raised his eyebrows.

"They've even got little knights made of cheese attacking it, and every so often, a little jet of flame shoots out of its mouth."

"You're jesting."

"It's over at the buffet."

"I've got to see that," said Philip and took off.

Thomas edged closer to Bane and the Baron, but as close as he dared get, he still couldn't make out any of their conversation. Bane shot a look at him, and that ended any hope of inconspicuous eavesdropping.

Thomas turned abruptly and nearly crashed into Philip returning from the buffet. He was carrying a knight-shaped piece of Wensleydale mounted on a tiny horse fashioned, somehow, from cranberries. "Check this out," he said.

Philip made the horse whinny.

"Very nice," said Thomas.

"You seem tense, Thomas."

"No kidding?" said Thomas and rolled his eyes.

"Oh dear," said Philip. "Look at that."

The wedding party had arrived.

In the history of weddings, there have been only two perfect brides. Guinevere wasn't one of them, but she could've been a third if the judging had been just the tiniest bit more accommodating.

She glowed. Arthur beamed. The Queen's Knights blinded people by reflecting the sun at them with their perfectly polished breastplates, and no one ever waited more exquisitely than Guinevere's Ladies in Waiting.

Thomas saw Chastity flash a smile at Philip, and Philip's face went bright pink. When the trumpet fanfare ceased and the applause faded, she made her way over.

"Whatcha got there Philip?"

"It's a... It's, um..."

"It's a cheesy knight," said Thomas.

Philip nodded. "Want one? There over–"

"I think I've already got one," said Chastity, and pulled him away through the crowd.

"Just keep him off ledges and high balconies," Thomas shouted after them. "And he doesn't take well to water..."

They completely ignored him.

There was a tap on his shoulder, and he turned to find a young woman looking at him with eyes that drove all thought right out of his head. Her hair was angelic. Her dress did things most clothes were too self-conscious to even consider, and her skin... While he couldn't see much, what he could see made him look back at her eyes and try not to think about it.

"Marie!" said Thomas, and it was clear that was about all he was going to be able to muster verbally for quite some time.

She smiled, and the orchestra began to play.

"Let's dance," she said.

Stark terror gave way to a simmering dread, which in turn fell to mild misgiving, and finally, a kind of uneasy acceptance as Thomas grew more comfortable dancing publicly, in front of people, while everyone watched. He tried to believe that the other wedding-goers were mostly paying attention to themselves and not him and Marie. Eventually he believed it. Time passed, they danced, and nothing terrible happened. Marie seemed to enjoy it immensely, and Thomas enjoyed her enjoying it.

The night was – Thomas had to admit to himself – rather nice. With everyone dressed as lavishly as they were and the music blanketing the whole, it felt magical – as if Father Time himself had shown up and decided things were special enough here and now to warrant the whole universe taking a rest. Being with Marie was probably part of it.

As they moved around the other dancers, Philip and Chastity spun by.

"Have you done it yet?" called Philip.

"Done what?" said Marie, smiling. "And more importantly, why have we stopped dancing?"

Thomas swallowed and spotted Arthur at the wine fountain. Arthur looked odd standing there. It took a moment for Thomas to realize it was the first time he'd ever seen him alone.

"I'm going to tell Arthur about Fogbottom and my brother," said Thomas.

"Oh!" said Marie. "Well, it's about time."

Thomas shot a look at her.

She raised her eyebrows, and then caught sight of Arthur herself.

"And look! There he is alone. Why are you still here?"

Thomas stammered, "I... But... We..." He took a breath. "I don't think you understand the gravity of the situation."

"Nonsense, you'll be fine," she said far too casually. "Go," she added, and she shoved him.

He frowned over his shoulder at her. In reply, she made a shooing motion and mouthed, "Now!"

King Arthur was sipping from his goblet and surveying the affair. He seemed as content a person there ever was. Thomas watched him watching Guinevere – Queen Guinevere now – for a moment, and then cleared his throat.

Arthur turned. "Sir Thomas," he paused with a mischievous grin, "...the Hesitant!" Arthur roared and slapped Thomas on the back. "See what I did there?"

Thomas bowed.

"My King," said Thomas.

"How doest the evening unfold for thee, my fortitudinous and stouthearted Less Valued Knight?"

Thomas stared, speechless.

Arthur kept a straight face for a second then bellowed a laugh. "I love talking like that. Merlin never lets me do it. He thinks I'm mocking him."

He sipped from his goblet and mumbled, "Come to think of it, maybe I am."

Thomas gave a nervous chuckle then tried to begin, "Your Majesty..."

Arthur seemed to be done entertaining himself for the moment. "Yes, Thomas?" he said.

"I have something to tell you, and something to ask, both of a bit of a sensitive nature."

Arthur raised his eyebrows. "Can it be spoken here?"

"Yes, I believe so, if done quickly."

"Well, out with it then." All bemusement was gone; Arthur waited on Thomas's words with such seriousness and sobriety Thomas found it a bit frightening. Thomas was suddenly very aware of the strength of the forces he could unleash with this one small conversation.

"As you know," said Thomas, "your servant the Baron Fogbottom rules my home, the village of Fogbottom."

Arthur nodded.

"For some time, the people of Fogbottom have been starving..."

"Yes, yes, there's a famine afoot if you haven't noticed," said Arthur.

"Of course, my Lord. But we believe, my brother and I, that the Baron has grain enough in his storehouses to feed the village yet he steadfastly refuses to do so."

Arthur shot a look past Thomas and quickly returned his gaze. There was a warning look in Arthur's expression, but Thomas dared not take his eyes off the King.

Thomas couldn't tell if the warning was *for* him or aimed *at* him. He decided all he could do was press on and have it all over with.

"To make matters worse," said Thomas, "we believe the Baron is up to something."

Arthur's expression remained unreadable, though his eyes searched Thomas's.

"We who?" was all he said.

Thomas was startled by the question. "Well, your majesty, myself and my brother William—"

A voice behind Thomas interrupted, "Your brother William is a rebel and a mug, and you'll do well to distance yourself from him young Farmer, as you have."

Thomas turned. It was the Baron.

"My King," said the Baron and bowed to Arthur.

"Baron Fogbottom," cried Arthur smiling. "Sir Thomas and I were just discussing how we're going to undo this curse the land is under."

"Oh were you?" The Baron shot a searching look at Thomas.

Arthur held up his goblet.

"The Grail. Of course," said the Baron looking relieved. "Has Merlin augured its location yet?" There was something condescending in the Baron's tone. To Thomas, he seemed far too comfortable in his manner with the King.

"In due time," said Arthur.

Guinevere appeared and attached herself to Arthur's arm. She whispered something in his ear, and Arthur smiled at her.

"I'm afraid I must take my leave, gentlemen. Baron, Thomas. Enjoy the evening," said Arthur and walked off with his bride.

Thomas's heart dropped so low at having lost his chance to petition for his brother that he didn't realize he'd been left alone with the Baron until it was too late.

"You'll do well, Farmer, to leave well enough alone. I don't know what your messing with here, playing at being a knight, tugging on Arthur's ear. But it will stop, or I warn you there will be consequences."

Thomas said nothing, and when he didn't avert his gaze, the Baron grinned. "Isn't your brother a guest of mine? Perhaps I should check on his accommodations... ensure that they are... adequate?"

Thomas bowed his head.

The Baron nodded. "Good," he said. "I'm glad we had this little chat, Farmer."

The Baron brushed past Thomas and disappeared into the crowd. Thomas stared at his feet and thought to himself that at least he'd gotten one thing right: this had all been a very bad idea.

Someone large stepped up next to him. Thomas looked up.

"Sir Marrok," said Thomas.

Marrok smiled but remained quiet. He nodded his head toward the Baron who was rejoining Bane in the crowd.

"Keep your friends close, and your enemies closer," he said.

Thomas watched the Baron mutter something to Bane. Both of them looked back at Thomas briefly.

"A quote from Sun Tzu, a Chinese General," said Marrok. "He also said, 'The supreme art of war is to subdue the enemy without fighting.'"

"Is that what this is then?" said Thomas. "War?"

Marrok took a deep breath. "Can I give you a piece of advice, Sir Thomas?"

Thomas nodded. "Of course, Sir."

"All Men suffer. Those who do not master their pain will find themselves driven by it." He rubbed absently at the scar on his arm. He pointed at Bane who was being pulled to the edge of the crowd by his father.

"Find that one's pain, and you'll find his drive."

Marrok's eyes were sad, but he smiled at Thomas.

There was a hubbub near the reception entrance where the Baron and Bane were headed. Thomas craned his neck and caught sight of the reason for both the hubbub and the Fogbottoms' convergence toward it.

Morgan le Fay had arrived.

She was dressed completely in black, and carried a feathery eye-mask attached to a long wand so that she could don it or remove it with a simple flick of her wrist. With her were her usual escort – King Uriens and their son Owain – and one other.

"Accolon," said Thomas.

A hand rested on Thomas's shoulder, and Thomas turned to find Marie looking up at him.

"That didn't look like it went well at all," she said.

Thomas gripped her hand.

"No," he said, "it didn't."

"I'm sorry, Thomas."

Bane and his father had reached Morgan. Bane looked like he was going to be ill. There were some pleasantries exchanged, and then Morgan said something that made the whole group burst out in laughter that was unmistakably cruel. Bane looked stunned. He turned on his heal and made his way out of the reception, skirting tables, shoving chairs, and bumping people out of the way.

"Sir Marrok," said Thomas, "do you think..."

But Marrok had disappeared.

Thomas glared at the retreating Bane.

"Thomas?" said Marie.

"I need to talk to Bane."

Marie made a noise somewhere between a laugh and a gasp.

"What... Really?" she said when Thomas didn't respond.

"I think I know what his problem is."

"We all know what his problem is," said Marie with one raised eyebrow.

"No I mean, really, I think I can get him to help."

Marie's face contorted into a look of such skepticism that Thomas had to laugh.

"Seriously. I think he just needs what any of us needs."

"And that is?" said Marie in a voice that made it clear she wasn't entirely sure she wanted to know.

"Respect," said Thomas.

"I have to go talk to him." Thomas couldn't stand still. Bane was about to disappear, but Thomas didn't want to leave Marie stranded at the wedding. Something in his gut that knew the little about girls that it did told him it would be a very, very bad idea to do so.

"Huh," said Marie. She looked impressed.

"Huh," she said again, searching Thomas's eyes.

She looked around the reception, glanced down at her dress, and shot a look at Chastity and Philip still whirling around amidst the other dancers.

Finally she shot a look back at Thomas and said, "What are you still doing here?"

Thomas blinked.

"Go!" she said, and shoved him again.

Thomas smiled at her.

"Now!" she said. She crossed her arms. "Before I change my mind."

Thomas went.

Thomas couldn't believe how hard it was to keep up with someone who didn't know he was being followed. Bane rounded a corner and Thomas hurried to keep him in sight. For a brief moment, he thought he'd lost Bane completely; then he saw a flash of Bane's cape entering the palace proper.

Thomas raced in and found an empty hall. He stopped and held his breath. With all of the normal palace-dwellers engaged in the festivities outside, the place was as quiet as a tomb. But there it was: footsteps, and then a heavy door opening and closing in the distance.

Thomas moved quickly down the hall and rounded a bend in the direction of the noise. He stopped at the first large door and listened.

"How *dare* they!"

It was Bane's voice, and it came from behind another set of enormous, iron-bound doors up ahead.

"The tables," whispered Thomas.

Thomas hesitated, wondering how to approach the situation and trying to figure out exactly what to say. Then a part of him he wasn't entirely familiar with decided to wing it, and he found himself throwing open the door and marching in without a plan.

Bane was pacing back and forth among the tables, but he froze when the doors opened.

"What are *you* doing here?" He was seething.

"I could ask the same of you, Bane," said Thomas in a strong voice that came from the same unfamiliar place that seemed to be making the decisions at the moment.

Bane was dangerous when he was calm, and here he was stalking around in a dark room in a rage. He glared at Thomas. Thomas was sure he was about to be leapt upon and pummeled mercilessly, but Bane suddenly turned his head and went back to pacing.

"I suppose you saw it all?" he said in a low voice.

"I saw enough."

"Then what do you want?" Bane stopped again. "Come to mock me like them? Come for paybacks? Take your shot, Farmer. Let's have it!"

All the frustration of the past few weeks swelled up in Thomas. He wanted to blame it all on Bane: William's imprisonment, his parent's wavering between complete lack of confidence and impossible expectations, Thomas's own lousy decision to put off a direct appeal to Arthur on his family's behalf so he could instead become a knight and try to save the world, and the carnival that was Camelot when he wanted, needed, expected so much more from his heroes.

In the midst of this storm of angry thought, Marrok's words softly but firmly spoke themselves. *All men suffer...*

"Master the pain," said Thomas under his breath.

"What?" Bane's fists were clenched.

Thomas sighed. All the anger washed out of him as quickly and effortlessly as a wave washing off the shore back into the ocean.

Thomas sat down.

"Bane, I know about Accolon. I know what you and your father planned. I know your father betrayed you."

"You... What? How?"

"It doesn't matter. The important thing is that it doesn't have to keep going like this. You have choices, Bane. You could be a great knight." Thomas couldn't believe the words coming out of his mouth.

"We all have to overcome these expectations people have of us," Thomas said.

Bane slumped in a chair and put his head in his hands. Thomas looked away and his eyes came to rest on the empty Round Table with its throne-like sieges.

Bane spoke from behind his hands. "You knew about Accolon, and you fought him anyway?"

"Well, no. No, I didn't know then. But I was pretty sure he was going to kick my butt."

Bane made a noise that could have been a laugh or a sob, and when he pulled his hands away, his face was red and his eyes looked exhausted.

"Why then? Why'd you do it?"

Thomas stared at the empty sieges and thought.

"Because as long as there's a chance, I've got to keep trying," he said. He turned to look at Bane who was calmly appraising Thomas.

"There's something else," said Thomas.

Bane's brow wrinkled slightly.

Thomas took a breath. "We know there's some sort of shipment leaving Fogbottom, and we suspect it's the village's grain."

Bane froze.

"Is it?" said Thomas.

Bane clenched his jaw, and instead of answering, stood up, made his way over to the scribe's corner and sat down at the small writing desk there. He lit a candle, pulled out some parchment and uncapped a bottle of ink.

"What are you doing?" said Thomas.

"What's it look like I'm doing?" said Bane.

He wrote some lines, then blew on the ink to dry it.

"This is a letter instructing the warden of Fogbottom Keep to release your brother."

Bane folded the paper, dribbled some wax on the seam and pressed his ring into it, sealing it. Thomas was afraid to make any sudden moves. If this was a dream, he didn't want to wake himself up.

"Bane, I... I don't know what to say."

"Don't say anything. Just take it," he said, and stood up and handed Thomas the letter.

Thomas took it and stood silently for a moment, searching Bane's face. He felt like hugging him, but he wasn't quite ready to go there yet. It was *Bane* after all.

"Go," said Bane. "The shipment leaves tomorrow."

Thomas stared at Bane for a moment in shock, then turned on his heel and fled the room. He carefully skirted the wedding reception, passed the barracks and made straight for the stables.

As the door swung slowly shut on the darkened table hall, Bane stood quietly grinning. It wasn't a friendly grin. If you came across a grin like that in a dark hall on a man standing by himself, you'd make an excuse and leave.

He rubbed some dried wax off his seal ring and glared at the Round Table. Moonlight was streaming in and illuminating a single, unclaimed siege. He bit his cheek and thought.

Drawing a dagger from his boot, he flipped it in his hand casually and moved to stand by the seat. He laughed once, shook his head, crawled under the table and started carving.

It took quite a bit of effort, and by the time he was finished he was sweating. He laid there in the moonlight in that quiet room appreciating his handiwork.

Bane was here.

After a while, he carefully cleaned up the mess of wood chips he'd made, and silently exited the hall.

CHAPTER XXI

WILLIAM

Thomas awoke to a cool morning with a bright but weak sun clipping the horizon. He was lying on his back under a saddle blanket and atop a pile of sticks and leaves he'd assembled the evening before. In his haste to get on the road, he'd brought little in the way of traveling gear, and he'd forgotten exactly how far Fogbottom was from Camelot. The horse he'd conscripted from the palace stables had begun to lag late in the night, and despite Thomas's overwhelming desire to press on, he'd been forced to stop out of consideration for the dark bay stallion with the white blaze on its head.

The horse stared at Thomas and made hungry noises. His father would've called the marking a bald face. The stable master had called it a war bonnet. It bothered Thomas that he could remember this but couldn't recall the horse's name.

"Pounder?" tried Thomas experimentally.

The horse didn't react.

"Prancer?"

Nothing.

"Protagonist." Thomas was sure that was it, until the horse simply looked away.

Thomas watched his breath curl up and away, in and out of the sunlight streaming between the trees. He could hear small forest creatures rummaging through the undergrowth. The world felt solid, and Thomas felt like he was finally on the right path. His stomach growled.

"Well, in any case, let's see what's in here," said Thomas as he pushed himself up onto his feet and rummaged through the saddlebags the stable master had insisted on packing. Impatient as he'd been the night before, he was glad for the stable master's insistence now. Inside one bag he found strips of peppered jerky and in another a bag of oats which he fastened around the horse's muzzle.

"Pepper?" said Thomas, hoping that wasn't right.

The horse chewed and looked sideways at him. Thomas got the distinct impression the horse was not at all impressed.

Thomas gathered up what little gear he had and broke camp while they ate. When the horse had its fill, he saddled him and took one last look around to make sure he wasn't forgetting anything.

The sun was higher now and strong enough to cast shadows on the forest floor. The frosted ground crunched under his boots as he moved about. He replayed a scene in his mind that he'd gone over countless times the night before: He and William ride down their lane to the Farmer cottage. His father sees them approach and drops what he's doing to stare, mouth wide. He yells something and his mother, his grandmother, and little Elizabeth pour out of the cottage. They cheer and hug and cry and everyone is glad to see William, but equally glad to see Thomas, amazed at who he's become and what he's accomplished. His father takes him aside and tells him he knew Thomas had it in him all along.

It was going to be a great day.

❧

That same morning, two men came galloping up the lane to the Farmer's cottage in Fogbottom. One was armored and escorted another who was rather smartly dressed, but road-worn, and his horse was laden with more saddlebags than seemed considerate from the horse's point of view.

Mr. Farmer was outside working, as usual, and he called to the Mrs. which brought not just Mrs. Farmer out, but Grandma and Elizabeth as well.

The smartly dressed man pulled a letter out of one of the saddlebags and read, "Mother and Father Farmer, Cottage at the End of the Road, Fogbottom?"

They looked at each other briefly.

"That'd be us," said Mr. Farmer.

"Sign for delivery please," said the man.

Elizabeth waved at the armored man, who tried to ignore her. "I like your horse's dress," she said.

The guard choked and glanced at the other adults. "It's not a *dress*, young miss. It's quilted armor." He looked horrified.

"Oh," said Elizabeth, "sorry. Well, anyway it's very pretty." She smiled reassuringly, but the man seemed inconsolable.

As the two men rode away, the Farmer's crowded around Mr. Farmer who carefully opened the letter and experimented with different distances between it and his eyes until he found one that suited him. He read:

Dear Mum and Dad,
  Working on it.
Love to you all,
Thomas

"That's it?" said Mrs. Farmer.

"Appears so," said Mr. Farmer.

"Well, there ye go," Grandma Farmer said and headed back inside.

∾

People addressed him with various names – Knuckles, Bones, Grandpa, Grumps, Old Man Chitterton, or just plain Old Man. No one could remember a Fogbottom without him. Every morning at half past ten, he showed up at the Brimful Kettle, ordered an orange pekoe "and keep 'em comin' miss," sat down – outside if it was nice and inside if it was otherwise – and set up either a chess board or a nine men's morris. There he'd sit, beating anyone who chose to have a go and speaking very little until seven that evening when the Kettle closed, at which point, Grumps would clear his table, pack up his board, and head home leaving a single silver coin on the table – enough to cover his tab for at least three days let alone one.

Grumps was very welcome at the Brimful Kettle.

No one asked him questions. Not because they didn't have any, but because he was so perfectly comfortable not answering them people grew comfortable not knowing.

At quarter to six, Grumps was eating a cucumber and cream cheese sandwich outside the Kettle and sitting three moves from checkmate with Chas Brightman who was sitting cross-armed, staring at the board and puffing on a pipe he'd carved himself.

"Let's go, champ, ain't got all day," said Grumps.

Chas guffawed. "Who're you kiddin'? All day is 'zactly what you've got old man."

"Hmpf," said Grumps, and chewed on his sandwich.

After a moment, he stopped, cocked his head and said "What's that?"

"That's the sound of Heaven's Chorus come to usher you on before you beat me again." Chas frowned inside the cloud of pipe smoke billowing around his head.

"Not that," said Grumps. "That!"

A bay charger bearing a war bonnet and a knight astride him shot round the corner, up the street, through the market, and out of sight.

Grumps popped the rest of the sandwich in his mouth, leaned back in his chair, and started packing his own pipe with tobacco. Chas peeled himself off the wall, righted the table and his chair, and began picking up chess pieces, grumbling all the while.

"What in God's green Earth... I oughta... Who do they think...? Give a man a... Rotten baron guards... Like they own the place!"

He sat down, brushed off his pipe, and stared moodily at Grumps.

"They do," said Grumps.

"Do what?"

"Own the place, indirectly. But that was no Baron's man."

"Well who was it then?"

"If I'm not mistaken," said Grumps, "that young man bore the marks of the Less Valued."

"The who?"

Grumps didn't answer, and Chas had learned long ago that it was no use pressing. Grumps answered what he wanted, when he wanted.

Grumps puffed slowly on his pipe and stared down the road after Thomas. At one point, he shifted and felt for the reassuring presence of the heavy leather chest armor he still wore every day under his tunic.

They called him lots of things: Grumps, Knuckles, Old Man; It had been a long time since anyone had called him Sir Chitterton. He packed up his belongings, bade good day to Chas, flipped a silver coin onto the table and headed home early.

Thomas crossed the drawbridge spanning Fogbottom Keep's empty moat. His horse's hooves pounded, hollow and jolting, until he was back on solid ground on the other side. He slowed and stopped as one of a pair of guards approached and took hold of his reins.

"Come from Camelot, sir? What news? Oi, Farmer? Is that you?"

Thomas dismounted. "Aye Wendsley, it's me."

Wendsley looked bigger than ever around the middle. The straps of his armor were strained and looked like they wouldn't hold much longer.

"Well, look at you!" said Wendsley. He stepped back and examined Thomas, head to foot and back. "What've ye gone and done to yerself? Workin' for Camelot now? Who's takin' care of yer Mum and Dad what with—"

Wendsley's face suddenly fell; he leaned in and lowered his voice. "Maybe ye don't know! Yer brother William's been locked up here for..."

Wendsley paused and screwed up his face. Thomas could see the mental strain, and when Wendsley started counting on his fingers, Thomas decided to save him the agony.

He pushed Bane's letter at Wendsley and said, "I know."

Wendsley took the letter, held it up in front of him, read the addressee, examined the seal, reread the addressee, and raised his eyebrows.

"I'm here to fix that," said Thomas.

"Well, right this way, sir," said Wendsley. The "sir" was said with a bit too much conviviality and too little sincerity for Thomas's taste at the moment. This was official business after all, and as a member of the Baron's militia, Wendsley was guilty by association as far as Thomas was concerned. Wendsley's chummy slap to his back didn't help either.

Wendsley put two fingers in his mouth and blew the kind of whistle Thomas had always thought was louder than a man had a right to make. A stable hand came running, accepted the reins, and led Thomas's horse away while Wendsley and Thomas entered the Keep proper.

They walked down a long hall, narrower and less decorated than the halls at Camelot. In fact, the only accoutrement Thomas saw was a single flag bearing the Baron's all too familiar livery: a white crescent moon on a red field. It marked the entrance to the Baron's throne room, which Thomas caught a glimpse of as they passed.

The throne room was stark. Above a chair that would've been painfully self-conscious in the presence of the Round Table's sieges, a pair of iron weapons hung: a mean looking mace and a longsword with an uninteresting hilt. The weapons looked more practical than decorative.

Thomas felt uneasy, but brushed it off. In a few minutes, he'd be reunited with his brother and they'd be on their way to deliver the good news, and themselves, home.

Wendsley took hold of a thick wooden knocker on a small, heavy door in a dark corner and rapped loudly. The sound echoed in the quiet keep. He stood back when he was finished and waited. After a moment, they could hear footsteps coming up stairs on the other side of the door, and a portal at head-height opened, revealing a puffy, scrunched up face not unlike Wendsley's.

"Password," said the face with a gruff voice.

Wendsley leaned in and whispered, "Despair."

"That was last week," said the face.

"Oh," said Wendsley, "right, um…" He pulled back and glanced at Thomas nervously. Counting with his fingers again, he mumbled to himself, "Despair, death, disease, disfigurement, dislocation, dis…

"Dismemberment!" he blurted.

The face screwed up even more and spat, "Shhh!" It shot a look at Thomas.

Wendsley grimaced, leaned back toward the door and whispered far too clearly, "Dismemberment!"

The face rolled its eyes, the portal slammed shut, and the door swung open revealing a narrow set of stairs curving down steeply into a musty dungeon.

Wendsley stood up straight and, in a voice that was as official-sounding as he could muster, addressed the guard to whom the scrunched up face from the portal belonged: "Sir Thomas Farmer to see the Warden on official business vis-à-vis the Baron's son, Bane of Fogbottom."

It sounded rehearsed, and knowing Wendsley, Thomas figured it had been rehearsed a lot.

"I know who the Baron's son is, Wendsley," grumbled the second guard. He turned to Thomas and did something horrible to his face. It took Thomas a moment to realize he was trying to stretch it into a welcoming smile.

"Right this way," said the guard, and gestured down the stairs. Wendsley led the way and Thomas followed while the second guard shut the small but heavy door, locked it, and lumbered after them.

The sound of the door locking gave Thomas an instant of perspective – seeing the dungeon from the point of view of someone taking up residence in it shot a pang of mixed feelings: horror for William who'd spent far too long imprisoned here simply for trying to help the village, anger at Bane and the Baron for their thoughtless cruelty to William and countless others, and trepidation at the thought of being locked up himself, which Thomas quickly brushed off as irrational. He craned his neck to make sure Wendsley still carried the letter from Bane. He did, and Thomas focused his thoughts on the job at hand: Talk to the warden, retrieve his brother, and get out.

They entered a small room dimly lit by torches fixed to the wall in plain, iron sconces. A table made from a single, thick board, a few solid, but otherwise unremarkable chairs, and a locked cabinet in the corner were the only furnishings. A deck of crudely detailed cards was strewn about the table.

A third guard rose from his seat. "I'll take that," he said, pointing at Thomas's sword.

Thomas gave Wendsley a questioning look.

"Standard procedure," said Wendsley. "Can't trust these pris'ners with sharp objects. Crazy, the lot of 'em.

"'Cept William, of course," he added hastily.

Thomas reluctantly handed over Ambrosia.

The third guard pulled out a ring of keys, unlocked the cabinet, and hung Thomas's sword inside among an assortment of similar but less remarkable implements.

The three guards looked at each other.

"I ain't gettin' him," said the second guard.

Wendsley looked at the guard with the keys.

"Uh-uh," said the third guard. "Me neither. Warden doesn't like to be n'trupted when he's med'tatin."

Wendsley sighed, drew himself up and knocked on a door on the far side of the small room.

There was a sound of something tumbling over, a cough, and then a voice yelled, "Who 'zit? Better be good!"

The door opened and an old, mean looking man glared from guard to guard to Wendsley to Thomas. He was short and disheveled, and Thomas got the immediate impression he blamed both those states on everyone else.

Wendsley opened his mouth to say something, but when the warden's head snapped in his direction, he instantly shut it again and thrust the letter at him.

He eyed Wendsley suspiciously, but took the letter and gave Thomas another hard look before examining it. He closed one eye and squinted at the seal before breaking it open, sighing, and reading the contents. His brow creased more and more as his eyes moved down the page. His eyes flicked up at Thomas when he finished.

"Right this way, sir," he said to Thomas. The warden motioned for Wendsley and the guard with the keys to follow, and they headed down a short hall, through a door, and into another hall with dozens of cell doors lining both sides.

"Your brother's in the last one on the left," growled the warden. Thomas hurried forward, registering the presence of a few other prisoners in the cells he passed. In the final cell, a figure hunched on a thin pile of dirty straw.

"William?" said Thomas. It didn't look like him at all.

The figure stirred, turned, and stood up. He was filthy, shirtless, and wide-eyed. His hair was matted together in some places and in others shot straight out from his head at odd angles. He had a beard.

Thomas stared, then finally, underneath it all, found his brother.

"William!" he shouted.

William shuffled forward and came to an abrupt halt. Thomas and William both looked down. A chain stretched between a bracket on the back wall and William's ankle.

"Remove that at once," Thomas said to the warden.

The warden gave a little bow that seemed infuriatingly unremorseful. In fact, he seemed to be enjoying something here immensely.

"Open the door," he said.

The guard with the keys moved toward William's cell door.

"Not that one," said the warden. He pointed to the cell door next to William's. "That one."

Thomas's mind raced. "What's going on?"

"In you go," said the warden. He shoved Thomas into the cell, snatched the keys from the guard – who looked as surprised as Thomas but not nearly as horrified – and locked the cell door.

"What are you doing? You're to free my brother..."

The warden unfurled Bane's letter, and Thomas's stomach sank.

"To the Warden of Fogbottom Keep from his Lord's son Bane, kindly inter the bearer of this note, Thomas

Farmer, a subject of the Baron of Fogbottom, for crimes against His Lordship and actions in conflict with the interest of Fogbottom. His term of incarceration shall last until such time as the Baron or his eldest and only son can be beset upon to administer justice in said matter.

"Signed, Bane, son of Fogbottom."

A wave of rage washed over Thomas, but as quickly as it came, it spilled away, and left him feeling simply cold and dark and empty. He'd been had. He gripped the iron bars of his cell, closed his eyes, and embraced what he knew his family had believed about him all along.

Thomas Farmer was a failure.

CHAPTER XXII

MIDDLINGS

Snowflakes the size of small coins floated down lazily on an otherwise still, quiet, and frozen day in Camelot. Philip had looked forward to the first snow every year since he was six. On a blustery, late fall day more than a decade ago, Philip's Dad had introduced him to a delectable treat called frozen custard. Life hadn't been the same since. The season's first blanket of snow meant that not only was it cold enough to make the stuff, but now you could jam the containers right into a nearby drift and it would keep.

Restaurants like The Fine Pickle began churning the dessert out by the barrel-full. This year, they'd added strawberry to the menu, but for the First Frozen, as Philip affectionately deemed it, he stuck with the tried and true: vanilla. He got it in a bowl made from some sort of thin cracker you could eat. The girl said it was new, and she called it an "edi-bowl". She giggled every time she said the word.

He had her ladle on chocolate syrup and whipped cream and then top it all off with a bright red cherry.

Philip paid her, picked up the dessert carefully, and headed to find a seat near the fire.

The Pickle was packed; Philip wasn't the only one who looked forward to frozen custard day. He had trouble finding a seat, but in the end managed to squeeze into a small table closer to the door and further from the warmth than he preferred. Glancing at the empty chair across from him, he wondered briefly what had become of Thomas; he hadn't seen him leave the wedding, and his bunk didn't look like it had been slept in – of course, they were trained to make their bunks look that way. Philip never understood this; why make the bed so carefully every morning if you were just going to sleep in it and mess it all up again?

He shrugged, picked up his spoon and dug in. It was delicious. He savored the first mouthful with his eyes closed, but was soon shoveling it in with vigor. He was about half way through when Marie walked in alone.

The Pickle was noisier than usual, but over it all she heard something that sounded vaguely like a wounded horse. She looked around and spotted Philip with his face a mess, his mouth full and his arms waving wildly in the air at her. He smiled, pointed at the empty seat and raised his eyebrows. She smiled back and after a brief wait and a discussion with the girl at the counter that involved the word "edi-bowl", some giggling, and this time even a snort, Marie joined Philip at the tiny table by the door.

"Ham oo eem ahmiff?" said Philip.

Marie laughed at the sight of Philip so unabashedly enjoying himself.

"Pardon?" she said.

Philip laughed at himself and held up a finger. Swallowing, he repeated, "Have you seen Thomas?"

"No," said Marie, suddenly serious. "I was hoping you knew what became of him after he chased off after that good-for-nothing son of Fogbottom."

Philip dropped his spoon. "He what?!"

Marie nodded. "Right before the whole thing with the wild hart and all those hounds crashing through the buffet tables."

"Oh that was something wasn't it?"

"Guinevere was horrified."

"That's the kind of thing that would happen to Sir Philip the Disadvantaged at *his* wedding," said Philip.

Marie laughed. "I do think Merlin exaggerated a bit. I mean, it was a terrible disruption, but as I told Lady – *Queen* Guinevere, no one was hurt, nothing irreplaceable was broken, and it'll give her a story to tell her grandchildren. I don't see how anyone's going to be glorified or doomed by an off-course hunting party, except of course the party-crashers themselves depending on how affronted Arthur feels."

The story did indeed grow over the years. Sources on the scene that day tell of a deer and several hounds crashing through the reception, and a huntress who was very distraught and fled the scene with an unknown knight in chase. The facts were quickly adapted to the meet the needs of the tellers including a victimized Guinevere, an irate Arthur, and Merlin. Five hounds became sixty, a cake covered deer became a magnificent white hart, the distraught huntress became a mysterious Lady of the Wood, and the Unknown Knight became an agent of a plot that was somehow all orchestrated by Morgan.

The reality, of course, was much less exciting; the aftermath even less so: When everything had come to rest and the whole reception stood silently waiting for the king's reaction, Arthur simply said, "Gawain, find the deer. Pellinore, find the lady." And then he stomped off with Guinevere in tow presumably to find someplace that behaved itself better in the presence of its king and queen.

Later tales tell not only a grander version of all the events, but also of Merlin's involvement in the more fanciful variety. In the end, it's impossible to say if the event had anything to do with Merlin's subsequent disappearance from Camelot, and in any case, that's a story for another time.

⊰

"Well..." said Philip, then looked as though he was thinking hard about something.

"What?" said Marie, curious.

"If there's one thing I've learned from being 'unlucky'," said Philip, making air quotes around the word unlucky, "it's that you can't ever tell what's going to come of something."

Marie paused with her spoon half way to her mouth. "Um," she said. "Thanks for that insight." She returned to her dessert.

"No, I mean—" Philip laughed at himself. "Right. For instance," he started over. "I call them triggers – these events that kind of kick things off. The trigger might seem horrible or just unfortunate or it can even seem like a good thing, at first. The important thing is to recognize it as a trigger, that's all. If you focus on the trigger itself, you're done for, because after the trigger, there'll be a series of events. These are the middlings..."

Marie was looking at him with a wary expression.

"Just bear with me." Philip slid his custard to the side so he could gesticulate safely.

"The middlings can be directly linked together – a ladder falling and scaring a cat that jumps on a man pushing a wheel barrow full of watermelons that spill and start rolling down the street..."

Marie raised her eyebrows.

"...Or they can seem completely unrelated until they collide at some point – a man arguing with a lady at a counter turns abruptly and bumps into a child chasing a runaway rolling-hoop who careens into a baker who's just walked out of his store carrying a large, delicate pastry – you get the idea."

Marie was completely engrossed. Her custard sat forgotten and melting on the table in front of her.

Across the street, an argument broke out between two men. One of them was brandishing a chicken and pointing at its feet.

"In any case, the middlings aren't important either. The trigger and the middlings are all leading up to the finish. The finish is what counts; that's what's going to tell you whether the trigger and the middlings were fortunate or unfortunate."

There was a sharp crack from up the street, and a sound of someone yelling. People in the Pickle began craning their necks to look out the windows.

"Now, the thing is," said Philip, clearly in his element, "the finish itself can be a trigger for another set or even a middling set up to collide with another set of middlings to form a bigger finish."

"You've thought about this a lot," said Marie.

"It's very complicated, being unlucky. Oh!" said Philip, "that's the other thing."

A horse came careening down the street headed straight toward the two men, oblivious, arguing over the chicken.

"Someone who you might call unlucky, I prefer to think of as more *cosmically involved*."

Marie gave him a puzzled look.

"Sure. Because you can't always tell how the finishes are going to turn out, being involved in the triggers or the middlings – while it might *seem* unfortunate–"

At the last minute, one of the arguing men looked over the other man's shoulder, saw the great beast hurtling down on them, grabbed the man holding the chicken, and pulled him out of the way. The second man dropped the chicken which headed straight for the door of the Pickle, which was slowly shutting after admitting the most recent customer. Both men got up and chased after the chicken.

"It just means you get to be a part of something bigger than yourself from time to time," Philip said. He picked up his bowl, and stuck a great big bite of half-melted vanilla custard covered in chocolate syrup and whipped cream in his mouth.

The chicken raced in, the door clicked shut, and Marie jumped. Philip's eyes darted to the window.

"Oh darn," he said around the spoon jammed in his mouth.

The two men shot into the Pickle, slamming the door into Philip's chair and knocking him forward. There was a great flurry of feathers, squawking, flailing of arms and yelling. In the chaos, something slipped out of Philip's coat, bounced onto the floor, spun and settled unnoticed by nearly everyone. The two men managed to snag the chicken and exited carrying the traumatized bird between them.

Philip sat motionless, vanilla custard, chocolate syrup, and whipped cream sliding leisurely down his front. Marie was frozen in the startled posture she'd assumed to protect her dessert from the fracas and herself from her dessert. She stared at Philip, then broke into hysterics.

"So," she said between laughs, "was that a fortunate or unfortunate finish?" She grinned ear to ear.

Philip gave her a scathing frown and said, "I'm going to go clean up."

He got up slowly and made his way to the restroom in as dignified a manner as possible. He caught several people chortling on the way and gave them looks intended to shut them up. This only added to their amusement.

In the washroom, Philip scraped the bulk of the errant confection off his clothes into a wastebasket, picked up a towel, wetted it and began to scrub at what was left.

"...the farmer rebellion..." he heard someone say.

Philip froze.

Hadn't heard of any rural discontent, thought Philip, *other than, well, the land dying and all. No outright rebellion in any case.*

He shrugged and started scrubbing again.

"...good to have them out of Camelot for a bit..."

Philip scrubbed slower and listened harder. The voices were coming through a window on the wall of the washroom. Philip leaned a bit and managed to catch a glimpse of two gruff looking men. One was wearing red and white, but Philip couldn't make out any other identifying marks.

"...don't know how you stand it," the colorless one said. "They're a rotten pair to work for."

"I'd quit if I had somewhere to go," said the one in colors. "I'm just glad I got the transfer out of Fogbottom, miserable pit that it is..."

Philip gasped. His mind raced and his eyes darted around the room.

"Not farmer – *Farmer,*" he said and gasped again. He threw down his towel, threw open the door, and smashed right into the linen closet. He backed up, closed that door, opened another that looked just like it, and rushed out of the washroom. On the way out of the Pickle, he grabbed a startled Marie by the arm and yelled, "C'mon, we've got to find Pyralis."

CHAPTER XXIII

THE FARMER REBELLION

*T*homas surveyed the cold, damp cell for a more comfortable place to sit. He'd already decided several times that there wasn't anything better – the whole cell was equally miserable – so he settled for shifting positions. He was surprised how torturous it was to simply be uncomfortable with no foreseeable relief.

He distracted himself from his physical discomfort with a mental one: trying to think of something he could say to his brother. Everything seemed inadequate. All he'd needed to do was to take the opportunity placed before him at the start of this whole mess and none of it would've happened. The Farmer's could've lived a nice, quiet life on the outskirts of Fogbottom, working the land, such as it was, and making do. Instead, Thomas had single-handedly disintegrated the family, wrecked any hope of relief for Fogbottom, and made an enormous fool of himself in Camelot. What had he been thinking, befriending people like Philip and Marie? They deserved so much better. He didn't even merit the company of a washed up evil wizard and a codependent giantess.

"I'm sorry," said William.

For a moment, Thomas thought his mouth had gone ahead and done the job his heart was working up to.

"Thomas," said William.

Thomas turned his head and saw William sitting in a similar fashion on his cell floor, staring at him with wet eyes in a face that was quite a bit hollower than he remembered.

"I'm sorry," he repeated.

Thomas stood up and went to the bars separating their cells.

"*You're* sorry? For what?"

"For getting us into this mess."

"But you didn't – I..."

And suddenly, Thomas was furious.

"There you go again! It's always about you. *William's* the hero. *William's* responsible–"

"Didn't you hear me? I said I screwed up!" William stood, and for the first time since Thomas had seen him in the dungeon, he reminded him of the William he knew.

Thomas poked himself in the chest. "No, William, this time I screwed up – I mean – Aaah!" Thomas pounded the bars in frustration.

"All *you* did," Thomas shouted, "was march up a stupid, little hill and get yourself thrown into prison. *I'm* the one who dealt with Mum and Dad. *I'm* the one who went to Camelot to petition Arthur for your release. *I'm* the one who traded the one chance to rectify it all for a shot at saving the world.

"Don't look at me like that. You'd have done the same." Thomas turned his back on William and slumped down on the floor.

"You did what now?" said William carefully.

Thomas sighed and told William his story.

❧

It was impossible in the windowless dungeon to tell how much time had passed while they talked. Thomas managed to forget where and how uncomfortable he was as he related all the events that had transpired between their incarcerations.

William interrupted frequently with growing admiration:

"A real giant?" he said.

"A giantess," Thomas corrected, and continued.

Later, William roared with laughter: "An egg right in Bane's face!"

And then with the kind of respect men gain for each other only when one of them does something very brave and very foolish: "You rode against him? The Black Knight? This... Accolon?"

Thomas nodded and continued. William wanted to hear everything about people like Arthur, Merlin, Guinevere, Gawain and Kay. Along the way, Thomas described Pyralis, Gorgella, and Sir Philip the Disadvantaged. He realized, fondly, what a bunch of misfits he and his friends and mentors all were.

He was recounting his experiences with Ox the Monosyllabic and Dedric the Diplopian at Madame Rhapsody's—

"Her cat's name is 'Sir Cuddlington'?"

"Mm-hmm," said Thomas. "Cuddles for short."

William groaned, and Thomas was glad to find himself connecting with his brother so effortlessly, but the moment was short-lived.

Sounds of some commotion filtered down the hall: a heavy door being thrown open, keys jangling, and voices. Thomas immediately recognized one of them as Bane's.

Bane strode toward them as if he owned the place which, indirectly, he did. He had a smug grin on his face the whole way, and when he stopped in front of Thomas's cell, he was having such a hard time containing his glee that he actually bounced on his toes.

"How are you doing Farmer?" Bane's voice dripped with twisted delight. An image flashed in Thomas's mind of Bane as a small boy torturing bugs.

"Can I get you anything? A blanket perhaps?"

"Bane," said Thomas through clenched teeth, "what's going on?"

"Why, Thomas, you're doing your duty to your lord of course. When Father found out I'd squashed the rebellion in Fogbottom and had the ringleader carrying his own sentence to our warden, he was overjoyed."

"What are you talking about? What rebellion?"

"Oh Thomas, stop pretending to be so innocent. The Baron told your brother he couldn't open the storehouses, William here wouldn't take 'No' for an answer, and when my Father did what he had to do maintain order—"

"Maintain order? My brother came to you in simple supplication for the good of your own lands!"

"This is exactly what I'm talking about. Who are you, Farmer, to decide what's good and bad for my – for my Father's land? And when he holds his ground against this insolence, off you go to Camelot to slander our name and push your own selfish agenda."

"Selfish agenda? Bane, the land is dying!"

Bane took a breath and when he spoke again he was dangerously calm. "What do you know about running a kingdom, Farmer?"

"I know enough not to trust someone who betrays me and then publicly humiliates me."

Bane's face went red with anger. He stared at Thomas and was clearly exerting great effort to contain his fury.

"Do you?" said Bane cryptically.

Thomas suddenly felt very cold.

"What do you mean?" he said.

"How did you wind up here Farmer? Did someone betray you? Someone who has publicly humiliated you?

Someone who intends to ensure that Fogbottom's needs are met?"

Thomas was no longer looking at a boy ripping wings off of insects. Somewhere, things had turned very dark and very serious. A few winters ago, Thomas had been out in the middle of a frozen lake, alone, enjoying the silence when an ominous crack sounded under his foot. Nothing had come of it, but his stomach was doing the same thing now as it had done then.

"What are you saying?" said Thomas.

A grin crawled across Bane's face – not the same gleeful grin he'd entered the dungeon with, this one was vicious. He spoke now as if addressing an audience.

"The Baron of Fogbottom hereby orders the execution of the Farmer rebels, tomorrow, at dawn, by hanging."

William stood up a bit too quickly, wobbled, and steadied himself on the iron bars of his cell.

Thomas stared at Bane in horror.

"Bane," he whispered. "Stop playing, this isn't – you can't be serious."

"Oh I assure you Farmer, Fogbottom's interests will be protected."

He leaned in close then and spoke softly and directly at Thomas's ear: "What possessed you to think we were cut from the same cloth, that we would ever drink from the same cup, that we should ever, *ever*, sit at the same table?"

He straightened up. "Camelot was a mistake for you Thomas. But don't worry. It's nothing I can't fix."

And with that, he turned on his heel and marched down the hall and through the door. For a brief moment, light from the entrance to the dungeon filtered in and illuminated the dank basement. Then the door slammed shut, and darkness returned.

After the fracas at the Fine Pickle had calmed down, and Philip had burst from the restroom and towed Marie out into the street, a tall knight with a sawtooth-shaped scar on his forearm got up from his table in the corner, and made his way casually to the table where Philip and Marie had been sitting.

He stooped and picked something up off the floor on the far side of Philip's chair. It flashed in the sunlight as he straightened and examined it. Glancing once out the window, he pocketed the object and exited the Pickle unnoticed.

※

At first, Marie thought Philip was playing at something, and she laughed as he dragged her out of the Pickle. But as they wound their way through the streets of Camelot, she began to realize something very serious was going on.

"Philip," she said, but she couldn't get his attention. They narrowly avoided being run over in rapid succession by a speeding carriage, a horse carrying a postman, and a woman leading a pack of oblivious children.

"Philip!" she yelled and tugged her own arm – the arm he still firmly gripped.

He glanced at her, but kept moving. The look she caught in his eyes frightened her.

"PHILIP!" she yelled and planted her feet. She wasn't able to stop him completely, but it was enough to get his attention. He spun around.

"What's – going – on?" She felt like punctuating each word with a stomp, but settled for yanking her arm out of Philip's grasp and punching him instead. Philip didn't even seem to notice. His furtive glances up and down the street reminded her of the deer that had found itself on Guinevere's wedding buffet.

"PHILIP!"

He looked at her again, and finally she saw some evidence of higher function behind his crazed eyes.

He blinked, and gave himself a little shake. He was breathing very hard.

"Philip," she said in as calm a voice as she could muster. "Did something happen in the restroom? Something you'd like to tell me about?" She wasn't sure there could ever be an answer to that pair of questions that anyone would want to hear.

Philip took a deep breath and related what he'd overheard.

"I think Thomas is in serious trouble," he finished.

Marie stared at him for a moment, her eyes beginning to mirror Philip's.

"Why are we standing here then?" she said.

"I don't know! C'mon!" said Philip, and they were off.

The sounds of pounding feet came from the stairs outside Pyralis's apartment. Gorgella froze in the act of affixing a small, metal bit to the end of another metal bit. There was a sparkly, black powder on her hands. Gorgella and Pyralis glanced at each other, then Gorgella set her bits down and Pyralis hastily threw a drape over the whole project. They faced the door and tried to look casual. Pyralis looked at Gorgella's hands and made a kind of nervous clicking sound with his cheek. She shoved them behind her back and recomposed herself just as the door burst open and Philip and Marie tumbled in.

"Ah," said Pyralis and breathed a sigh of relief, but Gorgella, oddly, redoubled her efforts to appear innocent.

"Pyralis," said Philip, breathing heavily. "And Gorgella, good, you're both here." He noticed Gorgella's strange look, but ignored it. "You've put on weight!" The words were out of his mouth before he could stop them. Marie stomped on his foot and glared at him, but Gorgella blushed and said, "Thank you."

It took only a few minutes to bring Pyralis and Gorgella up to speed. In the end, they needed no convincing; Pyralis began directing Gorgella to pack a bag with various implements, including a few odds and ends from under the drape. They packed those bits very carefully, taking their time, and mostly with their backs to Philip and Marie.

Finally, after what seemed like ages to Philip, Pyralis was ready. Gorgella heaved the pack over her shoulder and the four of them left the apartment.

"I need to borrow four horses, Rittenhouse," said Pyralis to a mildly surly stable master five minutes later.

"Four horses? Late for the apocalypse eh? I always thought ye looked like Death, Pyralis, but ye could've cast the other three better."

No one laughed.

Pyralis rummaged something from the pack, slipped it to Rittenhouse with a wink, and said, "Sorry, friend, we're in a bit of a hurry."

Rittenhouse eyed the thing Pyralis had given him suspiciously. "This won't blow up like the last batch, or melt the stove like the one before that, or turn into a–"

Pyralis shot a nervous look at his companions. "No, no, I've worked out all those issues. This'll do the trick, trust me."

"That's what ye said the last three times Pyralis."

Rittenhouse seemed to be mulling something over as he stared at Pyralis, then shrugged and said, "What've I got to lose, eh? Right this way."

He didn't move quickly, but he was efficient, and soon the four were perched atop their borrowed mounts.

"And which horseman might you be," Rittenhouse said to Gorgella. "Famine?"

Gorgella shot him a look and opened her mouth, but Pyralis rested a hand on her arm, and she stopped.

Rittenhouse laughed. He smacked the rump of her horse, and the four of them took off out of the stables.

"I'll send Hades on after ye when he shows up," he called.

"I think Hades might be where we're headed," said Philip.

They rode then as quickly as their horses could carry them, in silence and without break. In time, night fell, and they continued on with a full moon lighting their path.

CHAPTER XXIV

CHARMING DISARMAMENTS

William leaned back against the cell wall and slid slowly down onto the floor. Thomas still gripped the cell bars, staring at the door through which Bane had exited. Thomas felt strangely, sickeningly light. He could feel the cold iron in his palms, and the solid floor under his feet, but these sensations came to him too slowly, as if filtered through blankets. He felt detached.

I'm going to die.

The thought repeated itself slowly in his head.

A sound came from William that made Thomas turn. William's head was buried in his hands. His thick, curly hair that had been the object of so many girls' conversations hung limp and disheveled, obscuring what his hands didn't already hide. He was crying quietly but forcefully – his body rocked with each breath.

"I'm so," he said between sobs, "so sorry."

Thomas didn't move; he watched William cry for a moment, then went back to staring at the door.

"I shouldn't have..." continued William. "I shouldn't have come here. I thought...

"I thought..." he repeated, and trailed off into more quiet sobs.

A curious thing had begun inside Thomas's head. People were coming to mind in rapid flashes: Elizabeth holding out her tooth for Thomas to see, Grandma Farmer startled in her chair, Mr. Farmer turning to look at him from the wood pile, Pyralis dumping a bucket-load of stinking salve on a dirt floor, a bottle with a tiny, empty ship inside, Philip pointing out Camelot celebrities as Guinevere's company paraded by, Dedric and Ox, grinning and covered in smashed eggs, Marie at Guinevere's wedding.

"It doesn't end like this," he said softly.

There was a hitch in William's sob, but if he heard Thomas, he ignored him.

Other images began to present themselves to Thomas: Merlin frustrated with Arthur at the knighting ceremony, the black knight saluting the stands flippantly, Morgan grinning back wickedly, the Baron mocking his own son at Guinevere's wedding, and Bane simply looking down at him and Philip from his horse with a smile that made Thomas want to punch him.

"It doesn't," said Thomas, more forcefully this time, "end like this."

The feeling of detachment was gone. William looked up at him, his face streaked with tears and dirt.

"It's not your fault," said Thomas.

William shook his head in disagreement.

"It's not your fault. It's not my fault. It's not any of our *faults* that got us here William. We're the good guys.

"Look. What did Dad always say? To win, all evil needs is for good people to do nothing. Well, we're not doing *nothing* are we?"

William blinked and glanced around the cell. "Well," he said. "Not really much at the moment per se."

"I mean we're trying, William. It can't end like this, because... because we can't *let* it."

This wasn't coming out at all how Thomas had hoped. He took a breath and tried again.

"Listen," he said. "Remember when we'd talk about Camelot while we were cleaning out the Baron's stables, or hauling wood for Dad?"

William nodded.

"It's not like we imagined. It's filled with real people. Merlin's real. Arthur's real. Gawain and Kay and Pellinore... real people. They're just, you know, they've been involved a lot longer with what's going on. They make mistakes, they're downright foolish some of them, but they're trying to build something. Something good. Something right.

"If I learned one thing in Camelot, it's this: the only way to fail is to stop trying. There's always another chance."

William was giving Thomas a big-brother-look which meant he thought Thomas was missing something obvious that made everything Thomas was saying moot.

"What?" said Thomas, frustrated.

"If you haven't noticed," said William. "We're kind of locked in a dungeon here with no way out until our captors come and fetch us so they can *hang* us."

Thomas had to admit it was hard to be optimistic. He sat down with his back against the bars of the cell.

"If I've learned anything else," said Thomas, as much to himself as to William now, "we're not alone. We're never alone."

William gave him a quizzical look and opened his mouth to say something, but just then a tapping sound came from high up on the other side of Thomas's cell wall. It sounded like a metal hammer gently rapping against stone. It moved sideways, then back a bit, stopped briefly, then tapped twice rapidly in one spot.

They heard a muffled yell, and then silence. Thomas and William glanced at each other. William got up and moved toward the front of his own cell, closer to Thomas.

"What was–" said William, and the wall exploded.

⤎

Small rocks and dirt pelted Thomas's back and shoulders as he hunched by his cell door. Even partially deafened from the sound of the blast, he could hear larger rocks and building stone dropping and bouncing around on his cell floor. When it seemed the rain of debris had slowed enough to dare it, he squinted up at what was now a rather large, bright hole in the cell wall. A rush of clean air surprised him – he hadn't realized how quickly and easily he'd become accustomed to the dank, stale dungeon variety.

There were shapes moving in the light. They were yelling something, but with the ringing in his ears it just sounded like muffled grunts.

The shapes disappeared briefly, then one by one, Philip, Marie, Gorgella, and Pyralis dropped down into the cell. Philip got to Thomas first, lifted him up and gave him a great hug. Marie pulled him off and threw herself into Thomas's arms. Gorgella stood with her arms folded, looking proud, and Pyralis patted Thomas on the back.

The ringing was finally subsiding. "I can't tell you how happy I am to see you," said Thomas to all of them.

"WHAT WAS THAT?!" yelled William from the opposite corner of his cell. Thomas couldn't tell if he was still deafened, terrified, or both.

"William, it's okay," said Thomas. "These are my friends from Camelot." And he turned back to them, grinning.

"Pyralis, that's quite a piece of work," said Thomas pointing at the rubble.

"Oh no," said Pyralis, "that wasn't me." He put his hand on Gorgella's shoulder. She wore an enormous grin on her face and positively beamed with pride. Thomas thought she looked at least a foot taller.

Thomas raised his eyebrows in wonder. "You did that Gorgella? But how did you – have you been–"

Thomas shot a look at Pyralis. "Are you sure demolition is, you know, a good thing for someone in, er... a certain frame of mind."

Gorgella rolled her eyes.

"Not demolition my boy," said Pyralis.

"Rapid spontaneous deconstruction," said Gorgella. "There's lots of training and skill involved in knowing just where and how to knock something down safely, you know."

There was an ominous rumble behind her. Gorgella stopped and glanced backward. Pyralis didn't seem to notice.

"Quite true," he said, "and Gorgella here seems to have quite the knack for not only cobbling up the tools of the trade, but also surveying a work site, identifying load-bearing structures and..."

The rumble came again and some of the smaller rocks in the pile shifted.

"Um, Pyralis," said Gorgella. She took a step back from the rubble and pulled at Pyralis's sleeve.

Oblivious, Pyralis continued, "...undermining only those structures necessary to achieve the goals of the targeted deconstruction."

"Pyralis!" shouted Gorgella, and pulled him out of the way just in time as the larger rocks around the hole collapsed inward along with a great rush of gravel, dirt and racket. The five of them huddled near the cell door and watched their escape route disappear. When the dust had settled, Pyralis continued, stunned, "It's been a great boost to her self-worth."

"I'm so sorry," said Gorgella through her hands. Her pride was gone, replaced by horror as she glanced around at them.

The rest of them slowly turned as one to stare at the locked cell door. William started to laugh – he looked crazed. "Well, you were right Thomas. We're never alone. Good show, Camelot!" William fell over cackling.

Marie, still in Thomas's arms, looked up at him. "Thomas?" she said. Thomas, tears in his eyes, just slowly shook his head. They could hear shouting coming from outside, muted through the collapsed rubble, and down the hall, there was now an uproar in the guard room. They watched the door with dread.

After a moment, the din in the guard room settled, the door cracked open, and a gray muzzle poked out. There was a ring of keys in its jaws.

It sniffed twice, then shoved the door some more and a magnificent, silver wolf padded into the hall. The only blemish on its perfect hide was a conspicuous sawtooth-shaped scar on one foreleg. It headed straight for Thomas's cell, and squeezing its snout between the bars, shoved the keys up at Thomas.

Everyone looked from the wolf to Thomas.

Thomas simply said, "Thank you, sir. I guess this makes us even," and took the keys.

The wolf seemed to grin. There was a groan from the direction of the guard room, and the wolf's ears pricked. It snarled and took off down the hall.

Thomas quickly unlocked his cell and William's, and the six of them followed. Gorgella brought up the rear, towing a heavy-looking satchel.

"Um, Thomas," said Philip. "Is there something you'd like to tell us?"

"About what?" said Thomas.

"'About what?' he says. About your little friend there." Philip's voice trailed off as they pulled the guard room door the rest of the way open and surveyed the scene.

Two guards huddled in the corner, shaking. A third was pinned to the floor while the wolf snarled and growled atop him. The pinned guard struggled for a second, and then simply fainted.

The wolf swung its head toward the other two guards who looked as though they would crawl in between the cracks in the stone foundation if they could rather than tangle with the beast before them.

Thomas moved quickly to the cabinet, shuffled through the keys, and pulled the door open. He handed a dagger to Marie. Both Pyralis and Gorgella refused, and Philip was already armed. Inside the cabinet were two swords that put all the others to shame. One, of course, was Ambrosia, but Thomas didn't recognize the other. He lifted it out gently appreciating its weight and balance, then handed it to William. Finally, Thomas grabbed Ambrosia, and fastened her around his waist.

The sound of stomping feet came through the dungeon exit above. Philip rushed up the stairs. They heard a shout, a door slam, and Philip came charging back into the guard room.

"That way's no good," he said, eyeing the wolf, who was still growling menacingly at the huddled guards.

"*That* way," laughed William, "is the *only* way."

Philip frowned at him.

Out here where it was relatively light compared to the dungeon, Thomas finally got a good look at William. He looked absolutely dreadful. His cheeks were sunken. There were great black bags under his eyes. The eyes themselves were wide and yellowing. He was far too thin. He looked as crazed as he sounded.

Pyralis nudged Gorgella and nodded at the wall, but Gorgella just shook her head.

Thomas reached out and gripped her arm. "You can do it," he said.

Gorgella looked at him for a moment, then swallowed, set her pack down and pulled out a small hammer. She started tapping on the stones near the guard room ceiling, her eyes closed and her head bent.

After a minute, she seemed satisfied. She pulled a lump of something gray out of the pack and a long coil of black cord.

"Up you go," said Pyralis to the guards and herded them into the warden's office. Philip dragged the third, unconscious guard in after them, and then shut all three of them in. The wolf tugged on Thomas's shirt and started backing out of the room.

Thomas spoke slowly and clearly in as calm a voice as he could muster, "I think we'd better get around the corner now, William."

William was watching Gorgella, fascinated. "What? Oh, right," he said, and followed the rest of them back into the hall. After a moment, Gorgella backed into the hall as well, unrolling the cord.

"Three, two..." she said. Pyralis did something to the end of the cord that Thomas couldn't see.

There was an explosion in the guard room, and a shower of dirt and small stones hit the door in a fusillade and bounced into the hall, pelting their shins and feet.

When the debris came to rest, Gorgella gestured for them to stay put, and entered the room alone.

"It's safe," she called. The relief in her voice was plain to Thomas.

Thomas entered the space formerly known as the guard room. It was more of an open-air dugout now.

"It's amazing how a bit of light can change a room," said Marie entering behind Thomas, coughing lightly from the dust.

There was yelling from the courtyard above, and at the same time they heard something heavy hit the door at the top of the stairs. There was a loud crack as if the door had been ripped from its hinges, a resounding thud, and renewed yelling that was alarmingly less muffled.

William began giggling madly and started scrabbling up the rubble, but before he'd gotten half way, three armored heads poked into view.

"Halt right there, miscreants!"

Silhouetted against the sunlight it was hard to tell for certain, but Thomas got the distinct impression the Baron's guards were as frightened as he was.

There was pounding on the stairs and four more guards charged into the room. A girl screamed, and Thomas swung around ready to defend Marie, but she was standing calmly and pointing at Philip. Philip was aiming his sword at Sir Marrok who was standing half-naked where the wolf had been a minute ago.

"I'm going to need to borrow that," he said, and casually disarmed Philip.

The three guards above began to clamber down the rubble, three more appeared above them. William hastily backed down into the room, slipped as a rock turned, and rolled onto the floor gripping his ankle.

"You okay?" Thomas asked, lifting him up.

"Am I okay?" said William. "Am I okay," he repeated and incapacitated himself laughing.

The guards – ten in all now, with the sounds of more coming – surrounded Thomas's group, but stayed just out of arm's reach. Thomas didn't think they're standoffishness would last.

Gorgella began rummaging frantically in her pack.

"Drop it missy. And put down your weapons, all of you," commanded the best dressed of the guards.

"Do as I say, and no one gets hurt. Well, not yet anyway," he added with a wicked grin.

The detached feeling washed again over Thomas. He saw a vision of himself and his friends swarmed, tackled, and re-imprisoned. *Give up*, the feeling said. But as his heart fell, a weight pressed against his leg.

Ambrosia, he thought, and the detached feeling poured away as if he'd just climbed out of a pool. The world was solid and heavy again.

Thomas cleared his throat in an attempt to get his friends' attention. "Yo ho ho," he said, his hand on Ambrosia's hilt.

Philip shot a look at him.

"What did you say?" said the well-dressed guard.

"I said," repeated Thomas more forcefully.

"YO." He drew Ambrosia with one smooth motion. She made the kind of silky metal whisper a finely-crafted sword makes when it's drawn from a custom-fitted scabbard – the kind of sound that makes men want to be knights in the first place.

"HO." Thomas continued, and held Ambrosia aloft. She caught a ray of sunlight on her tip and lit up as bright as a small sun.

Comprehension dawned on Philip, Marie, and Marrok who'd all been in the room the day Thomas had demonstrated the sword's power to Arthur. They quickly grasped their noses. Philip shut his eyes tight – his face was already turning red, he was holding his breath so vigorously. Pyralis grinned and nonchalantly slipped his hand up to his face, delicately pinching the bridge of his nose just below his eyes. Gorgella looked around at them all, hesitated, then gripped her nose as well. William just stood there, eyeing everyone as if they were the mad ones.

Thomas couldn't wait anymore. Marie was trying to tell him something. She was blinking madly at him and flailing one hand, making repeated pinching motions. Two more guards bustled into the room from the stairs. One was very, very large.

"What's going on–" said the big guard.

"HO!" yelled Thomas. He brought Ambrosia down, point first and slammed her into the packed dirt floor. She slid smoothly into the ground, and when Thomas let go, she vibrated so fast she hummed.

In the midst of it all, despite the fact that they all might be captured and hung, or worse, Thomas thought he smelled doughnuts frying. It was a wonderful aroma, and his stomach growled. Frustrated, he shook his head. *Focus*, he thought to himself.

He turned toward the rubble pile and noticed all the guards, and William of course, who hadn't known to hold his breath, staring blankly into space. Some of them swayed slightly. Most had curious grins on their faces. A few were tossing their heads around like Thomas was.

Two thoughts struck Thomas at once: First, he'd forgotten to cover his own nose. And second, someone was grilling steak, and he really, really wanted one.

Thomas stumbled to the left and held his head in his hands. He flailed his hand in the direction of his nose and managed to grab it on the second try, but suddenly he wasn't in the guard room anymore...

He was at home. It was a bright summer day, and hundreds of blossoms from the cottonwood trees drifted lazily through the air. He was small, and he was reaching up and petting a black colt his father had brought 'round. The horse smelled like a horse – like the forest, like the fields, like Free Will. Its coat was warm from the sun...

He was ten. They'd stopped along the road on a hill outside of Camelot. They could see the palace towers jutting up over the battlements; bright blue pennants topped the towers and flapped in the high wind. Great, puffy clouds as big as mountains hung in the sky above. A knight had stopped and was talking to his father – the knight's sword flashed in the sun as he turned it over and pointed at something near the hilt. He handed Thomas his scabbard. The leather smelled like the earth, it smelled real, it smelled like Honor...

The guard room faded into view. William was on the ground. Marie was holding him by the shoulders and peering up into his face. She was wearing the dress she wore at Guinevere's wedding. She was gorgeous. The skin of her shoulders and neck was flawless. He sighed and breathed deeply of the perfume she wore. She smelled like summer. She smelled like mystery. She smelled like nothing else.

❧

A great splash of water hit Thomas hard. He sputtered, and jerked, and jumped to his feet. He swayed and turned and tried to back away from a half dozen shapes moving toward him.

"Thomas," said a familiar voice.

He blinked his eyes. It was Philip, and behind him, Marie, Pyralis, Gorgella, Marrok, and a prone and unconscious William.

"You forgot to hold your own nose, dummy," said Philip. They were all grinning at him.

Thomas rubbed at his face partly to clear the water away, partly to feel if everything was alright between his eyes. The water smelled like water. His dirty hand smelled like dirt. It was all good. He looked around.

"How'd we get here? Where are the guards?"

"We carried you two," said Marrok, gesturing to William as well. "And they'll be here shortly I'd imagine. As we were leaving, your friend the Baron showed up and was rousing them from Ambrosia's spell."

They were gathered around the fountain in the center of Fogbottom's village square. Philip had refilled his bucket and was carrying it toward William. William was smiling and mumbling something to himself. Then a tremendous wash of water hit him, and he was up, sputtering and swinging his sword wildly.

"Oh," he said after he'd come more fully to his senses. He found Thomas and stared at him suspiciously. "What was that?" There was wonder in his voice.

"It was like," he struggled to find the words, "...it was like all the best times of my life, one right after the other."

He shook his head. "I didn't want it to stop."

"The Baron's coming, William," said Thomas, "and he won't be happy."

William shook his head. "I'm so hungry," he said.

"We have to go," said Philip.

They gathered their few belongings and started for the far end of the square, but Thomas didn't budge. When she realized he wasn't with them, Marie turned back and came to him. The others paused.

"What's wrong Thomas?"

Thomas was simply standing there, gazing around the square. His internal struggle made it to his face, and he frowned.

"I want this to end," said Thomas.

"Want what to end?" said Marie.

"This—" he gestured at the town. "This fear. This... This... It's not *his*. None of it is his unless we give it to him. I'm tired of living at the Baron's behest. We've saved ourselves tonight, but..."

The others had returned and stood quietly listening. William had only come close enough to hear. He kept taking furtive glances toward the far end of the square – the direction the Baron would be coming from. Then he spotted Pyralis's saddlebag and said, "You wouldn't happen to have some jerky in there?"

"Help yourself," said Pyralis.

"It feels wrong to escape, and leave Fogbottom no better," said Marie, guessing at Thomas's feelings.

Thomas looked at her. "And knowing the Baron, probably even worse off because of our efforts," he said. All she did was look up at him, but he felt in that moment that no one understood him better.

"There are many ways to fight a battle," said Marrok. "Are you sure this is the best way to fight this one?"

Thomas didn't answer right away.

"You could die, Thomas Farmer," said Marrok.

Thomas gritted his teeth. He shook his head. Maybe it was exhaustion or shock or desperation but he rarely felt as sure as he did now. "It ends tonight," he said.

He looked back at Marie. "Go," he said softly. She shook her head.

Marrok laughed, and drew his sword. "If Sir Thomas stands, I stand," said Marrok.

Thomas felt a lump in his throat.

Gorgella dropped her pack and put her hands on her hips. "Me too," she said.

"As well do I," said Pyralis.

Philip swallowed and looked from person to person. "You guys are nuts," he said. But he drew his sword and stepped up to form a line with Thomas and Marrok.

Thomas, eyes watering, turned to William.

William shook his head, strode straight up to Thomas and held his sword out hilt first. Still chewing, he said, "Take this," and pushed the sword at him impatiently.

Thomas slowly reached out and took hold of the weapon.

"Stand strong," his brother said. Then turned and dashed out of the square without a backwards glance.

"You've got to be kidding me," said Philip after a moment of stunned silence.

Thomas was shocked, but he tried not to show it. "It's okay," he said.

"No it's ruddy well *not* okay," said Philip. "He's the reason we're here in the first place."

"But he's not the reason we're staying," said Marrok.

Philip shot a look at Marrok, and made as if to reply, then apparently thought better of it and clamped his mouth shut.

"How did you find us anyway?" said Philip.

Marrok laughed again. Thomas wished he could laugh like that while waiting for certain death.

"Well, the wolf-form has its advantages, but I had a little help from you before that."

Marrok pulled out a small, brass device and handed it to Philip. "I believe this is yours," he said.

"The compass?" said Philip, terribly confused. "But how did you–"

Pyralis plucked the compass from Philip's open hand. "I'll take that," he said.

Philip shot a look at Pyralis, who frowned back at him. "You mean to tell me," he rounded on Marrok, "that thing led you to us? No tricks? No," he waved his hands in the air, "tom foolery?"

Pyralis raised an eyebrow.

"What do you mean?" said Marrok.

Philip squinted at him, but Marrok seemed to Thomas to be telling the truth. In fact, Thomas wasn't sure it had ever crossed Marrok's mind that you could speak in any other way.

"The compass," said Pyralis, "has a pretty good sense of who is and who isn't fun to toy with."

Philip frowned, but said nothing more.

Marrok shrugged and twirled his sword in his hand.

Thomas looked at Marie to try to share a smile at Philip's expense, but Marie was staring up the road, dread spreading out from her wide eyes.

Thomas turned to see the Baron and Bane riding into the square with what had to be more than three dozen soldiers behind them.

CHAPTER XXV

A HERO BY ANY OTHER NAME

Thomas took two steps forward and planted himself in their path. Marrok and Philip fanned out behind him. Marie pulled a dagger from somewhere, and behind them, Pyralis drew a wand from his coat. Gorgella dropped her pack and stood clutching two more of the oddly-shaped mechanical devices, one in each hand.

The Baron trotted to a stop and held up a hand, commanding his troops to halt. Bane stopped beside him. His face was flush – he looked invigorated and sported the same wicked grin he'd worn earlier. Thomas found the Baron's stoic expression more alarming than Bane's open delight of the situation.

"I thought," said the Baron in a calm, cold voice, "we had an understanding, Farmer. I thought you knew, finally, where you stood."

"You thought wrong," said Thomas. "I stand for Fogbottom."

238

The Baron's dispassionate expression evaporated and was replaced by a look of such hatred that Thomas had to fight not to recoil from the fury of it alone.

"I *am* Fogbottom, boy," he spat.

Just as quickly as it had come, the hatred vanished and was replaced again by the cool, detached façade he'd worn previously.

"I find that most often, when people get themselves into trouble, it's because they've forgotten that one simple fact," he said.

Turning his head slightly, he addressed his soldiers. "Arrest him."

Gorgella cleared her throat, and the Baron seemed to notice Thomas's friends for the first time.

"Ah," he said, "and these would be the ones who damaged my home?" He squinted at them. "Two boys, two... women, a half-naked freak of nature, and an old man. Really, Stewart." He addressed a shorter, mean looking man that Thomas recognized as the Baron's warden. "I should have you strung up with them. Hold on..."

He turned back and peered at Pyralis, then laughed.

"Pyralis! Is that you?"

Thomas could feel Pyralis tense.

The Baron continued to laugh at a joke only he seemed to be getting. "This all makes sense now. What are you playing at you old worm?"

Thomas and the others turned to see Pyralis stammering. He glanced from Thomas to Marrok, then back to the Baron. He seemed to carefully ignore Gorgella's glare.

"Pyralis," said Thomas, "how does he—"

"Did you work for this cad, Pyralis?" said Philip. "I mean, evil wizard sure, but... the *Fogbottoms*?"

"Why is that so surprising?" shot Pyralis. He was frowning and shooting defensive looks at his companions in turn. "It's not like you can pick and choose your clientele when you're trying to get a business off the ground.

"Anyway," he said, "that was a long time ago. And just who do you think are the sort that hire evil wizards in the first place?"

Philip seemed to consider this for the first time. "Well, I suppose I assumed you could do fairly well making exploding pastries and liniments that, I don't know, surprised you in various ways."

Pyralis was glaring at him with such indignation that Philip seemed to find the Baron's crowd less threatening and turned back to face them instead.

The Baron was enjoying all of it immensely. "Exploding muffins! Is that what you've been about since we parted ways Pyralis?"

"I'm a healer now," said Pyralis through clenched teeth. He was pointing his wand at the Baron's chest. Thomas noticed his hand was shaking a bit and his knuckles were white.

"A what?" The Baron was laughing so hard he was beginning to stream tears from his eyes. Bane and the soldiers were laughing now too.

"A healer," said Pyralis. His wand had turned red at the tip and the glow was spreading backward.

"Oh that's rich," said the Baron. A few of the soldiers in the front of the crowd had noticed Pyralis's wand and were shifting in their saddles nervously.

The whole wand was gleaming now and the end pointed at the Baron had grown white. Pyralis was muttering something under his breath. It sounded like he was saying something backward, and he seemed to be inhaling rather than exhaling as he spoke.

Thomas took two steps, grabbed Pyralis's outstretched arm and said, "That's right, Pyralis. You're a healer now."

Pyralis, jerked as if he'd been struck. The wand immediately faded to its normal wooden hues. Pyralis breathed out, and a hot wind ruffled Thomas's hair. Most importantly, Thomas saw again the man he knew behind the eyes of the former evil wizard.

The Baron had stopped laughing and was squinting at the pair of them.

"Arrest them all." He said it so casually that it took a moment for the soldiers nearest him to realize he was talking to them.

"Arrest them all, I said!" and the soldiers jumped. They drew swords and fanned out to encircle them. Philip and Marrok stepped closer to Thomas, and he felt Marie press against him.

"It doesn't have to be this way," said Thomas, trying to sound charismatic, but his words sounded panicked even to himself.

The Baron smiled, and opened his mouth to say something, but was cut off by a yell from behind Thomas's group.

"Hey there, Fogbottom, what seems to be the trouble?"

It was William.

"What is he doing?" whispered Marie.

"I don't know," said Thomas, but his heart was soaring.

"The trouble—" began the Baron, but William cut him off again.

"I wasn't talking to you, ye festering windbag," he yelled. "I was talking to Fogbottom."

The Baron's face was nearly purple.

"I AM FOGBOTTOM," he roared.

"I think not," said William, and Mr. Farmer stepped around the corner followed by Old Man Chitterton.

They were joined by two more men that Thomas recognized as frequent hangers-on with Grumps at the Brimful Kettle. Then, Mrs. Farmer and Grandma Farmer stepped around the corner to join the others, and soon townspeople were pouring into the square.

Thomas recognized everyone: There were Mr. and Mrs. Applebutter from down the way – he carried a shovel and she sported a small rake – and the Chisel's from the west side of town with their son Jiminy who, it was rumored, could split a log with his fist. No one knew for certain how he'd escaped conscription into the Baron's troops, but Thomas had always attributed it to over-qualification. Smitty rounded the corner with a pair of boys that looked like miniature versions of the farrier himself. All three were wearing the leather aprons of their trade and carrying horseshoes like they were throwing axes. The Hunters appeared, and behind the Baron, their son Wendsley groaned audibly when he spied his mum and dad.

Even the Parson was there. He was a large man with fists the size of grapefruit, but Thomas had never seen him raise a hand in anger. The parson carried a copy of the Bible that was bigger than most six year olds and that proclaimed itself to be illustrated and "self-pronouncing". The first time Thomas had read that claim on its cover, he'd pictured the Parson lying in bed at night while the Bible sat on a table nearby, telling him stories in a deep, ostentatious voice.

As usual, William was in the center of a group of the most popular: Ackerly, Calvert, Royden, and Ward. Together with William, they'd invented a sport they called, creatively, Ball. Ball consisted mainly of one team trying to get a sack of flour, or a wheel, or anything heavy and unwieldy – and if breakable even better – from one end of a field to another. There weren't a lot of rules for Ball, and they almost never played using anything that actually resembled a ball. In any case, the five of them were undefeated.

"Father?" said Bane. Thomas couldn't recall ever seeing anything like apprehension in Bane's eyes before, but it was there now.

The Baron waved him away with a hand and commanded his soldiers. "Fan out. Surround them. End this display." Then he raised his voice and spoke to the crowd, "Disperse now or be arrested for illegal assembly and hang with these wretches. It makes no difference to me."

The numbers were in Thomas's favor now, but looking around, Thomas knew they were still in deep trouble. A man on foot swinging a battered old gardening tool was no match for an armored, armed, and mounted soldier. That was kind of the point of the armor, the arms, and the mount.

The soldiers encircled the square and began to close in. Several of the townspeople looked around for escape routes, but William caught sight of it and started them all chanting, "Fog–bot–tom." As the soldiers closed in, the crowd tightened rather than breaking, and a cold knot of fear dropped into Thomas's gut.

Then a familiar voice raised above the crowd, and the chanting died.

"Wendsley Cheston Hunter, is that you again?" said Grandma Farmer.

The rather portly Wendsley froze on his spot halfway round the circle of soldiers from the Baron and Thomas.

"What are you playing at, boy?"

Thomas would've laughed if he wasn't so scared.

Wendsley blushed and stammered.

"Wendsley, get off that horse this instant and come stand with your father," said another elderly lady.

"You listen to your nana," said Grandma Farmer. "And that goes for you too, Sedgley Sutton. I see you there. And your partner in crime – Mr. Buxton Yarlberry. You didn't get away with this monkey business in my schoolroom and you won't get away with it now. Are you three going to manhandle the women who gave you birth and fed you mashed peas when you couldn't even hold your own heads up?"

"They certainly are not," piped in Mrs. Sutton and Mrs. Yarlberry.

"And you..." continued Grandma Farmer, going one by one down the line of soldiers. Thomas stood and watched, astonished, as soldiers slid off their horses and joined their families in the crowd.

"You there!" shouted Bane at Grandma Farmer. She resolutely ignored him and persisted in her serial reprimands of soldiers twice her size.

Bane glanced at his father. The Baron was grinding his jaw and squinting from person to person around the crowd. Bane kicked at his horse's flanks and rode toward Grandma Farmer. "You there, old woman, step aside."

Thomas grabbed the reins as Bane passed and jerked the horse to a stop. Bane reached for his sword, and Thomas heard a sound of metal sliding on metal from the other side of the horse. Bane gasped and Marrok stepped into sight carrying both his and Bane's swords. Bane was rubbing his hand.

"Enough!" shouted the Baron. At least half of his soldiers had dismounted and abandoned him. They peppered the crowd, most standing sheepishly by their families, several looking rather relieved in spite of their embarrassment, and a small few actually throwing defiant looks at the Baron and his remaining guards.

"Unhand my son," the Baron commanded.

"You will release your hold on this town, leave, and never return," said Thomas.

The Baron looked as though this was the most preposterous idea he'd ever heard.

"You will hand over the keys to the keep and the storehouses." Thomas threw a stern look at Bane sitting above him. "And you will ride off with your son to a place of your choosing. But if you ever set foot in Fogbottom again—" Thomas took a breath. He couldn't believe he was saying these things to a pair of men who'd terrorized his life.

"You will be incarcerated and tried for trespassing."

The look on the Baron's face shifted from shock through disbelief and into open rage in the span of a few heartbeats.

He dismounted, drew his sword and marched toward Thomas.

"I told you, boy," he growled, "I am Fogbottom."

He raised his arm to swing.

There was a motion behind him and a man brushed roughly passed Thomas. He did something surprising and rather painful to Thomas's wrist that made him let go of his sword. The man caught it as it fell and, in one smooth motion, stepped in front of Thomas and ran the Baron straight through.

Everyone froze.

"No!" shouted Thomas.

The Baron's wide eyes drifted down from Thomas to the weapon buried in his midsection. He dropped his sword and fell to his knees, groping clumsily at the hilt protruding from his stomach.

"Father!" shouted Bane and dropped off his horse. Marrok caught him and held him.

Thomas looked at the man who'd run the Baron through. "Dad?" he said.

Mr. Farmer turned away from the Baron to look Thomas in the eye. "I'd had just about enough," said Mr. Farmer.

Thomas was flooded with a mix of love for his father, horror at the act, and distress at having the scene turn violent in the end after all.

The crowd was still. A few of the remaining Fogbottom guards slid off their mounts, but none of them made any hostile gesture.

Thomas dropped to his knee, supported the Baron with a hand on his shoulder and scanned the group wildly.

"Pyralis," he said. His mind raced.

"Pyralis, you can fix this."

Pyralis responded to Thomas with a look of unmistakable horror.

"Pyralis," pleaded Thomas. "You're a healer."

Pyralis's face relaxed a little, but his eyes darted around randomly. He seemed to be at a great struggle internally.

Gorgella reached out and touched his elbow. "You can do this," she said.

Marie knelt down with Thomas and wiped at the Baron's brow with a handkerchief. The Baron was sweating heavily and breathing in disturbing gasps, like a fish out of water.

Something seemed to break in Pyralis. He walked quickly over to the Baron. He knelt, put one hand on the Baron's shoulder, grabbed the hilt of the sword with the other and looked the Baron in the eye.

The Baron returned his gaze. "Please," he said.

Pyralis frowned, then closed his eyes and began muttering under his breath. Instead of the compressed feeling he'd felt around Pyralis when he's been about to destroy the Baron, this time there was an expansion and something that felt not unlike a soft wind moving *out*. There was an air about it of calm and comfort. Thomas felt himself relaxing.

Pyralis opened his eyes, said clearly, "*Soli Deo gloria*," and withdrew the sword with a quick pull. The force of the extraction pulled the Baron right up onto his feet. He wobbled there for a moment, gaining his balance, and staring at the place where the sword had hung so unnaturally just a moment ago. His clothing was sliced, and there was what looked like an old scar marring his abdomen, but he appeared otherwise unharmed.

The crowd didn't know who to stare at: the Baron standing there miraculously alive, or Pyralis who appeared to be as surprised as everyone else. The Parson made his way over to the former evil wizard and put a hand on his shoulder. He started to say something, changed his mind, and simply smiled at Pyralis who returned the grin with one of his own.

Marrok let go of Bane, and the boy rushed to his father. The Baron pushed him away, and began backing toward his horse eyeing the crowd suspiciously.

Surely, thought Thomas, this would change the Baron's heart. He took a step toward him but the Baron shot a wild look at him and yelled, "Stay back!"

He climbed onto his horse, and without another word, rode out of the square.

"Father!" shouted Bane, who scanned the crowd one last fearful time, mounted his own horse and followed the Baron out of sight.

The Fogbottomtons stood there for a moment, looking at each other. Then, one of the Baron's former guards threw his helmet in the air and cheered, and the crowd erupted in exuberant celebration. Wendsley Cheston Hunter marched straight over to Grandma Farmer and gave her a hug Thomas thought might kill her. Grandma looked a bit panicked herself at first, but quickly settled into it and patted Wendsley's back.

Mr. Farmer cornered Thomas, shook his hand, then pulled him into a wordless embrace, and that was that. In contrast, Mrs. Farmer couldn't seem to stop hugging her youngest son. Finally Thomas had to complain, at which point she simply moved on to William. Eventually she stopped with the squeezing altogether, but there was a smile pasted on her face that looked like it would never come off, and Thomas thought her eyes might be wet for the rest of her life.

William was looking better already. He still looked a shadow of his former self, but gone was the crazed look and air of death about him. Thomas was trying to decide if he'd actually taken the time to stop and comb his hair before rallying the townspeople when Ackerly and Royden hoisted William up on their shoulders and started the crowd cheering for him.

"This should be *your* moment Thomas," said Philip watching William.

Elizabeth came running into sight at that moment, spotted Thomas and rushed at him. She leapt into his arms and hugged him so hard he was afraid for a moment for the structural integrity of his neck.

"It *is* my moment, Philip," he said, and hugged Elizabeth back.

CHAPTER XXVI

THE SPOILS

It wasn't clear to Thomas what sparked it. There was a general, growing murmur and then someone shouted – possibly William or one of his friends – but suddenly the crowd was storming up the hill to Fogbottom Keep. Thomas, Marie, Philip, and the rest were swept along with it.

They reached the top and found the drawbridge lowered. The crowd swept over it, cheering and picking up speed. They headed en masse through the courtyard and round the bend to the grain storehouses where the entire mob stopped short with a collective gasp.

Bane and the Baron were tied up, sitting against the wall and looking rather chagrined. Three knights in full armor – each bearing their own crests but each also showing the colors of Camelot – were inspecting the contents of both the storehouses and a cart laden with sacks and boxes.

"The shipment," whispered Philip to Thomas.

The tallest knight abandoned his box and turned to address the crowd. "People of Fogbottom, fear not. Today your suffering ends!"

The crowd looked at itself and furrowed its brows.

Thomas recognized the knights immediately. He cleared his throat. "Sir Kay," he said bowing. "If I may be so bold, what brings Arthur's champions to our humble village?"

One of the other knights raised his visor.

"Timothy, is tha' you agin?"

"It's Thomas, Sir Gawain."

Gawain winked at him.

Thomas blinked.

"Good show, Thomas," whispered Kay to Thomas. Then he raised his voice and addressed the crowd, "You may not have been aware, but the one entrusted by Camelot with your land and yourselves' safekeeping and responsible stewardship was in fact—" He swung and pointed a long gauntleted finger at the Baron, "—a villain and a roustabout."

"A scheming despot," added the third knight.

"A donkey's— "

"I think they get the picture Gawain," said Kay. "Show them, Bedivere."

The third knight cracked open one of the larger boxes on the cart and pulled out a small, wrapped cake.

"Pastries?" said Philip.

"I should have known," said Pyralis.

Kay held the cake aloft and declared, "Poisoned pastries!"

"But I've been eating those," said William.

Bedivere made eye contact with Thomas and motioned him over. He led Thomas a short distance to the door of one of the storehouses. It was nearly but not completely empty.

"They're all like this," said Bedivere. "It's not much, but we don't believe the grain itself has been contaminated. It should last through the winter."

Thomas stared at the pile.

Bedivere slapped him on the back. "We weren't sure how we were going to pull this one off Thomas. Get inside the Baron's stronghold, apprehend him, and expose the plot. Then there was this explosion, and the next thing we knew his entire militia was streaming out the gate."

Bedivere laughed.

"I–" started Thomas. He wasn't sure where to begin. "I don't understand."

"We've been watching him for weeks. He planned on delivering these poisoned foods to Arthur's half-sister Morgan who, as I'm sure you know, has lost no love for her brother. She was going to distribute them throughout Camelot, and after everyone was sick, arrive on the scene, discredit Arthur, and produce the antidote.

"Thomas," continued Bedivere, "your part in foiling this plot is greatly appreciated."

"But I had no idea... He really poisoned all of our food?"

Bedivere winked.

"Ninth Article, isn't it?" said Bedivere. "Always make your betters look better or some such? Tuttle will be proud to hear how you've performed today, Sir Thomas."

"Performed? But it's no performance, Sir. I mean, we knew something was up, but it seemed like we were on our own... And there wasn't any proof besides, well, I guess besides my brother's condition now that I think about it..."

"Alright, let's not overplay it shall we?" said Bedivere and walked Thomas back to the crowd.

As they returned, Thomas saw Philip point Gawain toward William. Gawain made his way over and handed something to him. Something Gawain said caused William to shoot a look at Thomas. William grinned and nodded to Gawain, and then the three knights rode out of the

Keep towing the Baron, Bane, and the cart laden with contaminated confections.

William cleared his throat, and as usual for William, it was all it took to get the crowd's rapt attention.

"How does he do that?" said Thomas to no one in particular.

"People of Fogbottom," said William. "Sir Kay has left a task in our hands."

He grinned and held up the Baron's crown.

The crowd cheered and clapped.

"We are to name a temporary regent until such time as the king can appoint a new governor of these lands.

"And I," continued William as he stepped before Thomas, "can think of no one more deserving."

He dropped to one knee and lifted the crown up to Thomas. "If there be a better man to take on this mantle, to rule and guide, to safe-keep and steward Fogbottom..."

Thomas glanced at the crowd. Pyralis was beaming. Gorgella had her eyes wide and her hands clamped to her mouth, Elizabeth's jaw hung open, and Marie simply smiled. Mrs. Farmer wore a smile too large for her face. Grandma Farmer asked, "What's he got there?"

Thomas thought he caught an actual sparkle in Mr. Farmer's eye. "That's my boy," he said to Abraham Chisel who responded by slapping him hard on the back.

It seemed the whole crowd was smiling.

Thomas frowned and lifted the crown from William's fingers. It was beautifully crafted. There wasn't a hint of tarnish even in the crevices where the jewels were set. He blew on it and what little dust had settled on it lifted right off. It was heavier than it looked, but not too heavy. It weighed just enough to feel important, and despite the large, shining rubies on its front, it balanced perfectly in Thomas's fingers.

Thomas took a deep breath.

"Some time ago," he said, "a man made his way up this hill alone to petition the ruler of this land for supplication.

For mercy. For food. He was imprisoned and poisoned, but he didn't lose hope. All that time he thought only of how his actions might help his family, his friends, and his fellows.

"If there be a better man to take on this mantle, let *him* wear this crown," said Thomas and placed the crown on William's head. "I dub thee, William Farmer, Temporary Regent of the Village of Fogbottom."

For the second time that day the crowd gasped collectively. William shot a look up at Thomas.

Mr. Farmer said, "That's my other boy," and Chisel slapped him on the back again.

The crowd erupted in cheers. William stood and hugged Thomas. Elizabeth rushed up and hugged them both. The rest of the Farmers joined next, and soon the whole crowd was part of the embrace.

"I have to ask," said Thomas later when he and William were alone, "who is 'Wyb of Habab?'"

"Who is who?"

"Wyb... Here," said Thomas and pulled out William's letter, now rather worse for wear.

William read. "Oh!" he said and laughed. "Well now, look at that. It's nothing... Sometimes, you know, you run out of hidden message before you run out of important things to say."

CHAPTER XXVII

SOMNIA SALVEBIS

His eyes shut tight, Thomas stepped slowly through the stable with arms and hands outstretched. Several of the horses nickered. He made out the strong, deep voice of Solstice, and the friendly greetings of half a dozen others. They remembered him.

He stopped and with a contented smile playing at his lips said, "Noble steed and loyal friend..."

He had to laugh at himself; it sounded so foolish now, but he continued, "At the start and at the end..."

There was a sudden snort to his right and a large head pushed into his hand at just the right height.

"Booker," said Thomas, and opened his eyes.

Booker, the dilapidated gray workhorse with the oversized – and overactive – nostrils. Booker, the horse no knight in his right mind would adopt.

"Thomas!" yelled a voice outside.

"In here!" he yelled back. "In the stable." He stroked Booker's muzzle, and Booker turned his head sideways to look at Thomas's face with one large, weepy eye.

Philip appeared in the doorway, followed by Marie.

"There's a messenger here," said Marie.

"From Camelot," added Philip. Philip looked anxious.

"What's the matter?" Thomas stopped petting Booker, who pushed his head into Thomas's shoulder hard. Thomas fell sideways and caught himself, laughing.

A third person came into view. Dusty from travel, the blue and gold markings of Camelot were still clearly visible. He strode right up to Thomas.

"Sir Thomas the Hesitant?"

"Aye," said Thomas hesitantly, "I suppose that's me."

The man unfurled a short scroll and read, "Sir Tuttle the Authorized, on the orders of King Arthur, Lord of Britain, summons all Less Valued Knights to assemble in Camelot with the Round Table, the Knights Errant, and the Knights of the Watch in a matter of utmost urgency."

He furled the scroll with a flick, and turned to leave.

"Hold on," said Thomas. "What's this about?"

"Something about a magic cup that's gone missing," said the messenger, raising one eyebrow and giving a small shrug.

The man glanced at Booker and blurted, "Is that your mount, sir?"

Thomas looked Booker in the eye.

"Why yes," he said, after considering it a moment. "Yes he is."

Booker jerked his head nervously.

"Nonsense," said Thomas speaking to Booker, "you'll be fine."

EPILOGUE

Dear Reader,

A final word, if you will. You probably have many questions, as did I. What about the ring with the letters "LVK" and the phrase *Somnia Salvebis* for instance?

It seems the ring was given to Thomas by none other than Sir Tuttle the Authorized in honor of his outstanding service to the Table of Less Valued Knights. "Somnia, Salvebis" translates, of course, as "Nonsense, you'll be fine." It's doubtful, however, that the specific occasion for this award relates directly to the events in my grandfather's manuscript: Sir Thomas the Hesitant went on to do so many other important things.

And what of Marie? Or Sir Philip the Disadvantaged? Or young Elizabeth Abigail Farmer? These are all tales for another day.

Instead, I'd like to leave you with the message I gleaned from my grandfather's legacy. It is this: The best kept secret in the world may be no vast conspiracy, no grand hoodwink, no colossal ruse. It may be the simple fact that someone, all along, has been watching out for us.

Here's to the Less Valued.

Liam Bartholomew Perrin
April 29, 2008

The journey continues!
Turn the page to enjoy the first chapter of

FAYCALIBUR
A Less Valued Knights Novel #2

CHAPTER I

THE SENDING

"Watch," said Merlin.
    They watched.
    Nothing happened.
    This is not entirely accurate. Lots of things happened. For example, a candle flame danced and sputtered as it reveled in the cave's cool draft. A drop of water clung desperately to the tip of a stalactite, terrified, listening to the rhythmic demise of its brothers echo through the chamber. Mushrooms luminesced because, well, because they could. And the forces that hold the universe together delighted in the orderly molecular structure of the crystal at the center of the room.

    Merlin hit it hard with his staff.

    That's a wizard's job – perturbing the forces that hold the universe together. Merlin was good at it. He'd been good at it for a long time. He was tired now and looking forward to retirement.

    He'd trained his replacement, Nimue. He'd introduced her during Arthur's wedding in a manner of her choosing. It had been a bit flamboyant for his own taste with the mad hart and the braying hounds and the ruined desserts, but it was important she make it her own. He was ready to hand over the reins of this grand enterprise. Not the royal, governing, public reins. Those weren't his to give. No, the secret reins. The reins that steered not the coach, as it were, but the coachman.

But now this. He sighed. It was important they see this. There were things Nimue and her apprentice needed to learn – especially the apprentice. And that unlikely knight. Merlin frowned.

He hit the crystal again. A satisfying resonance accompanied the strike this time.

Images formed in the crystal. Fuzzy.

He hit it again.

The image focused:

Arthur in a battle for his life with a dark champion. Arthur driven back, near death, wielding a sword.

Nimue leaned in squinting. "What weapon is that?"

"Not Excalibur," said Merlin. "An impostor. Watch."

The impostor sword shatters. Arthur falls. The dark champion raises his sword.

The crystal went dark.

They watched.

Nothing else happened.

The candle flame was steady. The water drop swelled.

"There is a plot afoot," said Merlin gesturing at the empty crystal. "As you have seen."

"But," said Nimue, "How? Where is Excalibur?"

"He gave it to her," said Merlin.

"Morgan?"

Merlin nodded.

"But why?"

Merlin shrugged. "'Safekeeping,' he said."

Nimue's apprentice rolled her eyes.

Merlin draped a cloth over the crystal. "He'll soon learn she isn't to be trusted," he said. "I only hope he survives the lesson."

"We should put a stop to this," said Nimue.

Behind the beard and beneath the eyebrows Merlin could be quite expressive when he chose to be. But at times like this he was simply too lost in thought to bother operating his face for the benefit of others. Hotter heads often mistook his preoccupation for indifference, but if you wanted to know what was going on in Merlin's head it was best to ask, not guess.

Nimue's apprentice guessed. "You're not seriously going to let this happen. This isn't some life lesson or laboratory experiment where the student will learn best by being allowed to fail. This is Arthur being murdered. Surely it's Morgan behind this. We have to stop her!"

Merlin straightened.

"We," he said, "don't have to do anything."

He stared at her. She stared back.

Nimue's apprentice looked away. Her hands were balled in white-knuckled fists.

"Nimue," said Merlin. "Go to Morgan's court. Find what you can find. Unravel this plot."

"Yes," her apprentice hissed with excitement.

"Elisante," said Merlin.

The apprentice clenched her jaw. "I'm going too," she said.

Merlin nodded. "Find the one who bears the impostor sword, and do what you do best."

"And what is that exactly?" Elisante asked warily.

"Get in the way."

Merlin chuckled.

Nimue frowned.

Elisante glared.

Merlin cleared his throat. "Find Sir Thomas the Hesitant," he said. "And stop him."

Find out more about *Faycalibur* and the rest of the Less Valued Knights series at LiamPerrin.com.

ABOUT THE AUTHOR

Liam Perrin has been roughly geosynchronous for more than a few decades and likely will remain so. Most recently, he orbits the center of Earth from a position outside of Phoenix, Arizona where he tries to avoid collisions with his wife, one daughter, a miniature Australian shepherd, a Russian tortoise, and a 70-pound Sheprador who will love you to death. Seriously, she doesn't know when to stop. Unlike the author who figures he should stop right about... here.

Printed in Great Britain
by Amazon

87039724R00157